The Best British Mysteries III

The Best British Mysteries III

Edited by
Maxim Jakubowski

W F HOWES LTD

This large print edition published in 2006 by
W F Howes Ltd
Unit 4, Rearsby Business Park, Gaddesby Lane,
Rearsby, Leicester LE7 4YH

1 3 5 7 9 10 8 6 4 2

First published in the United Kingdom in 2006
by Allison & Busby Limited

A CIP catalogue record for this book is available
from the British Library

ISBN 1 84632 870 5

Typeset by Palimpsest Book Production Limited,
Grangemouth, Stirlingshire
Printed and bound in Great Britain
by Antony Rowe Ltd, Chippenham, Wilts.

CONTENTS

INTRODUCTION

Already our third volume presenting the best crime and mystery short stories written by British authors in the past year and it's another veritable cornucopia of thrills, dirty deeds, clever plots, evil villains, determined sleuths, psychological torment, confounding puzzles, and almost every shenanigan under the sun (or, in many instances, the moon . . .).

The ingenuity of crime writers never ceases to amaze me as they plumb the hidden depths of the human psyche and explore that tenuous territory that sometimes separates good and evil in which characters much like you and me can sometimes get away with it, or not, as the case may be. Murder, deceit and wrongdoing are fertile grounds, though, for splendid entertainment, as a recent statistic confirmed, showing that British library readers now read more mysteries than romance; the first time this has historically happened. Whether you read crime books for the intellectual crime-solving element, or for its often fascinating insight into human nature or, more simply, for the sheer pleasure of a good read where the plot effortlessly goes from A to Z with many a roadside attraction during the journey, there is no more satisfying form of entertainment and the mystery short story embodies all these virtues in a concentrated format which proves a challenge to good writers and a particular delight to readers. And, forgive me for just a touch of gentle chauvinism, British crime and mystery writers certainly rule the roost in this regard.

This year's batch of stories sees some grand names joining our ranks, who had not appeared in previous volumes: the delightful Alexander McCall Smith with, naturally, an African tale; the slick creator of Jack Reacher, British expatriate Lee Child, whose thrillers live on the bestseller list; the urbane Robert Goddard who actually seldom pens short stories; ex-Crime Writers' Association Chairperson Danuta Reah, whose story won the CWA Short Story Dagger this year, and the collaborative duo of Simon Avery and Ian Faulkner.

Last but not least, our always welcome repeat offenders, some of whom are making a dangerous habit of featuring in these pages: John Harvey, Ken Bruen, Gillian Linscott, Barbara Cleverly, Judith Cutler, Amy Myers, Peter Lovesey, Peter Turnbull.

A scintillating, if murderous menu . . .

Enjoy the fruits of their crimes.

Maxim Jakubowski

ACKNOWLEDGEMENTS

'Home' by John Harvey © 2005 by John Harvey. First appeared in *Ellery Queen Mystery Magazine*. Reprinted by permission of the author.

'The Greatest Trick of All' by Lee Child © 2005 by Lee Child. First appeared in *Greatest Hits*, edited by Robert Randisi. Reprinted by permission of the Avalon Publishing Group.

'He Loved to Go for Drives with His Father' by Alexander McCall Smith © 2005 by Alexander McCall Smith. First appeared in *A New Omnibus of Crime*, edited by Rosemary Herbert & Tony Hillerman. Reprinted by permission of the author's agent, David Higham Associates.

'Toupee for a Bald Tyre' by Robert Goddard © 2005 by Robert Goddard. First appeared in *The Detection Club Collection*, edited by Simon Brett. Reprinted by permission of the author and the Orion Publishing Group.

JOHN HARVEY

HOME

Resnick was unable to sleep. All those years of living alone, just the weight of the cats, one and occasionally more, pressing lightly down on the covers by his feet or in the V behind his legs, and now, with Lynn away for just forty-eight hours, he was lost without her by his side. The warmth of her body next to his, the small collisions as they turned from their respective dreams into a splay of legs, her arm sliding across his chest. 'Lay still, Charlie. Another five minutes, OK? Musk of her early morning breath.

He pushed away the sheet and swivelled round, then rose to his feet. Through an inch of open window, he could hear the slight swish of cars along the Woodborough Road. Not so many minutes short of two a.m.

Downstairs, Dizzy, the oldest of the four cats, a warrior no longer, raised his head from the fruit bowl he had long since appropriated as a bed, cocked a chewed and half-torn ear and regarded Resnick with a yellow eye.

Padding past, Resnick set the kettle to boil and slid a tin of coffee beans from the fridge. A flier announcing Lynn's course was pinned to the cork board on the wall – *Unzipping the Agenda: A Guide to Creative Management and Open Thinking*. Lynn and forty or so other officers from the East Midlands and East Anglia at a conference centre and hotel beside the A1 outside Stevenage. Promotion material. High fliers. When she had joined the Serious Crime Unit a little more than two years ago, it had been as a sergeant; an inspector now and barely thirty, unless somehow she blotted her copy book, the only way was up. Whereas for Resnick, who had turned down promotion and the chance to move onto a bigger stage, little more than a pension awaited once his years were in.

While the coffee dripped slowly through its filter, Resnick opened the back door into the garden and, as he did so, another of the cats, Pepper, slithered past his ankles. Beyond the allotments, the lights of the city burned dully through a haze of rain and mist. Down there, on the streets of St Ann's and the Meadows, armed officers patrolled with Walther P990s holstered at their hips. Drugs, of course, the cause of most of it, the cause and the core: all the way from after-dinner cocaine served at trendy middle-class dinner parties alongside the squares of Green and Black's dark organic choco- late, to twenty-five pound wraps of brown changing hands in the stairwells of dilapidated blocks of flats.

Bolting the door, he carried his coffee through into the living room, switched on the light and slid a CD into the stereo. *Art Pepper Meets the*

2

Rhythm Section, Los Angeles, January 19th, 1957. Pepper only months out of jail on drugs offences, his second term and still only thirty-two. And worse to come.

Resnick had seen him play in Leicester on the British leg of his European tour; Pepper older, wiser, allegedly straightened out, soon to be dead three years shy of sixty, a small miracle that he survived that long. That evening, in the function room of a nondescript pub, his playing had been melodic, and inventive, the tone piping and lean, its intensity controlled. Man earning a living, doing what he can.

Back in 'fifty-seven, in front of Miles Davis's rhythm section, he had glittered, half-afraid, inspired, alto saxophone dancing over the chords of half-remembered tunes. 'Star Eyes', 'Imagination,' 'Jazz Me Blues'. The track that Resnick would play again and again: 'You'd Be So Nice To Come Home To'.

For a moment Pepper's namesake cat appeared in the doorway, sniffed the air and turned away, presenting his fine tail.

Just time for Resnick, eyes closed, to conjure up a picture of Lynn, restlessly sleeping in a strange bed, before the phone began to ring.

It was the sergeant on duty, his voice stretched by tiredness: '. . . ten, fifteen minutes ago, sir. I thought you'd want to know.'

That stretch of the Ilkeston Road was a mixture of small shops and residential housing, old factories

3

put to new use, student accommodation. Police cars were parked, half on the kerb, either side of a black Ford Mondeo that, seemingly, had swerved wildly and collided, broadside-on, into a concrete post, amidst a welter of torn metal and splintered glass. Onlookers, some with overcoats pulled over their night clothes and carpet slippers on their feet, stood back behind hastily strung-out police tape, craning their necks. An ambulance and fire engine stood opposite, paramedics and fire officers mingling with uniformed police at the perimeter of the scene. Lights flashing, a second ambulance was pulling away as Resnick arrived.

Driving slowly past, he stopped outside a shop, long boarded-up, *High Class Butcher* in faded lettering on the brickwork above.

Anil Khan, once a DC in Resnick's squad and now a sergeant with Serious Crime, came briskly down to meet him and walked him back.

'One dead at the scene, sir, young female; one on his way to hospital, the driver. Female passenger, front near side, her leg's trapped against the door where it buckled in. Have to be cut out most likely. Oxyacetylene.'

Resnick could see the body now, stretched out against the lee of the wall beneath a dark grey blanket that was darker at the head.

'Impact?' Resnick said. 'Thrown forward against the windscreen?'

Khan shook his head. 'Shot.'

It stopped Resnick in his tracks.

'Another car, as best we can tell. Three shots, maybe four. One of them hit her in the neck. Must have nicked an artery. She was dead before we got her out.'

Illuminated by the street light above, Resnick could see the blood, sticky and bright, clinging to the upholstery like a second skin. Bending towards the body, he lifted back the blanket edge and looked down into the dead startled eyes of a girl of no more than sixteen.

Fifteen years and seven months. Alicia Ann Faye. She had lived with her mother, two younger sisters and an older brother in Radford. A bright and popular student, a lovely girl. She had been to an eighteenth-birthday party with her brother, Bradford, and his girlfriend, Marlee. Bradford driving.

They had been on their way home when the incident occurred, less than half a mile from where Alicia and Bradford lived. A blue BMW drew up alongside them at the lights before the turn into Ilkeston Road, revving its engine as if intent on racing. Anticipating the green, Bradford, responding to the challenge, accelerated downhill, the BMW in close pursuit; between the first set of lights and the old Radford Mill building, the BMW drew alongside, someone lowered the rear window, pushed a handgun through and fired four times. One shot ricocheted off the roof, another embedded itself in the rear of the front seat; one entered the fleshy part of Bradford's shoulder, causing him to swerve; the fourth and fatal shot struck Alicia low in side of the neck and exited close to her windpipe.

An impulse shooting, is that what this was? Or a case of mistaken identity?

In the October of the previous year a gunman had opened fire from a passing car, seemingly at random, into a group of young people on their way home from Goose Fair, and a fourteen-year-old girl had died. There were stories of gun gangs and blood feuds in the media, of areas of the inner city running out of control, turf wars over drugs. Flowers and sermons, blame and recriminations and in the heart of the city a minute's silence, many people wearing the dead girl's favourite colours; thousands lined the streets for the funeral, heads bowed in respect.

Now this.

Understaffed as they were, low on morale and resources, policing the city, Resnick knew, was becoming harder and harder. In the past eighteen months, violent crime had risen to double the national average; shootings had increased four-fold. In Radford, Jamaican Yardies controlled the trade in heroin and crack cocaine, while on the Bestwood estate, to the north, the mainly white criminal fraternity was forging an uneasy alliance with the Yardies, all the while fighting amongst themselves; at either side of the city centre, multiracial gangs from St Ann's and The

Meadows, Asian and Afro-Caribbean, fought out a constant battle for trade and respect.

So was Alicia simply another victim in the wrong place at the wrong time? Or something more? The search for the car was on: best chance it would be found on waste land, torched; ballistics were analysing the bullets from the scene; Bradford Faye and his family were being checked through records; friends would be questioned, neighbours. The public relations department had prepared a statement for the media, another for the Assistant Chief Constable. Resnick sat in the CID office in Canning Circus station with Anil Khan and Detective Inspector Maureen Price from Serious Crime. His patch, their concern. Their case more than his.

Outside the sky had lightened a little, but still their reflections as they sat were sharp against the window's plate glass.

Maureen Price was in her early forties, no nonsense, matter-of-fact, wearing loose-fitting grey trousers, a zip-up jacket, hair tied back. 'So what do we think? We think they were targeted or what?'

'The girl?'

'No, not the girl.'

'The brother, then?'

'That's what I'm thinking.' The computer print-out was in her hand. 'He was put under a super-vision order a little over two years back, offering to supply a class A drug.'

7

'That's when he'd be what?' Khan asked. 'Fifteen?'

'Sixteen. Just.'

'Anything since?'

'Not according to this.'

'You think he could still be involved?' Resnick said.

'I think it's possible, don't you?'

'And this was what? Some kind of pay-back?'

'Pay-back, warning, who knows? Maybe he was trying to step up into a different league, change his supplier, hold back his share of the cut, anything.'

'We've checked with the Drug Squad that he's a player?' Resnick asked.

Maureen Price looked over at Khan, who shook his head. 'Haven't been able to raise anyone so far.'

The detective inspector looked at her watch. 'Try again. Keep trying.'

Freeing his mobile from his pocket, Khan walked towards the far side of the room.

'How soon can we talk to Bradford, I wonder?' Resnick said.

'He's most likely still in surgery now. Mid-morning, I'd say. The earliest.'

'You want me to do that?'

'No, it's OK. I've asked them to call me from Queen's the minute he's out of recovery. There's an officer standing by.' She moved from the desk where she'd been sitting, stretching out her arms

8

and breathing in stale air. 'Maybe you could talk to the family?' She smiled. 'They're on your patch, Charlie, after all.'

There were bunches of flowers already tied to the post into which the car had crashed, some anonymous, some bearing hastily written words of sympathy. More flowers rested up against the low wall outside the house.

The victim support officer met Resnick at the door.

'How they holding up?' he asked.

'Good as can be expected, sir.'

Resnick nodded and followed the officer into a narrow hall.

'They're in back.'

Clarice Faye sat on a green high-backed settee, her youngest daughter cuddled up against her, face pressed to her mother's chest. The middle daughter, Jade, twelve or thirteen, sat close but not touching, head turned away. Clarice was slender, light-skinned, lighter than her daughters, shadows scored deep beneath her eyes. Resnick was reminded of a woman at sea, stubbornly holding on against the pitch and swell of the tide.

The room itself was neat and small, knick-knacks and framed photographs of the children, uniform smiles; a crucifix, metal on a wooden base, hung above the fireplace. The curtains, a heavy stripe, were still pulled part-way across.

Resnick introduced himself and expressed his

sympathy; accepted the chair that was offered, narrow with wooden arms, almost too narrow for his size.

'Bradford – have you heard from the hospital?'

'I saw my son this morning. He was sleeping. They told me to come home and get some rest.' She shook her head and squeezed her daughter's hand tight. 'As if I could.'

'He'll be all right?'

'He will live.'

The youngest child began to cry.

'He is a good boy, Bradford. Not wild. Not like some. Not any more. Why would anyone . . . ?' She stopped to sniff away a tear. 'He is going to join the army, you know that? Has been for an interview already, filled in the forms.' She pulled a tissue, screwed and damp, from her sleeve. 'A man now, you know? He makes me proud.'

Resnick's eyes ran round the photographs in the room. 'Alicia's father,' he ventured, 'is he . . . ?'

'He doesn't live with us any more.'

'But he's been told?'

'You think he cares?'

The older girl sprang to her feet and half-ran across the room.

'Jade, come back here.'

The door slammed hard against the frame.

Resnick leaned forward, drew his breath. 'Bradford and Alicia, last night, you know where they'd been?'

'The Meadows. A friend of Bradford's, his eighteenth.'

'Did they often go around together like that, Bradford and Alicia?'

'Sometimes, yes.'

'They were close then?'

'Of course.' An insult if it were otherwise, a slight.

'And his girlfriend, she didn't mind?'

'Marlee, no. She and Alicia, they were like mates. Pals.'

'Mum,' the younger girl said, raising her head. 'Licia didn't like her. Marlee. She didn't.'

'That's not so.'

'It is. She told me. She said she smelled.'

'Nonsense, child.' Clarice smiled indulgently and shook her head.

'How about Alicia?' Resnick asked. 'Did she have any boyfriends? Anyone special?'

The hesitation was perhaps a second too long. 'No. She was a serious girl. Serious about her studies. She didn't have time for that sort of thing. Besides, she was too young.'

'She was sixteen.'

'Too young for anything serious, that's what I mean.'

'But parties, like yesterday, that was OK?'

'Young people together, having fun. Besides, she had her brother to look after her . . .' Tears rushed to her face and she brushed them aside.

The phone rang and the victim support officer

11

answered it in the hall. 'It's Bradford,' he said from the doorway. 'They'll be taking him back up to the ward any time.'

'Quickly,' Clarice said to her daughter, bustling her off the settee. 'Coat and shoes.'

Resnick followed them out into the hall. Door open, Jade was sitting on one of the beds in the room she and Alicia had obviously shared. Aware that Resnick was looking at her, she swung her head sharply towards him, staring hard until he moved away.

Outside, clouds slid past in shades of grey; on the opposite side of the narrow street, a couple slowed as they walked by. Resnick waited while the family climbed into the support officer's car and drove away . . . *A good boy, Bradford. Not wild. Not any more.* The crucifix. The mother's words. Amazing, he thought, how we believe what we want to believe, all evidence aside.

On the Ilkeston Road, he stopped and crossed the street. There were more flowers now, and photographs of Alicia, covered in plastic against the coming rain. A large teddy bear with black ribbon in a bow around its neck. A dozen red roses wrapped in cellophane, the kind on sale in garage forecourts. Resnick stooped and looked at the card. *For Alicia. Our love will live forever. Michael.* Kisses, drawn in red biro in the shape of a heart, surrounded the words.

Resnick was putting the last touches of a salad together when he heard Lynn's key in the lock. A sauce of spicy sausage and tomato was simmering on the stove; a pan of gently bubbling water ready to receive the pasta.

'Hope you're good and hungry.'

'You know . . .' Her head appearing round the door. '. . . I'm not sure if I am.'

But she managed a good helping nonetheless, wiping the spare sauce from her plate with bread, washing it down with wine.

'So – how was it?' Resnick asked between mouthfuls.

'All right, I suppose.'

'Not brilliant then.'

'No, some of it was OK. Useful even.'

'Such as?'

'Oh, ways of avoiding tunnel vision. Stuff like that.'

Resnick poured more wine.

'I just wish,' Lynn said, 'they wouldn't get you to play these stupid games.'

'Games?'

'You know, if you were a vegetable, what vegetable would you be? If you were a car, what car?'

Resnick laughed. 'And what were you?'

'Vegetable or car?'

'Either.'

'A first crop potato, fresh out of the ground.'

'A bit mundane.'

'Come on, Charlie, born and brought up in Norfolk, what do you expect?'

'A turnip?'

She waited till he was looking at his plate, then clipped him round the head.

Later, in bed, when he pressed against her back and she turned inside his arms, her face close to his, she said: 'Better watch out, Charlie, I didn't tell you what kind of car.'

'Something moderately stylish, compact, not too fast?'

'A Maserati Coupé 4.2 in Azuro Blue with full cream leather upholstery.'

He was still laughing when she stopped his mouth with hers.

The bullet that had struck Bradford's shoulder was a 9mm, most likely from a plastic Glock. Patched up, replenished with blood, Bradford was sore, sullen, and little else. Aside from lucky. His girlfriend, Marlee, had twenty-seven stitches in a gash in her leg, several butterfly stitches to one side of her head and face and bruises galore. The BMW was found on open ground near railway tracks on the far side of Sneinton, burned out. No prints, no ejected shell cases, nothing of use. It took the best part of a week, but thirty-seven of the fifty or so people who had been at the party in The Meadows were traced, tracked down and questioned. For officers, rare and welcome overtime.

The Drug Squad had no recent information to suggest that Bradford was again dealing drugs, but there were several people at the party well known to them indeed. Troy James and Jason Fontaine in particular. Both had long been suspected of playing an active part in the trade in crack cocaine: suspected, arrested, interrogated, charged. James had served eighteen months of a three-year sentence before being released; Fontaine had been charged with possession of three kilos of amphetamine with intent to supply, but due to alleged contamination of evidence, the case against him had been dismissed. More recently, the pair of them had been suspected of breaking into a chemist's shop in Wilford and stealing several cases of cold remedies in order to manufacture crystal meth.

James and Fontaine were questioned in the street, questioned in their homes; brought into the police station and questioned again. Bradford spent as much as fourteen hours, broken over a number of sessions, talking to Maureen Price and Anil Khan.

Did he know Troy James and Jason Fontaine?

No.

He didn't know them?

No, not really.

Not really?

Not, you know, to talk to.

But they were at the party.

If you say so.

Well, they were there. James and Fontaine.

OK, so they were there. So what?

15

You and Fontaine, you had a conversation.

What conversation?

There are witnesses, claim to have seen you and Fontaine in conversation.

A few words, maybe. I don't remember.

A few words concerning . . . ?

Nothing important. Nothing.

How about an argument . . . a bit of pushing and shoving?

At the party?

At the party.

No.

Think. Think again. Take your time. It's easy to get confused.

Oh, that. Yeah. It was nothing, right? Someone's drink got spilled, knocked over. Happens all the time.

That's what it was about? The argument?

Yeah.

A few punches thrown?

Maybe.

By you?

Not by me.

By Fontaine?

Fontaine?

Yes. You and Fontaine, squaring up to one another.

No. No way.

'There's something there, Charlie,' Maureen Price said. 'Something between Bradford and Jason Fontaine.'

16

They were sitting in the Polish Diner on Derby Road, blueberry pancakes and coffee, Resnick's treat.

'Something personal?'

'To do with drugs, has to be. Best guess, Fontaine and Ford were using Bradford further down the chain and some way he held out on them, cut the stuff again with glucose, whatever. Either that, or he was trying to branch out on his own, their patch. Radford kid poaching in The Meadows, we all know how that goes down.'

'You'll keep on at him?'

'The girlfriend, too. She's pretty shaken up still. What happened to Alicia. Keeps thinking it could have been her, I shouldn't wonder. Flakey as anything. One of them'll break sooner or later.'

'You seem certain.'

Maureen paused, fork halfway to her mouth. 'It's all we've got, Charlie.'

Resnick nodded and reached for the maple syrup: maybe just a little touch more.

The flowers were wilting, starting to fade. One or two of the brighter bunches had been stolen. Rain had seeped down into plastic and cellophane, rendering the writing for the most part illegible.

Clarice Faye came to the door in a dark house-coat, belted tight across; there were shadows still around her eyes.

'I'm sorry to disturb you,' Resnick said.

A slight shake of the head: no move to invite him in.

'When we were talking before, you said Alicia didn't have any boyfriends, nobody special?'

'That's right.'

'Not Troy James?'

'I don't know that name?'

'How about Jason? Jason Fontaine?

The truth was there on her face, a small nerve twitching at the corner of her eye.

'She did go out with Jason Fontaine?'

'She saw him once or twice. The end of last year. He came round here in his car, calling for her. I told him, he wasn't suitable, not for her. Not for Alicia. He didn't bother her again.'

'And Alicia . . . ?'

'Alicia understood.' Clarice stepped back and began to close the door. 'If you'll excuse me now?'

'How about Michael?' Resnick said.

'I don't know no Michael.'

And the door closed quietly in his face.

He waited until Jade was on her way home from school, white shirt hanging out, coat open, skirt rolled high over dark tights, clumpy shoes. Her and three friends, loud across the pavement, one of them smoking a cigarette.

None of the others as much as noticed Resnick, gave him any heed.

'I won't keep you a minute,' Resnick said as Jade stopped, the others walking on, pace slowed, heads turned.

'Yeah, right.'

'You and Alicia, you shared a room.'

'So.'

'Secrets.'

'What secrets?'

'Jason Fontaine, was she seeing him any more?'

Jade tilted back her head, looked him in the eye. 'He was just a flash bastard, weren't he? Didn't care nothin' for her.'

'And Michael?'

'What about him?'

'You tell me.'

'He loved her, didn't he?'

Michael Draper was upstairs in his room: computer, stereo, books and folders from the course he was taking at City College, photographs of Alicia on the wall, Alicia and himself somewhere that might have been the Arboretum, on a bench in front of some trees, an old wall, Michael's skin alongside hers so white it seemed to bleed into the photo's edge.

'She was going to tell them, her mum and that, after her birthday. We were going to get engaged.'

'I'm sorry.'

The boy's eyes empty and raw from tears.

Maureen Price was out of the office, her mobile switched off. Khan wasn't sure where she was.

'Ask her to call me when she gets a chance,' Resnick said. 'She can get me at home.'

At home he made sure the chicken pieces had finished defrosting in the fridge, chopped parsley, squashed garlic cloves flat, opened a bottle of wine, saw to the cats, flicked through the pages of the *Post*, Alicia's murder now page four. Art Pepper again, turned up loud. Lynn was late, no later than usual, rushed, smiling, weary, a brush of lips against his cheek.

'I need a shower, Charlie, before anything else.'

'I'll get this started.' Knifing butter into the pan.

It had cost Bradford a hundred and fifteen, talked down from one twenty-five. A Brocock ME38 Magnum air pistol converted to fire live ammunition. .22 shells. Standing there at the edge of the car park, shadowed, he smiled: an eye for an eye. Fontaine's motor, his new one, another Beamer, was no more than thirty metres away, close to the light. He rubbed his hands and moved his feet against the cold, the rain that rattled against the hood of his parka, misted his eyes. Another fifteen minutes, no more, he'd be back out again, Fontaine, on with his rounds.

Less that fifteen, it was closer to ten.

Fontaine appeared at the side door of the pub, calling out to someone inside before raising a hand and turning away.

Bradford tensed, smelling his own stink, his own fear; waited until Fontaine had reached towards the handle of the car door, back turned.

'Wait,' Bradford said, stepping out of the dark.

Seeing him, seeing the pistol, Fontaine smiled. 'Bradford, my man.'

'Bastard,' Bradford said, moving closer. 'You killed my sister.'

'That slag!' Fontaine laughed. 'Down on her knees in front of any white meat she could find.'

Hands suddenly sticky, slick with sweat despite the cold, Bradford raised the gun and fired. The first shot missed, the second shattered the side window of the car, the third took Fontaine in the face splintering his jaw. Standing over him, Bradford fired twice more into his body as it slumped towards the ground, then ran.

After watching the news headlines, they decided on an early night. Lynn washed the dishes left over from dinner, while Resnick stacked away. He was locking the door when the phone went and Lynn picked it up. Ten twenty-three.

'Charlie,' she said, holding out the receiver. 'It's for you.'

LEE CHILD

THE GREATEST TRICK OF ALL

I could have shot you in one ear and out the other from a thousand yards. I could have brushed past you in a crowd and you wouldn't have known your throat was cut until you went to nod your head and it rolled down the street without you. I was the guy you were worrying about when you locked your doors and posted your guards and walked upstairs to bed, only to find me already up there before you, leaning on the dresser, just waiting in the dark.

I was the guy who always found a way.

I was the guy that couldn't be stopped.

But that's over now, I guess.

None of my stuff was original. I studied the best of the best, long ago. I learned from all of them. A move here, a move there, all stitched together. All the tricks. Including the greatest trick of all, which I learned from a man called Ryland. Back in the day Ryland worked all over, but mainly where there was oil, or white powder, or money, or girls, or high-stakes card games. Then he got old, and he slowly withdrew. Eventually he found the matrimonial market. Maybe he invented it, although I doubt that. But certainly he refined it. He turned it into a business. He was in the right place at the right time. Getting old and slowing down, just when all those Californian lawyers made divorce into a lottery win. Just when guys all over the hemisphere started to get nervous about it.

The theory was simple: a live wife goes to a lawyer, but a dead wife goes nowhere. Except the cemetery. Problem solved. A dead wife attracts a certain level of attention from the police, of course, but Ryland moved in a world where a guy would be a thousand times happier to get a call from a cop than a divorce lawyer. Cops would have to pussyfoot around the grief issue, and there was a general assumption that when it came to IQ cops were not the sharpest chisels in the box. Whereas lawyers were like razors. And, of course, part of the appeal of a guy like Ryland was that evidence was going to be very thin on the ground. No question, a wife dead at Ryland's hands was generally considered to be a lottery win in reverse.

He worked hard. Hit the microfilm and check it out. Check newspapers all over the States and Central and South America. Look at Europe, Germany, Italy, anyplace where there were substantial fortunes at stake. Look at how many women went missing. Look at how old they were, and how long they had been married. Then check the follow-up stories, the inside pages, the later paragraphs, and see how many hints there were about incipient marital strife. Check it out, and you'll see a pattern.

The cops saw a pattern too, of course. But Ryland was a ghost. He had survived oil and dope and money lending and hookers and gambling. No way was he going to get brought down by greedy husbands and bored wives. He flourished, and I bet his name was never written down in any cop's file. Not anywhere, not once. He was that good.

He was working back in the days when billionaires were rare. Back then, a hundred million was considered a threshold level. Below a hundred mil, you were poor. Above, you were respectable. People called a hundred mil a unit, and most of Ryland's clients were worth three or four units. And Ryland noticed something: rich husband, rich wife. The wives weren't rich in the sense their husbands were, of course. They didn't have units of their own. But they had spending cash. It stands to reason, Ryland said to me. Guys set them up with bank accounts and credit cards. Guys worth three or four units don't like to trouble themselves with trivia down at the six-figure level.

But the six-figure level was where Ryland worked.

And he noticed that the blood he was spilling was dripping all over minks and diamond chokers and Paris gowns and perforated leather seats in Mercedes Benzes. He started searching purses after a while. There were big checking balances in most of them, and platinum cards. He didn't steal anything, of course. That would have been fatal, and stupid, and Ryland wasn't stupid. Not stupid at all. But he was imaginative.

Or so he claimed.

Actually I like to be believe one of the women handed the idea to him. Maybe one a little feistier than normal. Maybe when it became clear what was about to transpire she put in a counter-offer. That's how I like to think it all started. Maybe she said: 'That rat bastard. I should pay you to off him instead.' I know Ryland's ears would have pricked up at that. Anything involving payment would have gotten him interested. He would have run the calculation at the same hyper speed he used for any calculation, from a bullet's trajectory to a risk assessment. He would have figured: this chick can afford a six-figure coat, so she can afford a six-figure hit.

Thus, the greatest trick of all.

Getting paid twice.

He told me about it after he got sick with cancer, and I took it as a kind of anointment. The nomination of an heir. The passing of the baton. He wanted me to be the new Ryland. That was OK with me. I also took it as a mute appeal not to let him linger and suffer. That was OK with me too. He was frail by then. He resisted the pillow like crazy, but the lights went out soon enough. And there it was. The old Ryland gone, and the new Ryland starting out with new energy.

First up was a stout forty-something from Essen in Germany. Married to a steel baron who had recently found her to be boring. A hundred grand in my pocket would save him a hundred million in hers. Classically, of course, you would hunt and strike before she ever knew you were on the planet. Previously, that would have been the hallmark of a job well done.

But not anymore.

I went with her to Gstaad. I didn't travel with her. I just showed up there the next day. Got to know her a little. She was a cow. I would have gladly killed her for free. But I didn't. I talked to her instead. I worked her around to the point where she said, 'My husband thinks I'm too old.' Then she looked up at me from under her lashes. It was the usual reassurance-seeking crap. She wanted me to say. 'You? Too old? How could he think that about such a beautiful woman?'

But I didn't say that.

Instead, I said, 'He wants to get rid of you.'

She took it as a question. She answered. 'Yes, I think he does.'

I said, 'No, I know he does. He offered me money to kill you.'

Think about it. How was she going to react? No screaming. No running to the Swiss cops. Just utter stunned silence, under the weight of the biggest single surprise she could have heard. First, of course, the conceptual question: 'You're an assassin?' She knew people like me existed. She had moved in her husband's world for a long time. Too long, according to him. Then eventually, of course, after all the other questions, the inevitable inquiry: 'How much did he offer you?'

Ryland had told me to exaggerate a little. In his opinion it gave the victims a little perverse pleasure to hear a big number. It gave them a last shot at feeling needed, in a backhanded kind of a way. They weren't wanted anymore, but at least it was costing a lot to get rid of them. Status, of a sort.

'Two hundred thousand US dollars,' I said.

The fat Essen bitch took that in and then started down the wrong road.

She said, 'I could give you that not to.'

'Wouldn't work for me,' I said. 'I can't leave a job undone. He would tell people, and my reputation would be shot. A guy like me, his reputation is all he's got.'

Gstaad was a good place to be having the conversation. It was isolated and other-worldly. It was like there was just her and me on the planet. I sat beside her and tried to radiate sympathy. Like a dentist maybe. When he has to drill a tooth. I'm sorry . . . but it's got to be done. Her anger built, a little slow, but it came. Eventually she got on the right road.

'You work for money,' she said.

I nodded.

'You work for anyone who can pay the freight,' she said.

'Like a taxicab,' I said.

She said, 'I'll pay you to kill him.'

There was anger there, of course, but there were also financial considerations. They were forming slowly in her mind, a little vaguely, but basically they were the exact obverse of the considerations I had seen in the husband's mind a week previously. People like that, it comes down to just four words: all the money, mine.

She asked, 'How much?'

'The same,' I said. 'Two hundred grand.'

We were in Switzerland, which made the banking part easy. I stuck with her, supportive, and watched her get her fat pink paws on two hundred thousand US dollars, crisp new bills from some European country's central reserve. She gave them to me and started to explain where her husband would be, and when.

'I know where he is,' I said. 'I have a rendezvous set up. For me to get paid.'

She giggled at the irony. Guaranteed access to the victim. She wasn't dumb. That was the single greatest strength of Ryland's idea.

We went for a walk, alone, on a snow-covered track rarely frequented by skiers. I killed her there by breaking her fat neck and leaving her in a position that suggested a slip and a fall. Then I took the train back to Essen and kept my rendezvous with the husband. Obviously he had gone to great lengths to keep our meetings secret. He was in a place he wouldn't normally go, alone and unobserved. I collected my fee and killed him too. A silenced .22, in the head. It was an article of faith for people like Ryland and me. If you get paid, you have to deliver.

So, two fees, and all those steel units cascading down to fractious heirs that would be calling me themselves, soon enough. All the money, mine.

It went on like that for two years. Check the microfilm. Check the papers. North America, Central, South, all over Europe. Cops in a lather about anarchists targeting rich couples. That was another strength of Ryland's idea. It rendered the motive inexplicable.

Then I got an offer from Brazil. I was kind of surprised. For some reason I imagined their divorce laws to be old-fashioned and traditional. I didn't think any Brazilian guy would need my kind of help. But someone reached out to me and I ended up face to face with a man who had big units from mineral deposits and an actress wife who was sleeping around. The guy was wounded about it. Maybe that's why he called me. He didn't strictly need to. But he wanted to.

He was rich and he was angry so I doubled my usual fee. That was no problem. I explained how it would work. Payment after the event at a discreet location, satisfaction guaranteed. Then he told me his wife was going to be on a train, some kind of a long private club-car journey through the mountains. That was a problem. There are no banks on trains. So I decided to pass on Ryland's trick, just this one time. I would go the traditional single-ended route. The old way. I checked a map and saw that I could get on the train late and get off early. The wife would be dead in her sleeper when it rolled into Rio. I would be long gone by then.

It was comforting to think about working the old way, just for once.

I spotted her on the train and kept well back. But even from a distance I saw the ring on her finger. It was a gigantic rock. A diamond so big they probably ran out of carat numbers to measure it with.

That was a bank right there, on her finger.

Traceable, theoretically, but not through certain parts of Amsterdam or Johannesburg or Freetown, Sierra Leone. Potentially a problem at customs posts, but I could swallow it.

I moved up the train.

She was a very beautiful woman. Skin like lavender honey, long black hair that shone, eyes like swimming pools. Long legs, a tiny waist, a rack that was popping out of her shirt. I took the armchair opposite her and said, 'Hello'. I figured a woman who sleeps around would at least give me a look. I have certain rough qualities. A few scars, the kind of unkempt appearance that suggests adventure. She didn't need money. She was married to it. Maybe all she needed was diversion.

It went well at first and I found a reason to move around the table and slide into the chair next to her. Then within an hour we were well into that train-journey thing where she was leaning left and I was leaning right and we were sharing intimacies over the rush of the wind and the clatter of the wheels. She talked about her marriage briefly and then changed the subject. I brought it back. I pointed to her ring and asked her about it. She spread her hand like a starfish and let me take a look.

'My husband gave it to me,' she said.

'So he should,' I said. 'He's a lucky man.'

'He's an angry man,' she said. 'I don't behave myself very well, I'm afraid.'

I said nothing.

She said, 'I think he wants to have me killed.'

So there it was, the opening that was often so hard to work around to. I should have said, 'He sure does,' and opened negotiations. But I didn't.

She said, 'I look at the men I meet and I wonder, is this the one?'

So then I got my mouth working and said, 'This is the one.'

'Really?' she said.

I nodded. 'I'm afraid so.'

'You're not the first,' she said.

That threw me a little. But I came back with, 'But I'm the best.'

'You are?'

'I'm the one who can't be stopped.'

'I carry insurance,' she said.

She raised her hand again and all I saw was the

31

diamond. Hard to blame myself, because the diamond was so big and the stiletto's blade was so slender. I really didn't see it at all. Wasn't aware of its existence until its tip went through my shirt and pierced my skin. Then she leaned on it with surprising strength and weight. It was cold. And long. A custom piece. It went right through me and pinned me to the chair. She used the heel of her hand and butted it firmly into place. Then she used my tie to wipe the handle clean of prints.

'Goodbye,' she said.

She got up and left me there. I was unable to move. An inch left or right would tear my insides out. I just sat and felt the spreading stain of blood reach my lap. I'm still sitting there, ten minutes later. Once I could have shot you in one ear and out the other from a thousand yards. Or I could have brushed past you in a crowd and you wouldn't have known your throat was cut until you went to nod your head and it rolled down the street without you. I was the guy you were worrying about when you locked your doors and posted your guards and walked upstairs to bed, only to find me already up there before you, leaning on the dresser, just waiting in the dark.

I was the guy who always found a way.

I was the guy that couldn't be stopped.

Then I met Ryland.

And that's all over now.

ALEXANDER MCCALL SMITH

HE LOVED TO GO FOR DRIVES WITH HIS FATHER

I

This took place some time ago, in a country called Swaziland, a small landlocked kingdom in southern Africa. It is a country of great beauty, rising from a swathe of low country in the south to highlands in the north-west. When viewed from a distance, these northern hills seem impossibly blue, fading into the sky as gently as mist shades into the contours of the land. Along the east side of the country there is a range of mountains, the Lebombo Mountains, from the ridge of which one may look down into Mozambique below, and beyond that, when conditions are right, to the line of blue which is the Indian Ocean.

At that time, which was in the nineteen fifties, the country was a British protectorate, presided over by a Paramount Chief, Sobhuza II, who was later to be referred to as the king. He was a man of considerable wisdom, much admired by his people, who were an offshoot of the Zulu nation and who were proud of their heritage.

The Paramount Chief lived in a sprawl of buildings between the two main towns of the country, Mbabane, which was the capital, and Manzini, which was close in to the airstrip and the few factories which the country had. The Paramount Chief's place was at the foot of a small group of hills which was sacred to the Swazi nation, being the place where leaders were traditionally buried in caves, wrapped in the hides of their finest oxen. Nobody was allowed to scale those hills except on the occasion of a royal burial or similar ceremony.

II

There was a Scottish doctor who took up a post as government medical officer in Manzini. He was based at the hospital there – a rambling collection of buildings next door to a hotel called the Uncle Charlie Hotel. This hotel, which had a bar and a long veranda, also boasted a dining room in which a striking mural had been painted. This mural showed a great African lake, with palm trees and mopani forests about its edges. Giraffe and zebra were depicted moving across the savanna. Nobody paid much attention to this mural, which had been painted as a shallow strip around the top of the walls, just below the ceiling, but every now and then a visitor who saw its merits would stand and stare at it. Such people said that for some reason the mural made them sad. 'It shows the beauty of Africa distilled,' said one such visitor. 'And it shows us what is being lost.'

The doctor had been allocated a house in the town, close to the tennis courts. It was a good house, commensurate with his position in the community, and it boasted a particularly attractive garden. The previous medical officer, who had been a bachelor, had spent all his spare time in the garden and had stocked it colourfully and imaginatively. He had been particularly fond of bougainvillea, which grew in profusion along the side of the house and around the kitchen garden. The local man who helped him in the garden did not like the bougainvillea, which he said attracted snakes. Nor did he like that doctor's collection of aloes, which he said were poisonous, and which he hoped would die of neglect. But aloes thrive on neglect, and they continued to grow.

The new doctor appreciated the garden but did not take a strong interest in it. He enjoyed playing chess, and he would sit for hours on the veranda, working out chess problems using a set made by Italian prisoners of war. His wife, who was not interested in chess, was a keen member of the tennis club. She was a strong player and would give lessons to any of the other tennis-playing wives who were eager to improve their game. She never played with her husband, who said that he found tennis a dull game after the first few services had been knocked over the net.

After chess, the doctor's other passion was cars.

He was something of an amateur mechanic, and he would sometimes spend the whole weekend tinkering with the engine of the old green Pontiac which he had bought in Cape Town and driven all the way up to Swaziland. This car was his pride and joy until it was badly damaged in an accident on the road that ran from Manzini to Mbabane. This was a notoriously dangerous road, with its hairpin bends, and numerous vehicles had simply dropped over the edge, careering down through the undergrowth until they came to a ruinous halt against a tree or a granite boulder. In the accident which destroyed the doctor's car, neither he nor his wife was seriously hurt, although they were both shaken by the event.

'I don't want to drive anywhere at night in this country,' said the doctor's wife to one of her tennis partners. 'It's just too dangerous.'

III

After the loss of his green Pontiac, the doctor was obliged to buy a much less interesting car, a Volkswagen, which, although reliable and well suited to the country's unpaved roads, was dull to drive. The engine was not very powerful, and the doctor liked to be able to accelerate more quickly in order to pass trucks. Trucks, particularly the large cattle trucks, threw up a large cloud of dust behind them, and the doctor hated having to drive in that. But there was not a very wide

36

choice of cars in Swaziland at that time, and the doctor could not lay his hands on anything more interesting.

Some months after the doctor's road accident, the manager of the Uncle Charlie Hotel went off to Johannesburg for a weekend. This man was a thin-faced Englishman whose wife had left him because she could not bear what she described as the boredom of living in a colonial backwater like Swaziland. She had gone to Nairobi, where she had a cousin, and where she soon met and married a wealthy farmer. The manager of the Uncle Charlie Hotel was philosophical about this. 'She never loved me, anyway,' he said. People who heard him talk this way were shocked into silence. It was difficult to know what to say in the face of such a personal revelation.

When he went off to Johannesburg for his weekend, the doctor's wife said: 'Poor man, he deserves a bit of fun after putting up with that flighty woman. Let's hope he meets somebody in Johannesburg.'

The hotel manager did not meet somebody in Johannesburg, but he did come back with a different car from the one in which he had set off. This was a Mercedes-Benz, which, although not new, was a car of considerable character and charm. It had beige leather seats and a marvellous wooden steering wheel. It was one of the most striking cars in the whole country, and it was even said that the Paramount Chief had seen in on the road and asked whose it was and had expressed a desire to have a car like that at some point.

Everybody talked about his new Mercedes-Benz. It stood parked in front of the Uncle Charlie Hotel, where one of the junior waiters was detailed to wash and polish it every day, paying particular attention to the shiny chrome bumpers and the silver three-point symbol at the top of the radiator.

The doctor was particularly taken with this car. A few days after its arrival he was seen by somebody in the dining room of the hotel to pull up beside it in his Volkswagen, get out, and peer through the window, like a schoolboy. And some time after that he was heard to say to the hospital pharmacist, 'I'd kill for a car like that. I really would.'

The doctor's wife was indifferent to vehicles of any sort. 'Men are ridiculous,' she observed at the tennis club one afternoon. 'They love those bits of machinery as if they were . . . as if they were women. It's ridiculous.'

'I'd prefer my husband to have a love affair with a car than another woman,' said one of the other tennis players.

'That's true,' said the doctor's wife. 'But I still wish that men would just grow up. They're so immature.'

IV

When the wife of the manager of the Uncle Charlie Hotel had gone off to Kenya, she had left behind a child. This was a boy of eleven, who suffered affected brain development. This boy could walk unaided, but could not utter more than a few words. But he was not troublesome. He did not scream or wail, as can happen with some of these distressing conditions. He merely gazed out of the window and pointed at birds and animals which attracted his attention. He took particular pleasure in looking at cattle and would make a mooing sound in imitation as he watched them. The manager of the Uncle Charlie Hotel would drive his son out in the Mercedes-Benz at the end of the working day and take him for a short spin along the Siteki Road, slowing down when they came to cattle grazing at the side of the road. Then they would drive back before it got dark, which happens so suddenly in those latitudes. One minute it will be light and the next the sun will have disappeared behind the hills and the night will be filled with the screech and chirrup of nocturnal insects.

The boy loved the Mercedes-Benz. He would stand beside it for hours, looking into its gleaming paintwork as if it were a mirror.

V

Six months after the manager had gone to Johannesburg to fetch the car, there was an awful row one morning at the Uncle Charlie Hotel. The Mercedes-Benz, which had been parked at the front of the hotel overnight, was missing from its place. The manager called the police immediately, and the police inspector himself came over within twenty minutes in his grey Land Rover.

'Car theft,' said the inspector. 'It happens, you know. It'll be over the border by now, I'm afraid, probably taken into South Africa, although it might have been spirited up to Lourenço Marques. I'm very sorry about this, but I fear that's that. Have you got the chassis number, by the way?'

The manager did not have the chassis number. He had bought the car in a private sale, and he had not been given proper registration documents. So there was no record of this vital piece of information.

'Then it will not be possible for us to get the cooperation of the people over the border,' said the police inspector. 'We wouldn't be able to prove that it was stolen, even if they found it.'

The manager of the Uncle Charlie Hotel swore violently when he received this news. This did not please the police inspector, who told him to watch his tongue. 'I understand how you feel,' he said. 'But you don't swear like that in front of me. Understand?'

Everybody sympathised with the manager over his loss.

'It's a terribly sad thing,' said one of the members of the tennis club. 'He used to take that boy of his for those runs on the Siteki Road. I saw them. It was rather touching, I thought, with that little boy sitting there looking out of the side and smiling in that way of his. Poignant really.'

'The insurance will pay up,' said another.

'Maybe. But you can't replace those cars just like that.'

'True. You can't.'

VI

The doctor's wife was aware of the fact that her husband was working on a project with his friend Ed, a mechanic who had a small garage on a dirt road that led to the Umbeluzi River. She had met this man once before and did not like him. There was something about his eyes which made her uncomfortable. The whites of his eyes looked yellow.

'Fatty deposits in the eyes,' said the doctor. 'His cholesterol is out of control.'

'I still don't like him,' she said.

The doctor shrugged. He did not like some of the women at the tennis club, but he did not think it helpful to say so. 'We're fiddling about with an engine,' he explained. 'It's an old Rover and we're stripping it right down and reboring it. Complicated stuff. But Ed's good at that sort of thing and he's teaching me a lot.'

She said nothing to this. She was not interested in that sort of thing and she did not mind if that is how he wanted to spend his spare time. It was better than drinking, which is what a lot of people did in the evenings, out of sheer boredom.

Then one evening the doctor announced to her that he had managed to acquire a new car through Ed. It was a Mercedes-Benz, he said, and he was sure that she would like it. It was the same model as the one which had belonged to the manager of the Uncle Charlie Hotel, but it was a different colour. The manager's car had been red; this one was black.

'How much did it cost?' she asked. 'Was it expensive?'

The doctor hesitated for a moment – just a moment. 'No,' he said. 'It was a very good bargain.'

He brought the car back to the house the following evening. He parked it in front of the veranda and invited her to inspect it.

'It runs beautifully,' he said. 'I'll take you up to Mbabane in it if you like. We could go right now.'

'No thanks,' she said. 'I don't want to travel at night. And you shouldn't either, or this one will end up down the hill like the Pontiac.'

VII

The manager of the Uncle Charlie Hotel was astonished when he saw the doctor driving around in the Mercedes-Benz. 'It's the same model as mine was,' he said. 'Different colour. But otherwise the same. He's lucky to get a car like that.'

He asked the doctor one day whether he would

mind if he had a look at his new car. 'I'm pretty envious of you, doc,' he said. 'You know I had one just the same as that. I know how nice they are to drive. Lovely cars.'

'Yes,' said the doctor. He did not seem to be enthusiastic about showing his car to the manager, but he could hardly refuse. He drove it around one Saturday afternoon, and let the manager sit behind the wheel.

'Lovely workmanship,' said the manager, caressing the steering wheel. 'Beautiful.'

'Built to last,' said the doctor. 'I loved that old Pontiac of mine, but this is in a different league.'

'Take good care of it,' said the manager, ruefully. 'These things get stolen. And I suppose it's pretty easy to whip them away and then repaint them.'

The doctor nodded. 'I'll be careful,' he said. 'I put it away in my garage at nights, you know. That's the safest thing to do. And when I take it to the hospital, I park it right outside the main entrance where the porter can keep an eye on it.'

'Very wise,' said the manager. He fingered the steering wheel again, as if making contact with an old friend – an old friend who had been lost and was much regretted.

VIII

The doctor's wife left the household finances to her husband, who was good with accounts. She did not have a head for figures and simply drew on the housekeeping accounts that they kept in a small lock-up cupboard in the doctor's study. But one afternoon she was in the study, looking for an envelope, when she came across a file of bank statements. She decided, out of idle curiosity, to look at the regular withdrawals for obvious purposes: the payment of the account at the general store, the payment of the insurance premiums, and so on. That was all unexceptional. But then it occurred to her that it was strange that there was no payment for the new car. The money from the sale of the Volkswagen had been paid in, but nothing had gone out to pay for its replacement.

She reflected on her discovery that afternoon, and it suddenly occurred to her that the only explanation was that the car had cost him nothing. And then, while she was standing on the veranda, looking at a frangipani tree, the thought struck her: her husband must have stolen the car, taken it to Ed's, and repainted it. All he would have had to pay for was the paint, with perhaps a small amount for Ed's time and connivance. He could have managed to pay that out of his normal pin money.

She stood quite still for a while, trying to reach another, less disturbing conclusion; but she could not. She went out into the garden and walked about in the daisies that had been planted by the previous doctor. She sought another answer in the flowers, but there was none to be had. It appalled her to think that she lived with a man who was prepared to do that. But then she thought: do I really know him all that well? He never talks to me about the things that really move him. He never does that. He is a stranger in so many ways. Men were a different continent, she thought; distant, unpredictable. Perhaps I should not be surprised.

Then she debated with herself what she should do. She could not tell the manager of the Uncle Charlie Hotel that they had his car. She could not bear the shame that would follow. She imagined what they would say at the tennis club, what would be said behind her back. It would be intolerable to be the subject of such gossip. She would rather die than be disgraced in that way.

She would have to punish him herself, she thought. She would have to show him that he could not get away with a crime like that. She would be the agent of justice.

IX

The doctor's wife was not a keen driver, but she did occasionally drive the Mercedes-Benz to the tennis club or into town to buy meat and vegetables. Now she said to the doctor, 'I'd like to drive up to Mbabane some time next week to visit Jennifer. She's not been well and I want to catch up with her.'

He said, 'That's fine. I'll get one of the hospital drivers to pick me up. You take the car.'

45

She went off that day. She drove up towards Mbabane and stopped near the top of the long incline, near a place where the road bent sharply. She got out to stretch her legs and looked down over the edge. The ground fell away sharply, down to a stand of eucalyptus trees far below. She heard the sound of their leaves in the wind, a sound that drifted up on the warm afternoon air. It was a beautiful country, she thought. There was so much beauty in Africa, but such wickedness too.

She returned to the car. The road was deserted, and so there was nobody to see her drive very slowly to the very edge of the road and then get out. She leaned against the car, the engine of which was still idling. She pushed, and very slowly it moved forward and then, in a sudden lurch, slipped over the edge. There was a crumbling of sand and dust from the edge of the road and a sound of crushing metal and the breaking of small trees. She watched as the car went down, turned over, and broke into flames. She leant down, picked up a handful of dust, and rubbed it into her face and hair. Then she tore her dress, and scratched at her arm with a stick until a small, bright line of blood appeared.

X

The doctor said to her, 'I'm so glad that you weren't hurt. It's you I care about. I don't care about the car.'

She said, 'You don't care about the car? Are you sure of that?'

He shook his head. 'No. Human life is more important than a machine. The important thing is that you weren't hurt. Well, hurt a tiny bit, but not much.'

She was silent for a moment. Then she said. 'You don't care about the car?' She paused, then, quite softly, as if remarking on something unimportant, she said, 'Well, I suppose it wasn't really your car in the first place, was it?'

The doctor said nothing. They had been sitting on the veranda and he now rose to his feet and walked over to peer at one of the bougainvillea bushes that twisted itself around one of the veranda pillars. Then he looked back at her. She saw that his face was drawn, aghast, uncomprehending.

'That poor little boy,' she said. 'He loved to go for drives with his father.'

ROBERT GODDARD

TOUPEE FOR A BALD TYRE

A Misadventure from the Motor Trade
Years of Harry Barnett

Swindon, 24 September 1970

If he had stayed in the pub, even for another five minutes, it probably would have been all right. Rillington had more or less said as much, which only made the thought more tantalising. Another five minutes; another pint; another gently blurred afternoon; for once, they would have added up to prudent business practice. Instead, Harry had returned dutifully, if far from soberly, to Barnchase Motors at half past two that afternoon – and found a visitor waiting for him.

'I was just about to give up on you, Mr Barnett,' Rillington explained, smiling thinly.

Harry sensed it was the only kind of smile that ever crossed his face. Rillington was a lean, sombre, narrow-eyed man of sixty or so, grey-suited, grey-haired, grey-*skinned*. On the early morning train journey to work that Harry imagined him taking, he would attact no one's attention, draw no one's glance, challenge no one's preconceptions. Yet here, seated stiffly on the other side of Harry's desk, brief-case clasped flatly in his lap, pursed lips empha-sising his trimmed moustache, he did pose some kind of challenge. That much was already certain.

'Your secretary didn't seem to think it was worth my while waiting.'

'No?' Harry caught Jackie's eye through the glass partition between his office and the outer room where she firted occasional typing and telephone-answering into her nail-filing regime. Her devot-edly plucked eyebrows arched meaningfully. 'She must have misunderstood. With my partner away for the day—'

'That would be Mr Chipchase.'

'Yes. He, er . . .'

'Is cheering on a horse at Newbury even as we speak, I dare say.'

'Ah, you—'

'Your secretary mentioned he was . . . enter-taining some clients at the races.'

Clients? If only, Harry thought. But all he said was, 'Quite,' grinning manfully and shooting a glare at Jackie, who by chance or contrivance was no longer looking in his direction. His gaze reverted glumly to Rillington's card, which lay before him on the blotter, forming a small oblong of orderly typography in a jungle of scrawled tele-phone numbers, jotted mark-up calculations and obscene doodles.

C E Rillington
Motor Repairs Standards Assessor
H M Ministry of Transport
St Christopher House
LONDON SE1
Tel: 01-928-7999

'So what can I . . . do for you, Mr Rillington?'

'I'd like you to clarify a few points for me, Mr Barnett.'

'Oh yes?' Harry lit a cigarette, hoping he would appear what the advertisement for the brand promised – as cool as a mountain stream – but gravely doubting it. 'Smoke?' He proffered the pack to Rillington.

'I prefer a pipe.'

'Well . . .'

'Shall we get on, Mr Barnett? I'm sure we're both busy people.'

'Right.' Harry took a spluttering draw on the cigarette. 'Of course.'

'I popped into your workshop while I was waiting.'

'You did?'

'Young fellow called Vince showed me around.'

'Excellent.' I'll strangle Vince with a fan-belt, thought Harry. Slowly. 'Helpful lad.'

'Indeed. Not that he could help me with the . . . statistics of your operation.'

'No?'

'Your province, I rather think. Yours and . . . Mr Chipchase's.'

'Statistics, Mr Rillington? I'm not . . .'

'They can be the very devil, I find. But they tell a story. There's been a push to apply them to my field in particular since this government came into office. Computers are the future, Mr Barnett. We're only nibbling at the edges of what they can achieve.'

'Really? I don't know much about that kind of—'

'Take the Korek, for example. Feed its findings to a computer and—'

'The what?'

'The Korek, Mr Barnett. Not heard of it?'

'Dr Who's latest enemy?'

'Very amusing.' Rillington looked anything *but* amused. 'It's a machine that pulls out crushed car bodies, using air-operated rams to reverse the effects of a crash. We can then check the manufacturer's dimensions against the final size and shape.'

'Amazing.'

'And revealing. If the car fails to reach those dimensions, it's generally because it never did. Now, why might that be, do you suppose?'

'Can't imagine.'

'You're aware of the disreputable practice of welding together the intact halves of two damaged cars to produce what looks, to a hapless buyer's eye, like a pristine ready-to-drive-away bargain?'

'Well, I . . .'

'The Korek finds that trick out every time.'

51

'Does it?' Harry distractedly tapped ash off his cigarette and locked eyes hopelessly with Monsieur Michelin, who beamed up at him from his perch on the rim of the ashtray. 'How very clever of it.'

'Now, taken together with a separate investigation of tyre blow-outs where the driver, if he or she is lucky enough to emerge in one piece, reports recently fitting remoulds which, upon inspection—'

'What have remoulds got to do with body welding?'

'At first glance, nothing, Mr Barnett. But therein lies the beauty of the computer. It correlates the statistics, you see. It crunches the numbers and spits out . . . overlaps.'

'Overlaps?'

'Common sources . . . of cars that fail the Korek test . . . and tyres that have been remoulded a couple of times too many. At *least* a couple of times.'

'I see.' Dimly and queasily, Harry did indeed begin to see. The blind eye he had long turned to Chipchase's profitable innovations on the repair front had suddenly descried a disturbing vision.

'Bad luck? Bad workmanship? Or something more sinister? That's what we're bound to ask ourselves when the statistics point us so compellingly to a particular garage.'

'Well, I . . .' Harry puffed out his cheeks. 'I suppose you would be.'

'Vince and his less talkative colleague . . . Joe is it?'

'That's right.'

'They both seemed competent enough to me. Capable, even. Well capable.'

'Oh . . . good.'

'And I don't believe in luck.'

'You don't?'

'Which brings us—'

'Here's that tea I promised you, Mr Rillington,' trilled Jackie, as she toed the door abruptly open and entered with a tray bearing two cups and saucers and a plate of digestive biscuits. 'And coffee for you, Mr Barnett.' *Mr Barnett?* Jackie was evidently on her best behaviour, a small mercy for which Harry could not summon much gratitude. 'Black, I reckoned. Was that right?'

'Spot on,' mumbled Harry, noticing as Jackie plonked the tray down on the desk that Rillington's gaze left him and slid appreciatively up Jackie's long and shapely legs to the hem of her miniskirt, which at that height Harry judged could scarcely be concealing very much. The man was evidently not immune to temptation. A chink in the armour, perhaps? But a small chink, in evidently thick armour.

Jackie minced out. Rillington's eyes swung back to Harry. 'Sugar?' Harry ventured.

'No thank you.'

'Biscuit?'

'Just the tea, I think.' Rillington took a sip.

'Righto.' A gulp of strong black coffee cleared the last of the fog from Harry's brain. But clarity did not furnish inspiration. 'So, where, er . . . were we?'

'How long have you and Mr Chipchase been in business together, Mr Barnett?'

'It's, er . . . five years now.'

'Did you take this place over from someone else?'

'Knight's Motorcycles. They, er . . . went bust.'

'And how long had *they* been in business?'

'Oh, seven or eight years. Until the late Fifties there were fields here. The Belmont Brewery used to graze their dray-horses—' Harry broke off, smiling awkwardly. 'I'm sure you don't want a local history lesson.'

Rillington turned and squinted out through the window into the serried ranks of Barnchase Motors' used cars, gleaming in the sunshine on the forecourt laid where Harry had once as a child fed carrot-tops to Belmont's magnificent beast of burden. 'Sounds like a veritable lost Eden,' Rillington murmured.

'I wouldn't go that far.'

'And we can't turn back the clock anyway, can we, Mr Barnett?'

'Fraid not.'

'Good Lord.' Rillington's squint honed itself into a concentrated peer. 'Is that an E-Type you have out there?'

'Yes. I, er . . . believe it is.' A midnight-blue 1962

Jaguar E-Type 3.8, to be precise. A snip at four hundred and ninety-nine guineas. A snip, indeed, at whatever price Rillington might be willing to pay. 'Fancy a test drive?' Harry asked impulsively.

'I wouldn't mind . . . taking a look.' A tinge of pleasurable anticipation had crossed Rillington's face. He sipped his tea, but his eyes remained fixed on the shimmering come-hither bonnet of the E-Type. Here was a second chink in his armour, one Harry was far better placed to exploit than the fleshy allurement of Jackie Fleetwood. 'I wouldn't mind at all.'

No more than a few minutes later, the two men were seated side by side in the car, Rillington's hands sliding slowly round the steering-wheel while Harry jingled the ignition key against the Jaguar's-head fob in what he judged to be a tempting tintinnabulation.

'Nought to sixty in seven seconds,' he purred. 'Top speed of a hundred and fifty. Really blows the cobwebs away.'

'I'm sure,' said Rillington.

'I could do a very special deal . . . for someone in your position.'

'No doubt.'

'What do you normally drive, Mr Rillington?'

'A Hillman Imp.'

'Well . . . need I say more?'

'Probably not.'

'Why don't you take her for a spin?'

'It's an idea.' Rillington smiled, less thinly than before, and moved his left hand from the steering-wheel towards the dangled ignition key. 'But not as good as *my* idea.' His hand froze.

'Sorry?'

'Once my report on this place hits the appropriate desk, you'll be for the high jump, Harry.' *Harry?* 'You and your race-going chum, Barry. It could be a police matter. It could be . . . the end of the line.'

Harry swallowed hard. 'Surely . . . not.'

'Oh yes.'

'But . . .'

'Cut as many corners as you have here and, sooner or later, you're bound to come to grief.'

'But . . .'

'Fortunately for you, there's a way out.'

'There is?'

'And it doesn't involve me taking this overpowered heap of junk off your hands.'

'No?'

'No. It involves something more . . . *recherché*. Which isn't French for remould.'

'I, er . . . don't . . .'

'Need to say a thing. Just listen. While I tell you a little story.' Rillington leant back in his seat. 'I used to do a bit of cycling, you know. Took it seriously. CTC membership. Fifty miles every weekend. Eighty every other. Proper racing bike. No half measures. Then, one Sunday morning, the bike let me down. The gears seized solid. There wasn't a thing I could do with it. I hadn't got far, so I wheeled it home, planning to strip it down in the garage. I got back several hours before I was due, of course. Bit of a surprise for the wife. More of one for me, though. I caught her with the husband of one of her Townswomen's Guild friends. In a compromising position, you might say. Very compromising. In fact, so compromising I'd never even thought of it. An eye-opener. Yes. You could certainly call it that. Now, why am I telling you this pitiful tale of the cuckolded suburbanite?' Good question, Harry thought. 'Well, you may be surprised to learn that Mrs Rillington and I are still together. It was a simple choice really. I preferred trying to satisfy her exotic tastes to indulging my hurt pride and turning into a bitter and lonely old man. To tell the truth, I *enjoyed* trying to satisfy her tastes. And, if I say so myself, I succeeded beyond her expectations. She no longer needed to look elsewhere. Oh my word no. But continued success required continuous innovation. Mrs Rillington has recently expressed her interest in unusual locations for lovemaking. Bearing in mind her enthusiasm for all things rubber, I think I may have found an ideal venue. Your workshop, Harry. Plenty of tyres, most of them bald enough to avoid tread marks, adaptable to any required height or juxtaposition. And plenty of authentic, grease-smeared, petroleum-scented atmosphere. I can see it now. I almost feel it now. As for Mrs Rillington . . .' Rillington

57

released a long, slow anticipatory breath. 'Enough said, I rather think.'

'You want to . . . use our workshop to . . .'

'It's her birthday tonight, Harry. We're making a long weekend of it. Starting tonight.'

'*Tonight?*'

'Why not?'

'Well, I . . .'

'Barnchase Motors can get a tick in every box from me. *If* you help me out. But if you're going to go all prissy on me . . .'

Harry smiled nervously. 'There's no question of that. I mean in this line of business, the customer is always right.'

'Glad to hear it. So . . .' Rillington flicked the still suspended ignition key with his forefinger. 'I don't think that's the right key. Do you?'

'Didn't think you'd get rid of him so easily,' said Jackie when Harry returned to the office after giving Rillington his key to the side-door of the workshop. 'I told Barry he had bad news written all over him.'

'Barry?'

'He phoned while you were out on the forecourt. Wanted to make sure everything was going smoothly, apparently.'

'I trust you told him it was.'

'Not exactly, no. Well, I didn't think it was, did I?'

'So, will Barry be rushing back to bale me out?'

'Didn't get that impression. Anyway, you don't need baling out now, do you?'

'No. As a matter of fact, I don't.'

'How *did* you get rid of him, then?'

'Who?' Harry countered coyly.

'Rillington. The guy with the wig.'

'Wig?'

'That hair's never natural. Didn't you notice?'

'Can't say I did.'

'Creepy, I'd call him. Could be a bit of a pervert on the quiet.'

'You reckon?'

'With that wig? And those X-ray eyes of his? Definitely kinky, I'd say.'

'Would you?' Harry yawned, exhaustion pouncing on him now the crisis was past. He could feel a doze coming on. 'Would you really?'

Harry was the last to leave Barnchase Motors that afternoon. Chipchase had not returned, which would have been unsurprising in the normal course of events but was utterly predictable given what Jackie had told him. MoT officials were not his company of choice. He was probably skulking in a pub in Newbury, fearing the worst. The thought gave Harry some small amount of pleasure. He would have to have a serious word with him about what Joe and Vince had been getting up to at his instigation. Harry would have to put his foot down. Firmly.

But that could wait. There was an evening of

gentle recuperation to be passed first. A pint at the Beehive; collection of dirty washing from his house; delivery thereof to his dear and doting mother, followed by consumption of one of her steak and kidney puddings; several more pints at the Glue Pot, and an earlyish night. Just the therapy his frayed nerves needed. As for what might be happening in the workshop back at Barnchase Motors while he was thus engaged, he could only imagine. With relief as well as incredulity.

Chipchase finally put in an appearance as Harry was nearing the end of his first pint at the Glue Pot, entering the bar with his coat collar turned up and the brim of his racing felt angled over his eyes as if he was intent on being taken for a fugitive.

'Hellfire, Harry,' he said as he sat down. 'Am I pleased to see you.'

'Worried about me, were you Barry?'

'You bet.'

'But not enough to hurry back and face the music with me?'

'Well, pulling the wool over some nitpicking bureaucrat's eyes is more your speciality than mine. I didn't want to cramp your style.'

'That a fact?'

'And you look chipper enough, so I'm guessing you got said bureaucrat off our backs.'

'You guess right.'

'How'd you manage that?'

'All in good time, Barry. Let's begin with *why* he was on our backs in the first place.'

Chipchase's response to Harry's account of Rillington's visit to Barnchase motors was a characteristic blend of bombast and blandishment: Harry had never wanted to know exactly how the profits he shared in had been generated and it was too late to start now, even supposing there was any substance to Rillington's accusations, which naturally there was not; but Harry's negotiation of a solution to the problem qualified as a redeeming masterstroke.

'Wouldn't mind being a fly on the workshop wall tonight, hey? You played a blinder there, Harry old cock, you really did.'

'I'm glad you think so.' Harry was finding censoriousness difficult to maintain as pint and lurid images filled his mind.

'Got a mental picture of Mrs Rillington, have you?'

'Big woman, I should think.'

'Yeah. With a bit of a spare tyre.'

Harry finally cracked at that and descended into tearful mirth. 'Several spare tyres tonight,' he managed to say.

'In all kinds of juxtapositions,' Barry hooted.

'Oh dear, oh dear.' Harry dried his eyes as best he could. 'I wonder if his toupee'll stay on.'

'I doubt it.'

'*Did you say toupee?*'

They did not at first appreciate that the question had come from a third party. Eventually, however, as the gale of their laughter blew itself out, they noticed a man staring at them round the corner of the settle. He was a small, shrunken, whey-faced fellow of indeterminate age, dressed in a threadbare ratcatcher's coat and a greasy pork-pie hat.

Without waiting for an answer, he slid round, Mackeson in hand and joined them at their table. 'Sounds like you could be talking about a mate of mine.'

'I doubt it,' said Harry.

'Fred Christie. Streaky, hawk-eyed bloke with a 'tache but not a strand of hair north of his eyebrows to call his own.'

'Never met him.'

'Are you sure about that? Only—'

'What does your mate do for a living?' put in Chipchase.

'How d'you mean?'

'Simple question, old cock. What's his line of work?'

'Well . . .'

'And what's yours, while we're about it?'

'Look . . .' The man leant forward and lowered his voice. 'I need to find Fred. Pronto. If you know where he is, I could, er, make it worth your while to point me in the right direction.'

'But Harry's already told you. We've never met him.'

'He, er, could be using a false name.'

'Oh yeah? Why might that be?'

'Let's just say . . . there are reasons.'

'Then we'd best be hearing what they are.'

'They're, er, private. Between him and me.'

'Not any more they aren't.' Chipchase gave the man a less than genial wink. 'Not if you want to get a chance to talk them over with Fred.'

'Are you saying you know where he is?'

'I'm saying we'll come clean if you'll come clean.'

The man squinted at each of them in turn. He did not look persuaded of the case for soul-baring.

'Have a think about it,' Chipchase continued. 'Harry and I are just off. We'll wait in my car. It's the Wolseley parked over the road. Two minutes.' He raised a pair of fingers. 'Then we skedaddle. So . . . don't think about it too long.'

'What are you playing at, Barry?' Harry demanded as soon as they were outside.

'Following my nose, Harry. Always a good policy.'

'You can't seriously think that creep really is a friend of Rillington's.'

'The description matched, didn't it?'

'That's rich. I was the one who met Rillington, not you.'

'Thin. Moustache. Toupee. You telling me that isn't Rillington?'

'I'm telling you—'

Chipchase whipped the driver's door open and flung himself in, slamming it behind him. Harry sighed heavily, opened the passenger door and clambered in.

'I'm telling you,' Harry resumed in a level tone, 'that there isn't a single good reason to believe a word this bloke says.'

'No?'

'Of course not.'

'How about your MoT man's choice of moniker?'

'What?'

'According to our friend, his real name's Christie.'

'So?'

'Like the murderer.'

'Like the actress too. And the whodunit writer. I don't see—'

'Never mind them. Where did Christie the *murderer* live, Harry? Tell me that. Surely you remember. It was all over the papers.'

Enlightenment dawned slowly on Harry in the Swindonian night. Christie the murderer. Of course. Harry had even flicked through a book about the case his mother had borrowed from the library. He really should have remembered the title. His pseudo-civil-servant visitor of earlier in the day clearly had. 'Ten Rillington Place,' he murmured.

'Exactly.'

'Bloody hell.'

'Looks like you've been had, Harry. And here comes the man who can tell us why.' A shadowy figure in a pork-pie hat had just emerged from the Glue Pot. He peered suspiciously about him, then headed towards them. 'Leave this to me.'

As the man slid into the seat behind them, Harry sensed all was not quite right.

Long before he could have said why, however, he felt something cold and hard pressing into the back of his neck.

'Yes, Harry, it's a gun,' Fred Christie, aka C E Rillington of the Ministry of Transport. 'One false move by you or Barry and your brains will be all over the windscreen.'

'Bloody hell.'

'Exactly. Very bloody indeed.'

'Calm down, mate,' said Chipchase, characteristically recommending a course of action he was obviously not following himself. 'There's no—'

'I'm not your mate, Barry. And I'm perfectly calm, thank you. But I *am* a little short of time and patience, so we'll dispense with the niceties. I tried the roundabout route and it didn't work. How much did Arnie tell you?'

'You mean the owner of that hat?'

'The very same.'

'Well, nothing really, except he knew you . . . and . . .'

'You weren't from the MoT,' Harry finished off, swallowing hard. 'We, er, stepped out here for a word in private.'

'And that's what we're having, Harry. Arnie's collecting his thoughts in the Gents. He'll be collecting them for quite a while, actually, so there's no immediate rush, but we do need to press on. Once I'd checked the workshop, I realised we'd have to resume our conversation on a more realistic basis. I asked after you at the pub where you take your liquid lunch and the mention of several other watering holes where I might find you. This was second on the list. I imagine Arnie came here because it's close to the station. He'd have been hoping to get some directions. Geography's not his strong point. Never was.'

'You and he . . . go back a long way, do you?'

'Too long. But let's get to the point. Where's my money?'

'Money?'

'Don't act dumb with me. I kept a careful mental note of the burial spot. It was a tricky exercise, pacing out across your yard and workshop what I originally paced out across a field. But there's not a shadow of a doubt. I checked and double-checked. The inspection pit is exactly where I buried the money – and several feet deeper than I dug. Well, Arnie did most of the digging, to tell the truth, but that doesn't give him any prior claims in my judgement, considering I went down for a longer stretch and we'd have been caught in possession, but for me thinking on my feet.

Now, you said Knight's Motorcycles owned the site before you, didn't you, Harry?'

'Yes,' came a hoarse response in what Harry barely recognised as his own voice.

'Did they have an inspection pit?'

'No.'

'So, you installed it?'

'Yes.'

'In that case, I return to my original question: where's my money?'

'We don't know,' said Chipchase.

'You dug the pit. Harry's just admitted it. You couldn't have avoided finding the money.'

'*We* didn't dig it. We got a builder in.'

'Sharland,' said Harry, his heart sinking as he realised the significance of the builder's identity.

'Now it was Chipchase's turn to say, 'Bloody hell.'

'What about Sharland?' snapped Christie.

'Our workshop was the last job he ever did,' Chipchase replied. 'He had a big Pools win straight after and retired.'

'A Pools win?'

'So he said.'

'And where did he retire to?'

'Spain, wasn't it, Harry?'

'Florida, I heard.'

'*Shut up.*' The pressure against Harry's neck increased. 'Why should I believe any of this?'

'Well, there's the fact that Sharland's bronzing himself in some palatial villa in the sun . . .' Chipchase began.

'While we're still stuck here in Swindon,' Harry rounded off.

'Bit of a choker for all of us,' Chipchase went on. 'No wonder the last time I saw the bloke he was grinning like the cat that's got the cream. Not that I know how much cream there was, of course.'

Christie said nothing. Harry's heart was thumping in his ears. A rivulet of sweat was inching down his temple. His breaths came fast and shallow.

'What now?' Chipchase asked eventually.

'Now?' Christie responded, as if from some more distant place than the rear seat of the car. 'You'd better start driving.'

'Where to?'

'Head west. Towards the motorway.'

'There's not a lot more we can—'

'*Just drive.*'

'OK, OK.'

The bleak thought formed in Harry's mind that this was likely to be a one-way journey. Either Christie believed them, in which case he was probably planning to kill them before going after Sharland. Or he did not believe them, in which case . . .

'That's funny.' Chipchase had got no response from the starter. He turned the ignition key off, then back on and tried the starter again. To no effect. 'The engine's dead.'

'Don't play games with me,' said Christie. 'Start the bloody car.'

'I can't.' There was another futile wrestle with ignition key and starter. 'It's dead as a doornail.'

'Do you take me for a fool? *Get this thing moving.*'

'I can't, I tell you.'

'Barry,' Harry put in, 'for God's sake—'

'I'm not kidding, Harry. It's kaput.'

'But you've just driven it from Newbury.'

'I know, I know. It doesn't make sense.' Chipchase glanced back at Christie. 'Why don't I take a look under the bonnet. There must be a loose connection.'

'There'd need to be a loose connection under *my* bonnet to fall for that one.'

'It's God's honest truth. I don't know what's the matter with the thing. Let me give it the once-over. You'll still have Harry as hostage. I'm not going to leg it with an old mate's life on the line, am I?'

Harry closed his eyes for a second, praying silently that Chipchase might once be relied upon.

'All right,' said Christie after a long and breathless moment's thought. 'Go ahead.' He pushed his door open. 'But remember: I'll have time to plug you as well as Harry if you try to scarper.'

'OK. Understood.' Chipchase climbed out, moved round to the front of the car and raised the bonnet, obscuring their view of him.

'*Stand where I can see you,*' shouted Christie.

Chipchase edged back into view round the near-side wing. He secured the bonnet-strut, then peered down into the engine.

'*Now you know how it feels.*'

The voice had carried distinctly through the still

night air, though where it had carried *from* Harry could not have said. His eyes swivelled in search of the source.

'That Zephyr you sold me conked out the second trip I took in it.' The source materialised in Harry's field of vision, striding towards Chipchase along the pavement. 'And what did that mealy mouthed partner of yours say? Not our problem. Well, it is *now*.' It was Mr Gifford, outraged and out-of-pocket buyer of one of Barnchase Motors' less durable used cars. Harry recalled a recent conversation with him. It had not ended harmoniously. 'Since I can't drive my car, I don't see why you should be able to drive yours, *Mr* Chipchase.'

Chipchase seemed lost for words. He glanced up at the approaching figure of Gifford – a bullet-headed, square-shouldered fellow carrying some weight he looked intent on throwing around – then gaped helplessly back at Harry through the windscreen.

'There's *Mr* Barnett as well,' roared Gifford, pointing an accusing finger at Harry. 'Get yourself out here and join the fun, why don't you?'

'Bloody hell,' murmured Harry.

'Come on.' Gifford yanked Harry's door open. 'Let's be having you.'

'Bugger it,' said Christie. Quietly and decisively.

Harry flinched at the words and closed his eyes, reckoning the odds were heavily weighted in favour of Christie pulling the trigger at that moment.

70

But he did not pull the trigger.

The pressure was suddenly removed from Harry's neck. There was a scuffling sound behind him. Then a pounding of running feet on paving stones. He opened his eyes. Both Chipchase and Gifford were looking past the car along the street. Harry turned to look in the same direction.

Just in time to see the pork-pie-hatted, toupee-sporting figure of Fred Christie vanishing at a trot round the corner into Faringdon Road.

'Who's that?' demanded Gifford.

'You don't want to know,' Chipchase replied, leaning back against the wing of the Wolseley and tipping up the brim of his hat to wipe the sweat off his brow. 'Believe me.'

'I thought . . . he was going to shoot me,' Harry said unevenly. He made to climb out of the bar, but his legs buckled beneath him. Gifford had to help him out in the end, frowning in puzzlement at his sudden conversion from saboteur to saviour.

'What's going on?' Gifford asked, almost solic-itously.

'Long story,' said Harry.

'He dropped the gun,' said Chipchase, pointing to a dark shape lying a few feet away in the gutter. 'Can you believe it? He dropped it and ran.'

'Gun?' Gifford stared at them in astonishment. 'You mean there are customers of yours even more pissed off than me?'

'In a sense,' mumbled Harry.

'But a *gun*? That's a bit strong.' Gifford stepped

towards the discarded weapon, then stopped – and laughed.

'What's so funny?' growled Chipchase.

'This gun.' Gifford stooped and picked it up.

'Be careful with it.'

'Don't worry. It's not connected.'

'Connected?'

'It's a petrol-pump nozzle.' Gifford held it up for them to see. And a petrol pump nozzle was indeed what they beheld. 'Gallon of thin air for you two?'

'Bloody hell,' said Harry.

'He must have filched it from the workshop,' said Chipchase.

'Let's hope that's all he filched.'

'*Where's he gone?*'

The shout had come from the doorway of the Glue Pot. They turned to see Arnie, bare-headed and even wobblier on his feet than Harry, staring blearily across at them and rubbing what was presumably a tender spot behind is left ear.

'That way,' said Harry and Barry in unison, pointing in the direction Christie had taken off in.

'He won't give me the slip this time,' Arnie declared optimistically before setting off in tepid pursuit.

A brief silence, borne of general disbelief, fell upon them. Then Chipchase said, 'Maybe we should phone the police.'

'Never thought I'd hear those words coming out of your mouth, Barry,' Harry responded, truthfully enough.

'Neither did I.' Chipchase shrugged. 'Anyway, I only said *maybe*.'

'What about my car?' Gifford cut in, seeming suddenly to remember his grievance.

'What about *mine*?' Chipchase countered.

'Listen.' Harry's spirits had revived sufficiently for him to assume the role of conciliator. 'Come to the office tomorrow, Mr Gifford, and I'll give you a full refund for the Zephyr, plus ten per cent for the inconvenience you've been put to.'

'If you think you can fob me off with a rubber cheque, you've got—'

'Cash in hand. And call it quits. Provided you replace whatever vital part you took out of this Wolseley, of course.'

'Well . . .' Gifford softened. 'I suppose . . . that'd be all right.'

'Hold up, Harry,' said Chipchase under his breath. 'I know you've just had a nasty experience, but don't you think you're getting a bit carried away? A *full refund*?'

'In the circumstances, I reckon we can afford to be generous.'

'Yeah? Well, there's generous and there's over-generous and then there's plain bloody crazy. We don't have to—'

'Tell you what, Barry. You can stay out here and haggle with Mr Gifford if you like. Or you can join me in the pub. But I need a drink. And it won't wait.'

So saying, Harry turned and steered a straightish

path across the street towards the Glue Pot, tossing back a concluding comment over his shoulder as he went.

'It's up to you.'

DANUTA REAH

NO FLIES ON FRANK

Frank Stout was a serial killer. He hadn't intended to be – he'd always planned to be an accountant. But instead, he became a serial killer who raised maggots.

This is how it happened.

Some of us – a few – are born to maggots. Some of us – most, in fact – achieve maggots eventually. And some of us have maggots thrust upon us. Frank's father, Harry Stout, achieved maggots earlier than most. He was thirty when he lost his job as a clerk in a local tax office. He read through his notice of redundancy with a growing sense of dread. He and his wife, Cynthia, had just bought, at more expense than Harry had ever imagined, a small semi on a modern housing estate at the edge of town. They would have to sell up. They would have to move, though Harry couldn't think where. Cynthia would not be happy.

She wasn't. Jobs were scarce, and Harry had not been able to find other employment. Cynthia was still expanding on her displeasure six weeks later over breakfast. 'It's no wonder no one wants to take you on,' she was saying as she cracked the shell of her egg with a sharp rap. 'Look at you. You're . . .'

The letter box rattled, and Harry escaped to collect the post. There were three letters, all addressed to him. Cynthia opened them. One was from a credit company offering to lend them improbable amounts of money at interest rates that were very small, at least as far as the font size went; a letter in a somewhat larger font telling them that if they didn't pay off their mortgage arrears they would be evicted; and there was a third letter. Cynthia studied the envelope. 'Cowlishaw and Thring,' she said. 'Solicitors.' She fixed her husband with a suspicious gaze. 'What have you been up to now, Harry?'

Harry concentrated on his cornflakes. She opened the envelope and slowly unfolded the sheets of paper inside.

Harry hadn't been up to anything. It was his uncle, Ted Stout, who had, or rather, who wouldn't be up to anything much any more. He had died, leaving his nephew as his sole surviving relative and the heir to his estate, the smallholding and farmhouse that Harry had visited when he was a child.

'Meadowsweet Farm,' Cynthia said, after she had read the letter. 'Meadowsweet Farm, Honeysuckle Lane, Lark Meadows . . .' She looked at her husband with more favour than she was generally given to. 'Well. I've never lived in the country. I suppose it will have to do.' And she consented to leave the tiny semi and move north to take over the tenancy of Meadowsweet Farm.

Harry had vague memories of the farm. As he, Cynthia and their six-year-old son, Frank, drove north, he let himself dream a little, about meadows full of wild flowers and hills in a misty blue distance. He was a man who had yet to learn the danger in dreams.

Times had changed since his childhood visits. The road that led to the farm was still called Honeysuckle Lane, the area where the farm stood was still called Lark Meadows, but the signpost pointing in the direction of the farm said, perhaps unintentionally, all that was needed: Municipal Dump.

The fields had vanished under industrial shacks, the hedgerows had been grubbed out, the lanes had become roads, and the pastures where the cows used to graze had become a landfill site, run by Meadowlands Waste Management, plc.

'You've made me move to a rubbish tip,' Cynthia sobbed to her husband as he unpacked their bags from the car. 'My mother told me you'd never amount to anything, but I didn't listen to her, fool that I was!'

Uncle Stout's old dog, Mortimer, uncurled from the blanket under the sink where he slept, and crept out, roused by the noise. 'And you can get rid of that!' Cynthia wept, pointing at him.

Mortimer sat back on his hind legs and started scratching with a *scruff, scruff* sound. Frank, curious, reached out his hand and touched the rough hair. His mother screamed in horror. 'Frank! Don't touch that filthy animal!' Her face was red and her eyes bulged with emotion. She turned on her husband. 'Get rid of it! Tie a brick round its neck and throw it in the canal!' She grabbed Frank's wrist and hauled him away. 'I'm taking Frank and I'm going to my mother's.' She dragged the bewildered Frank to the car, and drove off, leaving Harry alone.

He stood in the doorway and looked at the derelict farm, at the sheds with the sagging corrugated roofs, and the rutted yard in front of the house, and his shoulders drooped. Something cold thrust itself into his hand. He looked down. Mortimer blinked up at him with rheumy eyes. 'I'm sorry, old boy,' Harry said. 'She'll not tolerate you, not at any price.' He gave Mortimer away to a man he met in the pub, an old man who liked to sit in a dark corner and drink beer, and was happy to have a dog as a drinking companion.

Day and night, trucks passed the farm gate on their way to the landfill, their engines throbbing as they laboured up the hill, heavy with their load. They cruised past on their way back, their rusty, high-sided dumpers empty. Harry read the legend on the sides of the trucks: Meadowlands – managing waste for *you*.

Harry walked the bounds of the farm. It consisted of the yard, the farmhouse, the outbuildings and some scrubland that had once been a field. All the rest had vanished under the landfill. There was a wall at the edge of the field, marking the boundary between Harry's land and that of Meadowlands Waste. Water seeped under the wall and trickled into the drainage ditch that was choked with a grey, slimy weed. Nothing grew in the field. Nothing grew anywhere. The land was dead.

He approached Meadowlands Waste. He thought they might like to buy the farm and have more space to dump more waste. The agent's voice was cool as he explained the situation to Harry. Yes, the owners of the site would like to buy the farm. He told Harry the sum they were willing to pay. Harry protested, and the agent smiled. 'Who else will buy it?' he said.

Harry got out his life insurance policy and read it carefully. Then he went to the cupboard under the stairs and took out the shotgun that his uncle had kept illegally for years. It was probably a good thing that, before he took any drastic action, he checked his bank statement to see what funds, if any, he would leave to his family apart from the insurance payout. The overdraft was impressive, but what was even more impressive was the fact that the bank had not paid the insurance premium for the last six months. The policy had lapsed.

It was the end. He could think of nothing else to do.

He looked around the yard. Nothing grew. No birds sang. Nothing could live near the landfill.

Except the rats. They seemed to thrive for a while, but then even they died. One of the corpses lay rotting in the yard. Moodily, he turned it over with his foot. A cloud of bluebottles rose from it, their buzzing making a high-pitched, sticky sound. He looked at the heaving mass of maggots that was already infesting the corpse.

It is in moments of true darkness that the real mettle of a man is tested. When life gives you lemons, make lemonade. He saw in front of him, like a vision, the rivers and the canals, the streams and the lakes, the waterways of Britain. And in his vision, he saw ranks of men standing on the river banks and tow paths, rods raised, lines running out into the water, thousands upon thousands. He could see the expanding ripples in the water where the fish had jumped. It was an epiphany.

There *was* something that could live on this land.

Six months later, he drove to his mother-in-law's, his brand new BMW dominating the road. He pulled up outside the house, jumped down from the driver's seat and marched up to the front door. He rapped smartly on the glass.

Cynthia had been peering round the curtains to observe Harry's arrival. She opened the door and looked at her husband with disapproval. 'What have you been getting up to now?' she said.

Under his wife's cold eye, Harry's newly found confidence dwindled. He looked at his feet. 'What you asked me to, dear,' he said. 'Fixing the place up. Providing for you. Please come and see.'

Cynthia stood in thought. Harry was Harry, but her mother was getting on her nerves. And the car was the latest model. 'Alright,' she said, after a moment. They collected Frank from school – it was only a short walk away, but she insisted they take the car – and Harry drove his family back up north.

When they arrived at Meadowsweet Farm, Cynthia stepped out the car. She looked round, and her eyes narrowed. 'What's that?' she said. She was looking at a new shed, a huge, corrugated iron construction that stood, dark and silent against the evening sky. 'Well?' She eyed her husband narrowly.

The breeze blew towards them, and for a moment, they were enveloped in an appalling stench. 'I'm going nowhere till I know what you've got in there,' she said, folding her arms.

'Magg . . . mushrooms!' he said. 'Lots of money in mushrooms. White gold. Don't you worry about it, dear. Please come back. And tomorrow, we can go shopping.'

Ten years passed. Frank, at his mother's insistence, had been sent away to school. He didn't like it. It was the kind of school where the boys were supposed to be good at sport, at rowing and rugby and cricket. He was good at maths. But he grew up biddable and well-spoken. His mother was pleased.

On his sixteenth birthday, he came home for

the summer so that his father could show him the family business. 'This is how it works, son,' Harry said, proudly. Every morning, trucks came up the lane, but not to Meadowlands Waste plc. Meadowlands Waste had been sued for breaching environmental regulations and had been closed down. The trucks came to Meadowsweet Farm now. They pulled into the yard and dumped their loads into the sheds that stood in the once derelict field. Frank gagged at the smell that rose up.

'Ragmeat,' Harry said, rubbing his hands with satisfaction. 'Where do the farmers get rid of their dead chickens? Their diseased cows and sheep? Easy. They pay me, they bring them here, and my little beauties do the rest. Come on, son.'

He took Frank into the first shed. Frank held his scarf over his nose, and looked at the mound of dead and decaying flesh on the floor. A movement caught his eye. He leaned forward and saw the whole pile was gently heaving. Tentatively, he reached out with his foot and turned it over. He recoiled. It was a white, seething mass.

'My beauties,' his father said. 'My white gold. Now come and meet my queens.'

Frank looked into Harry's shining eyes, and decided that his father must have gone insane some years ago. He caught his breath, feeling an unspoken apprehension rising up in him as he followed Harry to the door of the next shed. His father pushed it open and Frank looked in. He could see a dim room with walls that were dark and iridescent.

As they stepped through, a shrill chorus filled the air as the walls took flight. Fat bluebottles launched themselves into space and flew madly around in the shadows, their bodies making a tinny noise as they batted against the walls and the roof. Something landed on Frank's cheek, something else on the lids of his swiftly closed eyes. Something explored his lips, something tried to explore his nostril. He blew out through his nose and gripped it, began to open his mouth to breathe, closed it again. He wanted to scream.

'My queens,' his father said proudly. 'Here, Bess! Here!'

Frank looked round in the dim light, blinking his eyes to keep away the questing flies. Bess? Had his father brought a dog in with them? But his father was standing with his hand raised, a hand that slowly vanished under an iridescent glove. 'Good girls,' his father said. 'Good girls.'

Frank returned to school with his mind made up. His visit home had decided him. He was going to be an accountant. His headmaster, apprised of his plans, looked resigned. He didn't expect his boys to become accountants. He expected them to become captains of industry, to employ accountants, teams of accountants. In one of two cases, they employed so much time of so many accountants that their names appeared in the Sunday papers and they had to take long holidays in certain South American states.

On the other hand . . . He contemplated the youth in front of him, noting the pale skin that always looked slightly damp. He noted the pink-rimmed eyes, blinking a little as though the light was too bright. He noted the thin, mousy hair. An accountant.

'Very well, Stout,' he said, his voice kind.

But it was just a few weeks into term that Frank was summoned to the headmaster's study again. He edged nervously through the door, and saw to his alarm his mother sitting there, snuffling into a lacy handkerchief.

The headmaster looked up and cleared his throat. 'Ah, Stout,' he said. 'Very bad show. Dreadful news. You must take care of your mother, lad.'

And to Frank's deep and abiding horror, his mother fell on his shoulder with a howl of anguish. 'Frank!' she sobbed. 'My Frankie. My poor, fatherless boy!' From this, Frank gathered that his father had died, but it was some days before he found out the circumstances of his death, suffocated under a delivery of ragmeat as he was checking the welfare of his latest clutch of maggots.

'You must come home with me,' his mother wept. 'You must be the man of the house now.' She looked at the headmaster. 'We'll expect a rebate on this term's fees.'

'Our policy is no remission of fees,' the headmaster said automatically. 'You can take it up with our accountants, if you wish.'

So Frank had maggots thrust upon him.

He remembered his father's pride in his work and he tried to cultivate – if not love, at least respect for the bluebottle, and its offspring. But it was as if they knew that the person who had cared for them was gone. It was as if they knew that no matter how meticulously Frank attended to their welfare, he wasn't a true maggot man. The number and quality of larvae deteriorated. They were smaller. They were less plump and juicy. They weren't so lively as bait, less inclined to wriggle alluringly on the end of a hook, enticing the fish to swallow the barb. Sales began to drop off. Frank proposed to his mother that she sell the maggot farm, and he would take his accountancy exams.

His mother was horrified. 'Sell your father's farm? His life's work? What kind of son are you? Shame on you Frank.'

So the years went by and Frank continued to raise maggots.

One rainy afternoon after the delivery truck had been, he was working on the accounts for Meadowsweet Farm. It was the one task that gave him real pleasure. He was absorbed in the books, when the door opened and a young woman came in. 'Oh,' she said in surprise. She was carrying a heavy box full of cleaning equipment, as well as the old-fashioned vacuum cleaner that his mother had never bothered replacing. 'I'm so sorry. I didn't mean to disturb you.'

Frank leapt to his feet. 'Let me help you with those,' he said. 'You aren't disturbing me,' he added. He realised at once who she was. She was his mother's most recent cleaner. His mother seemed to get through cleaners rather quickly. This one was small and pretty, and she told him that her name was Sheena.

Later that afternoon, when she'd finished her work, she brought him a cup of tea, and seemed inclined to talk. They talked about Frank's exams and about Sheena's career as an actress. She worked as a cleaner because she earned very little money from acting, and wasn't trained to do anything else. 'I wasn't very clever at school,' she confided. She had, however, just been offered a part in the Christmas pantomime at the small theatre in town. 'It could be my big break,' she told him. 'Juliet LeJoy is starring.'

Frank had never heard of Juliet LeJoy, but Sheena seemed excited so he smiled and nodded. He thought that he had never before seen a girl as pretty as Sheena.

She looked at her watch, and her face flushed a beautiful pink. 'Oh, my goodness,' she said. 'Look at the time.' She hurried out. Frank looked at the clock. They'd been talking for an hour.

After that, he looked forward to the days she

worked. They got into the habit of having lunch together. Sheena would make sandwiches, and then they would sit at the old farmhouse table where Frank did the accounts, and talk. Frank had never really talked to a girl before. They didn't seem to notice him. Sheena did.

She listened to everything he said with wide-eyed fascination. He even told her about his dreams of becoming an accountant. 'You're so clever,' she sighed.

And in the week before Christmas, she brought some mistletoe to the gloomy farmhouse – Cynthia had decided that they couldn't possibly celebrate Christmas in the years since her husband had died – and held it above Frank's head. She stood on tiptoe, and touched his cheek with her lips. 'See you in the New Year,' she whispered. Frank's face was scarlet, and his head was spinning.

He didn't notice Cynthia watching the exchange from the door of her room.

When the festive season was over, the day came for Sheena's return. Frank lingered over breakfast, then, wanting some activity that would keep him in the house, he set to work putting up some shelves in the kitchen. He was aware of his mother's eyes on him as he wielded the powerful cordless drill.

'It's very inconsiderate of you to make a mess in here today,' she said after a while. 'Mrs Mason isn't coming until Thursday.'

'I'll clear up,' Frank said. He had no intention of leaving the mess for Sheena. Then he realised what his mother had said. 'Who's Mrs Mason?'

His mother lifted her tea cup to her mouth, and drank before she answered. 'You don't make the tea strong enough, Frank. Mrs Mason is our new cleaner. She's starting on Thursday.'

The drill felt heavy in Frank's hands. 'What about Sheena?'

Cynthia's lips thinned. 'I sacked her,' she said.

'You can't sack her.' Frank stepped towards her, his hands held out. 'Please, mother. I love her.' He hadn't realised it before, but as soon as he said it, he knew it was true.

'Love her,' his mother scoffed. 'She was just making up to you because she's after your money. I said so in the letter. Well,' she sipped her tea again, '*you* did. It was one of the letters you signed last week.' She pushed her chair away from the table and stood up.

'Mother! You've got to tell her . . .'

She ignored him and went to leave the room. Frank reached out to stop her, forgetting that he had the drill in his hands. He flinched as she tried to push past him, and his finger tightened inadvertently on the trigger. The drill howled and his mother shrieked – once.

It is a fact that Frank was probably aware of, but to which he hadn't until that moment given much thought, that the human eyeball does not require something as powerful as a Bosch drill with a masonry bit to penetrate it. A simple hand drill would have sufficed.

'Mother?' he said, apprehensively. He looked at the body on the floor, then he looked at the drill in his hand. He wasn't stupid. He knew how this would look.

As he stood there, frozen, the phone rang. He picked it up. 'Meadowsweet Bait,' he said automatically. It was the delivery firm. They wouldn't be able to bring the truck load of carcasses until the next day. After he had rung off, Frank stood there staring at the wall. He'd killed his mother. Her body was in the kitchen. But he had more important things to deal with. The truck wasn't coming. The maggots would go hungry, and then some of them would die. His father would never have allowed that to happen.

He looked at the phone. He looked at his mother's body. He looked at the maggot shed.

And he had an idea.

The maggot farm was thriving again. Somehow, Frank had become attuned to the bluebottles, and to their larvae. He owed them a debt of gratitude for saving him from considerable embarrassment. Two weeks after his mother's unfortunate accident, he collected the clean, white bones – how strange that his all-powerful mother should really have been so small – and dropped them down the well in the middle of the yard. The run-off from the landfill site had poisoned the well a long time ago, leaving the water toxic and corrosive. He thought it would suit his mother very well.

He decided that he would probably be best advised not to use a cordless drill again – the manufacturers do warn against the possibility of accidents – so he stowed it in his car with a view to getting rid of it some time.

He told himself he was happy. But he was lonely. He missed Sheena. He'd tried phoning her, but she'd put down the phone. He'd sent a letter, but she'd returned it unopened. He needed to talk to her, to explain to her that it hadn't been him that had written to her in such a hurtful way, to tell her that he would think it an honour if she were to accept his hand, and his fortune.

He waited outside her flat, but he didn't have the courage to approach her. He followed her to the theatre, where he saw the huge posters adorning the walls: *Juliet LeJoy in Aladdin! With Bobby Beaver as Widow Twankey!* The names didn't mean anything to him, but he noticed that the show was running until the end of January. He went to the box office at once, and bought a ticket for every night.

That evening, he sat at the front of the dress circle, entranced by the brilliance of the stage. The curtain drew back, the dancers came on and there, tiny and airy and graceful was Sheena, more beautiful than he had remembered. To Frank, she was the star of the show, the light that illuminated the stage, though in truth, he had to twist in his seat and peer to even see her, because Juliet LeJoy, a strapping woman with yellow hair, seemed always to be between Sheena and the audience, seemed to edge her off the stage, and to cut her few moments of performance short. Frank didn't care. He had seen Sheena again.

After that first night, he went to the best florist in town and ordered the biggest and the most expensive bouquet they could produce. He stood in the shadows outside the stage door that evening, waiting for her to arrive. But when she came, she was with a young man, looking up at him as they walked, listening with that intent, serious expression Frank remembered so well. His heart twisted, and he stepped back into the shadows.

Every evening, it was the same. He would wait with a new bouquet, but even though, after that first evening, Sheena arrived alone, he couldn't screw up the courage to approach her. It was almost the end of January, and the last performance loomed. Frank waited, determined that this time, he would speak to her. But when she arrived, she was on the arm of the young man. He stood there in despair. He'd lost her. He was turning to leave – he couldn't bear to watch her in her last performance – when a car pulled up at the stage door. 'Take it round to my parking space,' the driver ordered the doorman as she got out. 'And don't make a mess of it this time.'

Frank realised it was Juliet LeJoy, the star of the show. She worked with Sheena. She would see

Sheena in just a few moments. He cleared his throat. 'Excuse me,' he said.

She raised her eyebrows as she ran her eyes up and down him. 'Yes?' Her voice wasn't friendly.

'I wondered,' Frank said timidly, 'if you would give these flowers to Sheena . . .' His voice trailed off as he realised his mistake.

'How dare . . .' She began, then her eyes narrowed as she looked at the bouquet. It was the most expensive the flower shop could provide – roses and maidenhair fern and orchids and lilies. Her eyes studied Frank more closely, looked past him to his brand new Toyota Land Cruiser V6 300 turbo inter-cooler. She gave him a dazzling smile. Her teeth had a porcelain whiteness that reminded him of the sheen on a bluebottle's egg. 'I'll see what I can do,' she said, and took the bouquet into the theatre with her.

Frank sat in his accustomed place, rigid with tension. The music played, the dancers swirled. Sheena glittered in her small part. And then at the end of the show, the cast lined up to take a final bow. Frank could see a stagehand waiting in the wings, carrying a magnificent bouquet, the bouquet that he had bought for Sheena. He watched, not breathing, waiting for Sheena's face to light up when she was presented with the flowers. She would read the card and know that he was there. And when she looked round the theatre, he would bow and she would see him, and after the show when she came out of the stage door, he would step out of the shadows, and . . .

The stagehand stepped forward. He raised the bouquet, and laid it reverentially in the arms of Juliet LeJoy. She gasped with manufactured pleasure and read the card. Then she looked directly at Frank and blew him a kiss. And at the same time, Sheena looked up and saw him sitting there. She gave him a sad smile that pierced his heart.

Disconsolate, he walked slowly to the stage door, and found Juliet LeJoy waiting for him. 'I'm so sorry,' she said, 'but Sheena was upset about the flowers. She was afraid that her fiancé – did you know she's engaged to be married? – her fiancé would be terribly angry if a man sent her a bouquet like that. So I promised her I would pretend they were for me.'

Frank felt as though his heart had been torn in two.

'You're the man who owns Meadowsweet Farm, aren't you?' Juliet LeJoy went on. 'She told me about you. We could go for a drink, if you like.' Frank, numb with grief, barely heard what she was saying. She climbed into his car, then looked at him with surprised impatience. 'Come on,' she said.

Slowly, he sat behind the wheel. 'Where do you want to go?' he said.

Soon, they were sitting in the plush bar of the only five star hotel in the area. Frank sipped orange juice while Juliet drank something called a Slippery Nipple, and talked.

She told him how famous she was, except people didn't appreciate her any more. She told him how expensive it was to buy the clothes she needed for public appearances, how she needed someone to invest in a show in which she would star.

When they left the hotel, she snuggled up to him and asked him if he would drive her home. He didn't want to, but he didn't seem to have a choice. They drove for a while, then she directed him to park his car in a secluded lane. Frank looked out at the dark landscape. 'You live here?' he said. He couldn't see any houses.

Before he could say anything else, he was seized in a violent embrace. Juliet pressed her lips against his astonished gape, her tongue flopping in his mouth like a netted goldfish. She fell back onto the car seat, and pulled him down on top of her. She seemed to have double the usual complement of hands that found their way through every weak spot the barrier of his clothes presented. 'Frank!' she moaned.

Then she pushed his head down, down below her protuberant chest, below her belt, below . . . His mouth fell open in panic. He felt a pair of thighs muffle his cars as her heels landed against his shoulders and her calves tightened round the back of his neck. He took a terrified gasp and then he was choking and smothering in a claustrophobic nightmare beyond anything he'd ever imagined.

He was, more literally than he might have realised, going down for the third time, when there was a sudden, shrill whining noise. Juliet jerked violently. The vice around his neck released and he sprang free, gasping for breath and wiping his mouth. He leaped out of the car and was about to escape into the night, when he realised that Juliet was lying very still and very silent. He went back. He averted his eyes and pulled her skirt down over her knees, then looked more closely.

He saw at once what had happened. The drill – the Bosch drill with the masonry bit, the drill with which he had already had one unfortunate accident, was wedged down the side of the seat. Juliet's weight must have been enough to trigger it. It had drilled a neat size 8 hole through the back of her neck, probably a neater hole than Frank would have managed had he been holding the drill himself. It had proved the manufacturer's claims about the robustness of the tool. It had also proved fatal.

Frank drove home in a state of confusion. It was pitch dark by the time he got back to Meadowsweet Farm. He looked at Juliet, still slumped in the seat beside him.

He looked at the maggot shed.

He was just negotiating Juliet out of the car, when he heard a sound. It was like a muffled sob. Cautiously, he pushed Juliet back into the car and closed the door, then peered through the darkness. The sob came again. He followed the sound until he came to his front door. There was someone huddled against it, weeping silently, just the occasional sob escaping to reveal that she was there.

He knew at once who it was. 'Sheena?' he said.

'Frank?' Her voice, quivering with tears, was as soft and beautiful as he remembered. 'I'm going away tomorrow, and I had to see you just once more.'

Slowly, hesitantly, he put his arms round her. He could see the white of her neck glimmering in the darkness as she drooped her head onto his shoulder.

'Sheena, I love you,' he said. And before she could pull away, he told her about his mother's letter, about his attempts to contact her, about the bouquet he'd asked Juliet to give her.

As she listened, Sheena stopped crying. 'Oh, Frank,' she said. 'Juliet was lying. I'm not engaged. She told me you had been waiting for her every night to give her flowers. I saw you drive off with her tonight. I've been so unhappy.'

'You don't need to be,' Frank said gallantly, but he was becoming uncomfortably aware of Juliet as an unwanted third party on the scene. He couldn't bear to lose Sheena now.

'I've been so stupid,' she said. 'I should never have doubted you. And now it's too late.'

'Too late?' he said.

'I've got a job touring the Middle East,' she said. 'I auditioned for a part with the company here. I almost got it, but they gave it to Juliet instead.'

All at once, everything became clear to Frank. 'Don't go,' he said. 'Stay. I have a feeling it's all going to work out.'

She mopped her eyes with a tissue. 'All right, Frank.'

He felt the surge of triumph he'd felt that day before Christmas when she'd held up the mistletoe and kissed his cheek. 'Will you marry me?' he said.

'Oh, Frank, of course I will. But what about your mother?' She looked at him with wide eyes.

'Oh, she's gone away.' Frank had more or less forgotten about his mother. 'You go into the house,' he said. 'I'll just – er – put the car away.'

The disappearance of Juliet LeJoy was a bit of a nine-day-wonder. Her career had been going downhill rapidly. Her agent let it be known that she owed him money – rather a lot of money. A friend, in between expressing her concern and anxiety, expanded on Juliet's earlier career when her foray into artistic film had been – well – artistic. There were videos. For a brief time, Juliet LeJoy was a bigger star that she had been for years, but then newer stories emerged to fill the headlines.

Sheena got a place in the repertory theatre. She wasn't given lead roles – those went to an ex-soap star whose career had taken a downward turn, but whose name could still be relied on to attract a provincial audience.

Sheena moved into the farmhouse. She tore down the heavy paper with which Cynthia had covered the walls, and painted them white. She put vases full of flowers on the tables. She took down all the net curtains that were shutting out the light. The old, dark house was transformed, and Frank and Sheena were happy.

But one day, she came back from the theatre in tears. The ex-soap star was angry because she said that the director favoured Sheena. 'He says he can't afford to offend her,' Sheena wept. 'He's very sorry, but he says I'll have to go.'

Frank patted her absent-mindedly on the shoulder. He'd been a bit worried that morning, as he'd done his rounds. He'd spent time with the maggots, and he could see that they were – not ailing, but not as content as he would like them to be. He knew that they needed something they weren't getting, and he had been turning the problem over in his mind. And suddenly he had an idea.

'Don't worry, dearest,' he said.

Sheena, surprised by the change in his tone, looked up. 'But it's so hard to get work. I'll have to leave,' she said, her eyes still brimming with tears. 'I'll have to join the tour in the Middle East.'

'Oh, I don't think so.' Frank smiled his re-assurance at her. 'But I've got to go out. I won't be long. I need to pick up a food supplement for the . . . mushrooms.'

The rise to fame of Sheena Stout was legendary. Her picture smiled out from magazine covers, from posters, from celebrity columns in news-papers. 'I've been very lucky. But I couldn't have done it without Frank,' she murmured when she was interviewed by Richard and Judy. In fact, the only thing that marred her story was the trail of mystery and disaster that seemed to dog her co-stars, who had a tendency to vanish without trace in a cloud of ill-feeling and bad debt.

Frank, back home at Meadowsweet Farm, was happy. His wife was successful. His maggots were thriving. Every morning, he went into the sheds and watched the mass of white bodies squirming and growing fat, glowing with health and contentment.

Every day, he went into the shed where the iridescent insects laid the eggs that hatched the white gold. The blue-black bodies would swarm around his head. Sometimes, one of the flies would land on his outstretched fingers and gaze at him with her multi-faceted eyes. She would rub her front legs together, her gauze wings trembling, then she would take off to join the joyous flight of her companions. 'Bees,' he would whisper. He no longer wanted to be an accountant. He knew that he owed them his happiness.

And locked away in the attic was the cordless drill with the masonry bit. Who knew when it might be needed again? After all, every man, even a man as happy as Frank, needs some insurance against misfortune.

SIMON BRETT

CAIN WAS INNOCENT

I t was a quiet afternoon in Heaven. This was not unusual. It's always afternoon in Heaven and, by definition, it's always quiet. Inspector Gabriel was bored. He was still glad he had gone to Heaven rather than The Other Place, but after his first fifty years of Eternity, he was beginning to learn the truth of the old saying that you could have too much of a good thing. OK, the Big Man had been generous to him. Given him his own precinct, just like he'd had on earth, and put him in charge of solving every crime that happened in Heaven. But, though initially gratifying, the appointment carried with it an in-built contradiction. Indeed, it joined all those other jokes about being a fashion designer in a nudist colony, or trying to make it as a straight actor in New York, or being George W Bush's conscience. There actually wasn't much of a job there.

So Inspector Gabriel had precisely nothing to do. And the same went for his sidekick, Sergeant Uriel. They'd done out the station more or less as they wanted it, though they did have a real problem recapturing in Heaven the essential shabbiness of the working environments they'd been used to on earth. But they lacked cases to work on. They had reached the goal towards which every terrestrial cop aspired. Heaven really was a crime-free zone.

They looked out of their windows – far too clean to have been part of any real-life station – and watched golf. White-clad figures with golden clubs addressed their green balls on the undulating cloudscape. Mostly newcomers – they had to be – who still got a kick out of holes-in-one from every tee.

In the same way, the people sipping vintage nectar on the terrace of St Raphael's Bar had to be recent arrivals. However good the liquor, the fact that in Heaven no one ever got drunk or had a hangover rather took away the point of drinking.

'Do you reckon I should go and check out the back alleys?' suggested the Sergeant. 'See if there's been a murder . . . ? Even a mugging . . . ? Someone making a rude gesture . . . ?'

Inspector Gabriel sighed. 'Uriel, you know full well there aren't any back alleys in Heaven. And no rude gestures either . . . let alone the more extreme crimes you enumerated.'

'Yeah, I know.' A wistful shake of the head. 'I kinda miss them, you know.'

'You're not the only one.' the Inspector looked out over the vista of perfect white. A moment of silence hung between them before he vocalised an idea that had been brooding inside him for a long time. 'Maybe we should start looking at old cases . . .'

'How'd you mean, boss?'

'Well, look, we could spend a long time sitting here in Heaven waiting for a new crime to be committed . . .'

'We could spend Eternity.'

'Right, Uriel. Funny, till you get up here, you never really have a concept of Eternity. I mean, you may kind of get a feeling of it, if you've watched golf . . . or baseball . . . or cricket, but up here it's the real deal.'

'Yup,' the Sergeant agreed. 'Eternity's a hell of a long time.' He looked shrewdly across at his boss. 'You mentioned looking at old cases. You mean crimes that happened on earth? Like murders?'

'That's right. Most of the victims end up here, and if you wait long enough most of the suspects will also arrive eventually.'

'Hm.' Sergeant Uriel nodded his grizzled head thoughtfully. 'There is one drawback, though.'

'What's that?'

'Well, we won't get the villains coming up to Heaven. By definition, the actual perps are going to end up in The Other Place, aren't they?'

'Oh, come on, Uriel. You know how many murder investigations end up fingering the wrong guy. People who're capable of getting away with murder down on earth are not going to have too much of a problem blagging their way into Heaven, are they?'

'I guess not. So you're saying there actually are a lot of murderers walking round up here?'

'Of course there are. Well, there's Cain, for a start.'

'The Daddy of all murderers. Yeah, we see plenty of him.'

'Constantly maundering on. Complaining about that Mark on his forehead. And insisting that he was stitched up for the case, that he never laid a finger on Abel.'

Sergeant Ariel let out a harsh laugh. 'Still, you hear that from every villain, don't you? They all claim they're innocent.'

'Yes.' Gabriel gave his white beard a thoughtful rub. 'Mind you, it is odd that he's up here, though, isn't it? I mean, the Bible says he did it. The Word of God. There's never been much doubt that he did. And yet here he is in Heaven, boring everyone to tears by constantly saying he didn't do it. Why? The Big Man doesn't usually make mistakes on that scale.'

'No. I'd always assumed that Cain came up from The Other Place in one of the amnesties. You know, when they redefined the crimes that you had to go to Hell for. I mean, way back everyone who got executed went straight to The Other Place – never any question about whether they were guilty or not.'

'I heard about that, Uriel. All those poor little Cockney kids who'd stolen handkerchiefs.'

'Right. Well, I figured Cain got a transfer up here as part of one of those amnesties.'

'Yes. Except his crime is still murder. That's about the biggest rap you can take.' There was a gleam of incipient interest in Inspector Gabriel's eye. 'I definitely think there's something odd about it. Something worthy of investigation. If we could prove that Cain was innocent . . .'

Uriel was catching his boss's enthusiasm, but still felt it his duty to throw a wet blanket over such speculation. 'It'd be a very difficult case.'

'We've cracked difficult cases before. What makes this one so different?'

'It's all a long time ago.'

'A very long time ago. In fact, by definition, about as long ago as it possibly could be.'

'Yeah. Then again, boss, we've got a problem with lack of suspects. We start off with Adam and Eve, then they have kids, who are Cain and Abel. Abel gets killed so he's kind of out of the equation, unless we get into the suicide area . . .'

'Don't go there.'

'No, I don't want to.'

'I've been thinking about this for a while,' said Gabriel, 'and doing a bit of research. The obvious thing to do, of course, would be to ask Abel, but the funny thing is, nobody up here seems to know where he is. Which is odd. I mean, he wouldn't have gone to The Other Place, would he?'

'Unless he *did* commit suicide.'

The Inspector dismissed the idea with a weary

shake of the head. 'I'm sure we'll find him some-where up here.'

'So, boss, going back . . . we've just got the three suspects. Cain, who took the rap for it . . .'

'Not just the rap. He took the Mark too. Don't forget the Mark.'

'Could I? The Mark's the thing he keeps beefing on about. But the fact remains, given our current level of information, we've only got three suspects. Cain, Adam and Eve.'

'And the Serpent. What happened to the Serpent?'

'I don't know, boss. He probably just slipped away.'

'Like a snake in the grass. But he's important, Uriel. I mean, with any list of suspects, the first thing you ask is: who's got form? Adam, Eve – just been created. Cain – just been born. When have they had a chance to mix with bad company?'

'And how do you *find* bad company in Eden?'

'Ah, but remember, they weren't in Eden when it happened. Adam and Eve had been kicked out by the Big Man.'

'For eating the Apple. Yeah, that was a crime. So they've got form too.'

'But not the form on the scale that the Serpent has. God recognized him straight away, knew the kind of stuff he got up to. I mean, come on, this guy's Satan! Also, he's in disguise, which is not the kind of behaviour you expect from the average denizen of Paradise. And, second, he was responsible at that time for all the evil in the known world – though, granted, not much of it was known then – but this Satan was still one nasty piece of work. So far as I'm concerned, the Serpent's definitely on the suspect list.'

'And he'd have been clever enough to frame Cain and make him take the rap.'

'Be meat and drink to him, that kind of stuff.'

Sergeant Uriel nodded agreement. 'So what do we do? Go after the Serpent?'

'Call him by his proper name. He's Satan.'

'Aka Lucifer.'

'Yeah, but that was a long time back.'

'OK. So we go after Satan? That's going to involve a trip down to The Other Place.'

'Not necessarily, Uriel. He comes up here for conferences and things, you know, ever since the Big Man got more ecumenical and He started reaching out to embrace other faith groups.'

'Yeah. I'm afraid that still sticks in my craw – the idea of Satan coming up to Heaven.'

'Now you mustn't be old-fashioned. We've got to try and build bridges towards these people. Maybe they aren't so different from us.'

'Huh.' The Sergeant's hunched body language showed how much the idea appealed to him.

'Anyway, Satan's not our first port of call in this investigation.'

'No? So who is?'

'Cain, obviously. As you say, he's always maundering on about how he didn't do it. Now for the first time, we'll actually *listen* to what he's saying. Let's go find him.'

'OK.' Sergeant Uriel eased his massive but weightless bulk off his white stool. 'And when we talk to him, boss, what . . . ? We used the old Good Cop routine?'

'Do we have any alternative, Uriel?'

Cain was sitting in a white armchair in the corner of St Raphael's Bar. Alone. He was nearly always alone. His one-track conversation tended to drive people away.

As ever, in front of him stood a bottle of the finest two-thousand-year-old malt whisky, from which he constantly topped off his chalice. The conventional wisdom in Heaven was that, however much you drank, you never got intoxicated. Cain didn't buy that. He reckoned that somewhere in infinity was the magic moment when the alcohol would kick in and do its stuff. He drank like he was determined to find that moment.

The two cops idled up to the bar. They didn't want to make a big thing of their entrance. Inspector Gabriel ordered the first lot of drinks. Even though no payment was involved in St Raphael's Bar, there was a strictly observed protocol as to whose round it was.

Sergeant Uriel asked for a beer. Gabriel ordered it from St Raphael, adding, 'And I'll have an alcohol-free one, thanks.' It didn't make any difference, but it did make for variety.

They stayed leaning against the counter and looked across the bar towards Cain. It was the mid-afternoon lull, but then it always was the mid-afternoon lull in St Raphael's Bar. Knots of newcomers at a few tables enthused about how great it was to be there, how relieved they were not to be at The Other Place and how really nice Heaven was. They all looked white and squeaky clean against the white and gold furniture.

The only bright colour visible in the room was the Mark on Cain's forehead.

The sight would have settled a lot of ancestral arguments amongst biblical commentators and freemasons. The Bible remains tantalisingly unspecific about the nature of 'The Mark of Cain'. Some authorities maintain that it was the name of God etched across the miscreant's forehead. Others thought that it was dark skin and that Cain was the father of all the world's people of colour. Some rabbinical experts even identified it with leprosy. (And it is also, incidentally, the name of an Australian rock band.)

But all the theorists would have been silenced by the neat red cross tattooed above Cain's eyes.

'I never understood,' said Uriel, 'why he didn't have that removed in C & P.'

'C & P' stood for 'Cleansing and Purification'. It was a service offered to all new souls as soon as they had finished their Pearly Gates paperwork. The nature of the dying process meant that few arrived looking their best, but C & P gave them the chance of a complete makeover and the opportunity to select their 'Heaven Age', the stage of their lives at which they would like to stay for all Eternity.

It was hardly surprising that a lot of souls – particularly women – chose to look a good few decades younger than their death age. Not Gabriel and Uriel, though. They'd opted to stay the way they'd looked just before the car-chase which had brought them up to Heaven – though they'd had their actual injuries tidied up. They reckoned the grizzled look added gravitas to their image as cops.

'I mean,' Uriel went on, 'those C & P boys can do wonders with facial blemishes. And some of the stuff they've done with reassembling organ transplant recipients with their donors . . . it's just stunning. For them, a little thing like Cain's forehead wouldn't present problems.'

'You're missing the point, Uriel. Cain wants to keep it.'

'Yeah?'

'Sure. Until his innocence is proved, it's part of his identity. And it's a conversation piece. I mean, anyone incautious enough to ask, 'What's that Mark on your forehead? . . . ?'

'Gets the full spiel.'

'Exactly. And that's what we're about to do.'

'I mean, how many more times have I got to say this?'

Not many more – please, thought Inspector

Gabriel. They'd been talking to Cain for three-quarters of an hour and he'd already said his bit at least a dozen times. Trouble was, the bit he'd said lacked detail. When you stripped away the grievances about the millennia he had spent with a Mark on his forehead, being shunned by all and sundry, Cain's monologue still consisted of just the one assertion: 'I didn't do it.'

Inspector Gabriel tried again. 'Can you be a bit more specific? We have it on good authority that—'

'What authority?'

'The best authority available. The Bible. Holy Writ. The Word of God.'

'Oh, forget that. The Word of God has never been more than just a whitewash job. Public Relations. Spin.'

'According to the Bible,' the Inspector persisted, '"it came to pass, when they were in the field, that Cain rose up against Abel his brother, and slew him."'

'I was never in the damned field!'

'Ah, but you were. Only just before the incident you had "brought of the fruit of the ground an offering unto the Lord."' Gabriel was rather pleased with his logic. 'How could you have got "the fruit of the ground" if you were never in the field?'

'It was a different field! Abel was killed in the field from which he took his offering, "the firstlings of his flock and of the fat thereof." It was a different kind of field, a different kind of farming. I was arable. Abel was "a keeper of sheep". I was just "a tiller of the ground". I never went into his field. I'm allergic to sheep!'

'It doesn't say in the Bible which field Abel was slain in.'

'There's a lot of things about the case that aren't mentioned in the Bible. The guys who wrote the Old Testament, these bozos who claimed to be transcribing the Word of God, all they wanted was everything neat – nice open-and-shut case, no loose ends. "Cain slew Abel," that's easy, isn't it? They'd rather have that than the truth.'

'So what is the truth?'

'I didn't do it!'

Inspector Gabriel had difficulty suppressing his exasperation. 'So why didn't you say that when God challenged you about the murder?'

''Cause I was taken by surprise, that's why. Suddenly He's asking me where Abel is. I don't know, do I? I haven't seen him for a while. We're not that close and, apart from anything else, he always smells of sheep and, like I say, I'm allergic to—'

'Yes, yes, yes. But why didn't you tell God you didn't do it?'

'He didn't give me the chance! He asks me where Abel, my brother is, and I say "I know not: am I my brother's keeper?' And at this stage I don't even know anything's happened to the guy, so why should I be worried? But immediately God's saying that "the voice of the brother's blood crieth

111

unto me from the ground" and then that I'm "cursed from the earth, which hath opened her mouth to receive they brother's blood from thy hand". I mean, when do I get the chance to tell my side of the story?'

There was silence. Sergeant Uriel, who'd been feeling a bit left out of the conversation, was the one to break it. 'But you don't have anything else? You haven't got an alibi for the time when the homicide took place?'

'I was in my field. The field where I grow "the fruit of the ground". That's what I do. I'm a tiller.'

Uriel looked bewildered. 'I thought he was a Hun.'

'Who?'

'Attila.'

Inspector Gabriel tactfully intervened. 'Don't worry. We have a slight misunderstanding here. So, Cain, nobody actually saw you in your field at the relevant time? Nobody could stand up in court and give you an alibi?'

A weary shake of the head. 'Only the vegetables.'

'I don't think they're going to be much help. After all this time, maybe the best thing would be,' the Inspector went on, 'for us to have a word with Abel. Except nobody seems to have seen him recently. Do you know where he is, Cain?'

'Oh, don't you start!' And he shouted, 'I know not: am I my brother's keeper?'

'Sorry. I didn't mean to do that.'

'I should bloody hope not.'

'But Cain,' asked Uriel urgently, 'if you don't have an alibi, maybe you saw someone? Someone who might have been the perp? Someone who went into that field with your brother?'

'I tell you, I was nowhere near Abel's field. I didn't see a soul.'

The two cops exchanged looks. The Sergeant's long experience read the message in his superior's eyes: we've got all we're going to get here, time to move on.

'Yes, well, thank you Cain, this has been—'

'Have you the beginning of an idea what it's like going through life with a thing like this stuck on your forehead? Everyone convinced you're guilty of a crime you didn't commit? It wreaks havoc with your family life, for a start. You know, after I was framed for Abel's death, I went into the Land of Nod, and I knew my wife "and she conceived and bore Enoch . . . And unto Enoch was born Irad: and Irad begat Mehujael: and Mehujael begat Methusael: and Methusael begat Lamech. And Lamech took unto him two wives: the name of the one was—"'

'Yeah, we get it,' said Inspector Gabriel. 'You have a big family. What exactly is your point?'

'Just that they're all up here and, because I got this Mark on my forehead, none of them ever comes to visit.'

'*Cherchez la femme*,' said the Inspector as they wafted back to the station.

113

'I'm sorry. I don't speak foreign.'

'"Look for the woman." Old-fashioned bit of advice, but sometimes old-fashioned is good.'

'What, boss? You're suggesting we check out Cain's old lady? The one who conceived and bore Enoch?'

'No, no. We may get to her eventually, but she's not where we go next.'

'Then who?'

'Look, Uriel, Cain and Abel were brothers. Bit of sibling rivalry there I'd say. In fact, if Cain did actually do it, the ultimate sibling rivalry. And who's going to know those two boys best? Who was around all the time they were growing up?'

'Eve? You mean Eve?'

'You bet your life I do.'

Officially, there wasn't any pecking order in Heaven. Everyone was entitled to exactly the same amount of celestial bliss. That was the theory anyway, but some souls, by virtue of the profile they'd had on earth, did get special attention. Gabriel and Uriel were made well aware of that as they entered Eve's eternal home.

The décor was very feminine. Clouds, which are by their nature fluffy, had never been fluffier, and Eve herself moved around in her own nimbus. She had selected for her body image the moment when she first sprang from Adam's rib and, although she was now clothed, the diaphanous white catsuit, through which a fig-leaf *cache-sexe* could be clearly seen, left no ambiguity about the precise definition of her contours. The two detectives could not repress within them a vague stirring which they distantly remembered as lust.

Eve was surrounded by other female souls, similarly dressed. Their main purpose was apparently to worship her, but there seemed little doubt that, if the need arose, they would protect her too.

She was one of the souls whose position in Heaven had undergone radical reassessment. After Cain and Abel, Eve had given birth to Seth. 'And the days of Adam after he had begotten Seth were eight hundred years: and he begat sons and daughters. And all the days that Adam lived were nine hundred and thirty years: and he died.' So, though Eve did slightly predecease her husband, she had had a busy life and, at the time of her death, she was very tired.

And then, when she arrived at the Pearly Gates, there had been a rather unseemly altercation. St Peter, a Judaco-Christian traditionalist, blamed Eve for Original Sin, and was not about to let in a soul who, to his mind, had corrupted the purity of humankind for all Eternity. The Big Man himself had to intervene before the newcomer was admitted, and for a good few millennia, Eve suffered from a certain amount of misogynistic prejudice.

It was only when Sixties feminists – particularly American ones – started dying that her status changed. The new generation of female souls entering Heaven saw Eve as an icon. Her eating of the Apple and persuading Adam to do the same was no longer a shameful betrayal of the human race; it was now viewed as an act of female empowerment. Eve had resisted the phallocentric dictates of the traditional male establishment and asserted herself as a woman. So far as her newly arrived acolytes were concerned, she could do no wrong. For them, she was an Earth Mother . . . in every sense.

Uriel may not have been, but Inspector Gabriel was aware of this recent reassessment, and accordingly circumspect as he began his questioning.

'I'm sorry to go into ancient history, Eve . . .'

'It's not about the Apple again, is it?'

'No, no. Nothing to do with the Apple, I promise.'

'Thank the Lord! I've done so many interviews on that subject that I'm totally Appled out.'

The expression was greeted by a ripple of sycophantic appreciation from her acolytes.

'The Apple won't be mentioned.'

'Good.' She gave Gabriel a shrewd, calculating gaze. 'So does that mean it's sex?'

'No, not even sex.'

She started to look interested. 'There's a novelty. I tell you, the number of times I've to talk about sex to *OT Magazine* or *Halo*, well, you just wouldn't believe it.'

'No, I want to talk about your kids.'

'Which ones? There were quite a few of them. Remember for over nine hundred years Adam was a serial begetter.'

'It's the first two we're interested in. Cain and Abel.'

'Ah.' Eve looked thoughtful. 'Those boys have a hell of a lot to answer for.'

'Not least giving Jeffrey Archer an idea for an novel,' Sergeant Uriel mumbled.

His boss ignored him. 'The thing is, we all know the official story. As printed in the Bible. I just wondered, Eve, what with you having been on the scene at the time, do you agree with what's written there?'

'It's the Word of God. That was there in the beginning. Holy Writ. Doesn't pay to argue with the Word of God.'

'I wasn't asking you whether it paid.' Inspector Gabriel's voice took on the harder note he'd used to employ in interrogations. It sounded pleasingly nostalgic. 'I was asking whether you agree that Genesis, Chapter Four, is an accurate account of what took place in that field.'

'I was never in the field.'

'No. Cain says he wasn't either.'

'Oh.'

'I mean, when he was growing up, was Cain a truthful kid?'

'Yeah, I did my best to teach all of them the value of honesty.'

'The knowledge of right and wrong?'

'I thought I made it clear, Inspector Gabriel, that the Apple was off-bounds.'

'Oh, sure. Sorry. Listen, Eve, what were Cain

and Abel like? What kind of kids? Did they have similar personalities?'

'No way!' She grinned wryly at the recollection. 'No, no, no. Abel was very anal. You know, the way he kept those sheep, all neat in little folds, clearing up after them all the time with a pooper-scooper. Whereas Cain was more laid-back, bit of a slob really. OK, he'd occasionally till the fields, but not like his life depended on it. Tilling – he could take it or leave it.

'I mean, when they presented God with the offerings, that was typical of their characters. Abel got all "the firstlings of his flock" groomed with little bows round their necks "and the fat thereof" in neat little packages. That's Abel all over. But when Cain comes up, well, for a start he's late, and "the fruit of the ground" is a few root vegetables still covered in earth, like they'd just been pulled up that morning, which of course they had.

'So it was no wonder the Big Man went for Abel's offering rather than Cain's . . . as Abel had planned He would.'

'But did the incident cause dissension between the two boys?'

Eve shrugged. 'Not that I was aware of. Cain knew Abel was always going to be the arse-licker, he was cool with that.'

'And yet, according to the Bible, he still slew his brother.'

Eve looked uncomfortable. 'Yeah, well, he must've had a rush of blood to the head.' She fell back on the old formula. 'It's the Word of God. You can't argue with that.' Her manner became brusque. 'Now I'm afraid I really must get on. Another feminist historical revisionist has just died and we girls are organising a Welcome Party for her at the Pearly Gates.'

'Yeah, just a couple of things before you go . . .'

'What?' Her patience with him was wearing thin.

'I wondered if you knew where I could find Abel?'

'No one has seen him since he came up here, assuming, that is, he did come up here.'

'Doesn't that seem odd?'

Another shrug from the archetypal shoulders. 'I've found it doesn't do to question too many things that happen up here. The Big Man knows what he's doing. We get very well looked after. Doesn't do to rock the boat. Just trust the Word of God.'

'And what about Adam? Will it be easy for me to find Adam?'

She let out a sardonic chuckle. 'Oh yeah, easy to find him. Probably not so easy to get any sense out of him.'

'Why? What's he—?'

But Inspector Gabriel had had all the time Eve was going to allot him. She looked around at her acolytes. 'Now let's get this party organised.'

Her words were greeted by an enthusiastic simpering of dead American feminists, through which Inspector Gabriel managed to ask, 'One last question. Did Cain have any allergies?'

'What?'

'Was there anything he was allergic to?'

'Oh, we're talking a long time ago now. A long, long time ago. You're asking a lot for me to remember that. I mean, after all those kids . . .' Eve's heavenly brows wrinkled with the effort of recollection. 'Yeah, maybe there was something, though . . .'

'Can you remember what?'

'No, I . . . Oh, just a minute.' A beam of satisfaction spread across the original female face. 'Yeah, there was one thing that used to bring him out in this really nasty rash, not helped of course by his clothes being made of leaves, and there weren't any antihistamines around then or—'

'I'm sorry, I must interrupt you. What was the thing that Cain was allergic to?'

'Sheep,' said Eve.

'It sounds to me like he was telling the truth,' said Sergeant Uriel, suddenly loquacious after taking a backseat during the interviews with Cain and Eve. 'I mean, his own Mom's confirmed Cain had this allergy, so he's not going to go near Abel's field, is he? Not if it's full of sheep.'

'I wouldn't be so sure.' Inspector Gabriel shook his head solemnly. 'I've dealt with enough murderers to know how strong the urge to kill can be. A guy who's set his mind on topping someone is not going to be put off by the thought of getting itchy skin.'

120

'Maybe, boss, but I'm still having problems seeing Cain as our murderer.'

'Me too. But we don't have any other very convincing scenario, do we? I mean, if only we could prove that Cain had an alibi. But there once again we're up against one of the big problems of the time period we're dealing with.'

'How'dya mean?'

'It's like with the suspects, Uriel. Not a lot of people around, either to commit the murder or to give someone an alibi to prove they didn't commit the murder.'

'Yeah. We're back to Cain, Eve and Adam.'

'And the Serpent. Never forget the Serpent, Uriel.'

'I won't.' The Sergeant shrugged hopefully. 'Oh well, maybe we'll get the vital lead from Adam.'

'Maybe. I wonder what Eve meant about it not being easy to get any sense out of him.'

It soon became clear why his former rib had lowered her expectations of coherence from her husband. Adam was seriously old. When he grew up longevity was highly prized, and he got a charge from being the oldest man to have died in the world (though, had he thought about it, he would have received the same accolade by dying at ninety-eight, or forty-three, or seventeen, or one week). So he had selected the moment of death as his Heaven Age . . . and no one looks their best at nine hundred and thirty.

He was, of course, very well looked after. Some deceased nurses, who'd really got a charge out of their caring profession on earth, were in Seventh Heaven with Adam to look after.

But, as a subject for police interrogation, he left a lot to be desired. All he did was sit in a wheeleloud and chuckle to himself, saying over and over again, 'I'm the Daddy of them all.'

Gabriel and Uriel didn't bother staying with him long.

Back at the station a pall of despondence hung between them as they yet again went through the evidence.

'Every minute I'm getting more convinced of Cain's innocence,' said the Inspector, 'but I just can't see who else is in the frame.'

'There's still the Serpent.'

'Yes, sure. I checked. Satan's coming up here for an Interfaith Symposium in a couple of weeks. He's giving a paper on "George W Bush and the Religious Wrong." We could probably get a word with him then, but . . .' Inspector Gabriel's lower lip curled with lack of conviction.

'Why have you suddenly turned against Satan as a suspect? Come on, he's the Prince of Darkness. He's responsible for all the bad things in the world. Slaying one keeper of sheep here or there isn't going to be a big deal to a guy like that.'

'No, but that's why I'm going off him. It's too

small a crime. There's no way Satan would bother with killing Abel. Or if he did it, he'd certainly claim the credit.'

'Yeah, but his old boss God had just started His big new idea – Mankind. Satan wants to screw that up, so he kills Abel and makes it look like Cain did it.'

'But if he wanted to destroy Mankind, why did he stop there? Why didn't he slay the other three humans?'

'Erm, well . . .' Theological debate had never been Sergeant Uriel's strong suit. He'd always been better at splaying hoods across their automobiles and getting them to spill the beans. 'Maybe he slays Abel, because that way he brings evil into the world?'

'He'd already brought evil into the world by making Eve eat the Apple.'

'But . . .'

'No, no, quiet, Uriel.' Inspector Gabriel scratched at his grizzled brow while he tried to shape his thoughts. 'I think we've got to go right back to the beginning.'

'The beginning of the case?'

'The beginning of the world. What's the first thing that happens in the Bible?'

'"In the beginning God created the heaven and the earth,"' quoted Sergeant Uriel, who had been to Sunday school.

'OK, that's Genesis. But we have another description of the beginning.'

'Do we, boss? Where?'

'First verse of The Gospel According to Saint John. "In the beginning was the Word, and the Word was with God, and the Word was God. The same was in the beginning with God." What does that sound like to you, Uriel?'

'I don't know. It's kinda neatly written.' The Sergeant thought about the words a bit more. 'Sounds kinda like an advertising slogan.'

'Yes.' Gabriel nodded with satisfaction. 'That's exactly what it sounds like. And what did Cain say? "The Word of God has never been more than a whitewash job. Public Relations. Spin."'

'Yeah, but he would say that, wouldn't he? If he was the murderer, he'd say it.'

'But if he wasn't the murderer, why would he say it then?'

'Because, but for the Word of God, he wouldn't have had to go through life with something on his forehead that makes him look like an ambulance.'

Inspector Gabriel tapped a reflective finger against the bridge of his nose. 'That might be the reason. Other possibility is that he said it because it was true . . .'

'Sorry?'

'That it all was just a whitewash. PR. Spin.'

Obviously, though there were no secrets in Heaven – that would have gone against the whole spirit of the place – some things weren't particularly advertised. Where the Big Man lived was one of them. The precise location was never defined, for security reasons of course. Though He wouldn't have been at risk from any of the usual denizens of Heaven, there had been considerable slackening of border controls in recent years, and the increase of Cultural Exchange Programmes with The Other Place brought its own hazards.

In the same way, the whole administrative apparatus of Heaven was, well, not overt. This was for no sinister reason. Most people had spent far too much of their time on earth organizing things, and longed for an Eternity which was totally without responsibilities. Too much evidence of the stage management of Heaven would only have brought back tedious memories for them.

But everything was, of course, above board, and totally transparent. Any soul who wished to find out some detail of the celestial management would instantly have been given the information required. It was just that very few people ever bothered to ask.

This was borne in upon Inspector Gabriel when he first began enquiring about The Word. Most of the souls he talked to claimed ignorance of where he'd find it, so he went to ask Raphael, who heard all the heavenly gossip in his bar. But the Saint was uncharacteristically evasive. '"The Word of God?" That's always been around. The "Logos" from the Greek, you know.'

'But you don't know where it actually is?'

Mine Heavenly Host shook his head. 'I've always

thought of it more as a metaphysical concept than a concrete one.' You did get a high class of bar room chat at St Raphael's.

But it was in the bar that Inspector Gabriel found the clue. There was a list of regulations pinned up on the wall. They weren't there because they were likely to be infringed, but for a lot of souls a bar didn't feel like a bar without a list of regulations. So there were a few prohibitions like 'Thou shalt not spit on the floor', 'Thou shalt not wear muddy boots in the bar' and 'Thou shalt put thy drinks on the nectar-mats supplied.' At the bottom of the list, though, as Gabriel pointed out triumphantly to Uriel, was printed: 'A Word of God Publication', followed by an address many clouds away.

It was a huge white tower block, with 'The Word of God' on the tiniest, most discreet gold plate by the front door. The receptionist wore smart business wings and a huge professional smile. 'How can I help you, gentlemen?'

'There's something we want to inquire about the Word of God,' said Inspector Gabriel.

'May I ask what is the nature of your inquiry? Is it Purely Factual, are you looking for an Informed Commentary on the Text, tracing your family history through the Begetting Lists or Challenging the Accuracy of Holy Writ?' Her voice contained no disapproval of any of these possibilities.

'I guess it'd be the last.'

Sergeant Uriel spelled it out. 'Yes, we're Challenging the Accuracy of Holy Writ.'

'Very well,' said the girl, with another omni-competent smile. 'You'll need to speak to someone in Doctrinal Spin.' She leant forward to the keyboard in front of her. 'Let me see who's free.'

The man who was free had chosen thirty-five as his Heaven Age. He was neat and punctilious, and his character was reflected in a neat and punctil-ious office. Pens and papers were laid out on his desk with geometric precision.

'Cain and Abel,' he said. 'Goodness, you are going back a long way.'

'Nearly to the beginning of time. I hope your records go back that far.'

'Don't have any worries on that score,' he said with a patronising laugh. 'Remember, "In the beginning was the Word". These offices have been here right from the start.'

'Even before "God created the heaven and the earth"?' asked Sergeant Uriel.

'Oh yes. Long before that. It was here that the whole department strategy for the creation of the heaven and the earth was devised.'

'So this is where the Big Man did the planning?'

'This is where He was advised on the most appropriate ways of planning, yes. And, inciden-tally, in these offices we still refer to Him as 'God'. The 'Big Man' initiative was only developed in the last century to make him sound more approachable and user-friendly.'

'OK,' said Gabriel. 'So you're kind of strategic thinkers and advisers to God?'

'That's exactly what we are.'

'Right then, can you tell us the strategic thinking behind the Cain and Abel story?'

The young man pursed his lips unwillingly. 'I won't deny that I'd rather not tell you. My personal view is that some secrets should be kept secret. In the same way, I can't claim to be an enthusiast of all these Interfaith Dialogues with The Other Place.'

'Maybe not, but since the Freedom of Heavenly Information Act, you are obliged to—'

'I am fully aware of my obligations, thank you,' he snapped. 'Yes, the new buzz word in Heaven is transparency. All records are available to whoever wants to see them.'

'And presumably,' said Inspector Gabriel, 'it was God who brought in that policy?'

'Goodness, no, God doesn't bring in any policies. The Think Tanks here at The Word of God recommend policies to Him. In the past those policies have been extremely sensible. But in recent years there has been a younger element recruited here' – his lip curled with distaste – 'who have brought in these modern notions of transparency and accountability. I was always more in favour of keeping some mystery about Heaven. Nothing wrong with a bit of ignorance, you know.

But these new, so-called Young Turks have no respect for tradition and keep trying to make God trendy, and I'm afraid to say He listens to them in a way that—'

Inspector Gabriel stemmed this flood of bitchy office politics. 'Can we get back to Cain and Abel, please?'

The young man's lips were tightened as if by a drawstring. 'Very well.' Unwillingly he summoned up a file to his computer screen. 'What precisely do you wish to know?'

'Whether Cain was the perp or not,' Uriel replied.

'You have to set this in context,' said the young man primly. 'The creation of the heaven and the earth and light and the firmament and the waters and the dry land and the seeds and the fruit and the sun and the moon and every living creature after their kind and man was a very considerable achievement – particularly inside a week. But obviously it wasn't perfect. Corners had been cut so inevitably shortcomings were discovered, and in the ensuing weeks and years a certain level of adjustment was required.

'The really big problem was that of good and evil.'

'But I thought that was sorted out in the Garden of Eden. Adam and Eve got the knowledge of good and evil after the Serpent had persuaded her—'

'Inspector Gabriel, will you please let me finish!

Having the knowledge of good and evil was not enough. Even outside the Garden of Eden, Adam and Eve's lives were still pretty idyllic. The Think Tanks here reckoned a more vivid demonstration of human evil was required. So a rather brilliant young copywriter had the idea—'

'Copywriter? You have copywriters here?'

'How else do you think the Word of God got written? Of course we have copywriters. Anyway, this rather brilliant young man had the idea of creating a really archetypal act of evil.'

There was an inevitability about it. 'The murder of Abel by Cain.'

'You're ahead of me, Inspector,' the official said sourly. 'Yes. If this murder was recorded in Holy Writ, then it would serve to all mankind as an example of human evil. And we had to get more evil into the world somehow. The people in this building had to look ahead. George W Bush was going to need people to bomb. How can you bomb people unless you can convince other people that they are evil? Paradise – even the paradise that Adam and Eve found after they'd been evicted from Eden – was just a bit too good, not viable in the long term, you know.' He snickered smugly. 'Setting up an apparent murder solved that problem at a stroke.'

'You say an "apparent murder".'

'Yes, and I say that quite deliberately, Inspector.'

'You mean' – Sergeant Uriel pieced things together – 'Abel wasn't actually killed?'

'His death was recorded in Holy Writ. That was all that mattered. There was no need for him to actually die.'

'So Cain didn't do it?'

'No,' the man agreed smugly, 'but everyone thought he did it, so the aim of that rather bright young copywriter was achieved. The world now contained evil, which in the future could provide a justification for . . . absolutely anything.'

'So what happened to Abel? Adam and Eve and Cain would have noticed if he was still around, wouldn't they?'

'Yes, Inspector. The people here at the Word of God did a deal with him. They offered him an early exit from earth and a good job up here, where he could keep to himself and wouldn't have to mix with all the other riff-raff. Who's going to turn down that kind of package? And all this was the work' – an even more complacent smile spread across his face – 'of one very bright young copy-writer.'

'I get it,' said Inspector Gabriel. 'You're that bright young copywriter, aren't you?'

'No,' came the reply. 'I'm Abel.'

The cops were surprised by Cain's reaction to the findings of their investigation. They thought he'd be ecstatic finally to have his innocence proved.

But no, he asked them to keep quiet about the whole business. Take away his claim not to have killed his brother, and he wouldn't have anything to talk about.

Besides, he was getting rather fond of the Mark on his forehead.

KEN BRUEN

PUNK

D on't give me shit about ghosts.
Things that go bump in the night
The fuck are you kidding?
I've seen enough monsters walking around to
give any tough guy nightmares and the sooner
they got put in the ground, the better

When I hit sixty, I got out . . . my line of work,
you kill people for a living, it takes it's toll and
you know what, it was getting stale, kind of lame,
no buzz there no more. Sure, it was a regular gig,
I'm not bitching, let's get that clear from the off,
I want to whine, you'll know.

But I had the bucks stashed, nice little invest-
ment plan and figured, enjoy.

My roots are Irish, I'm not saying it helps to be
a Mick in the killing business, we don't have the
edge in it, ask the Italians, but I like to think I
brought certain poetry to my work, an artist if you
will

Truth to tell, and I always tell the truth, I cant
abide a liar, give me any scumbag, don't care what
he's done, he fronts up, I can cut him some slack
but a liar, whoa, don't get me started, the thing

is, I was getting slow, the old reflexes were zoning out.

And I just didn't have the taste for it, you got to love what you do, am I right. Don't read me wrong here, you listening. I didn't love *killing* . . . I'm not some psycho. I relished the details, the planning, and the clean efficiency of despatch.

My Mom was Irish, came over on the boat, got a job as a cleaning lady and then met my old man, all he ever cleaned was his plate. She was from Galway, reared me to stories of The Claddagh, the swans, the old streets of the what used to be a Spanish town and the music, ah the wild mix of bodhrans, uileann pipes, spoons, fiddle, and the keening voice.

Jeez, she'd a grand voice, hear her sing . . . Carrickfergus, fuck, that was like a prayer in action. She was real hot on religion, mass every Sunday, confession, the whole nine

Get this, my old man was an atheist, believed in nothing, especially not work, he wasn't violent, just feckless, found a woman who'd pay the freight and let go. When I was 17, big and OK, a little mean, I slung his ass on out, him whining

'Where am I going to go?'

I said

'Try the track, you spend most of your life there anyway.'

My Mom would have taken him back, Irish women, that demented loyalty, but I was running the show and she was real proud of the money I was producing. I heard he got him some other woman in Canarsie, like I give a fuck

Good riddance

I'd done my first job for Mr Dunne, he'd told me

'Kid, I got a guy giving me lots of grief, you got any ideas on that?'

I did

The guy is in the East River

Mr Dunne never asked for details, just handed me a wedge of serious change, said

'You're my boy.'

I was

He used me sparingly, a full year before he had another problem and I took care of that too.

Automobile accident.

Grimaldi's was the place back then and he took me out for dinner there, said, handing me an envelope,

'Get a good suit, we're putting on the Ritz.'

He talked kind of odd but I respected him

The staff there, falling over him and he said

'See kid, this is juice and you . . . you're my main supply.'

I was mid bite on the biggest steak I'd ever seen and swallowed it sweet, asked

'Really?'

He was drinking wine, lots of it, I never cared for it, give me a cold one, I'm good, and a nice shot of Jameson to round out the evening, what more do you need? He said

'See, I don't have to do a whole lot now, I hint . . . you want the kid on your sorry ass and presto, the problem's gone.'

He ate a half mountain of mashed potato, awash in gravy, then said

'You've a dark future ahead of you kid but you need to be real careful.'

I pledged that I would.

And I was

My Mom got sick last year, the cancer, and on her last night, she took off her wedding band, the gold Claddagh, put it on my finger, croaked

'Go to Ireland for me gasun (son)'

I tried to give her back the ring, me heart was torn in a hundred ways and she near screamed

'I worked hard for that piece of gold, you think I'm letting it sit in a box in the cold ground.'

It's on my right hand, the heart pointing out, means I'm on the lookout

I'm not

Women talk

I don't talk

My last job, I don't really like to dwell on, it was before Mr Dunne got his, a two bit loan shark gutted him, left him spilling his mashed potatoes all over East 33rd and Second.

Mr Dunne has summoned me, looked bothered, said

'Frank, I have a real delicate situation.'

'I was no longer the kid, had moved too far along for that. He lit a cigar, his face serious, continued

'There's a teenager, seventeen years of age, name of Gerry Kane, he's knocked up my niece and is fond of hitting her, I want him brought to his senses, nothing major, you understand how to behave, you reading me?'

I had thought I was

It went south, badly

I'd given him a few slaps, the way you do and the punk, he pulled a knife

Can you fucking believe it?

A knife . . .

On me?

Didn't he know anything

And it got away from me, first time ever, I lost it, big time, they say I scalped him and other stuff

I'm not making excuses, trying me own self or nothing but I'd been doing a lot of speed, you think you can just kill people and get by on the odd brew with a Jameson chaser

Grow up

He had the most amazing blond mop of hair, like Brian Jones before the swimming pool and wait til you hear this, he was seventeen, right? And on his right arm, was the tattoo, *Semper Fi* . . . the little bastard, I had my buddy buy the farm in Desert Storm and this piece of shit, this trash, this *nothing*, was wearing it . . . for fashion?

That section of skin, I threw in a dumpster on Flatbush

The shit hit the fan, naturally and maybe it was

just as well that Mr Dunne got diced by the loan shark.

I was finished in the biz.

So, I made my move, liquidised my assets, sold my Mom's house and flew to the West of Ireland

Rented a little cottage in Oranmore, a beautiful village on the outskirts of the city.

There's a little river runs right by my window and get this, you can fish it, got me some nice trout and cooked the suckers me own self.

My cottage looks just like the one in *The Quiet Man* and the locals, they're real friendly, the one place in the world where they love Yanks. They're not too nosy, I go to the local on a Saturday night, buy for the house and they like me a lot, well, they like my dollars

Same difference.

They even try some matchmaking, a widow named Theresa, she comes round after the pub on Sat and I give her a workout, she thinks I'm very quiet but her, she could talk for Ireland, and does

I like to read . . . you're going to laugh your socks off but I read poetry, that guy Yeats, the fucker had it . . . sings to me, there's a small book-store, mainly second hand stuff and they keep any poetry for me.

I'm getting me an education

I was reading . . . *A terrible beauty . . .*

Jeez, like some awful omen that

I had that marked with my Mums memorial card

when . . . when . . . how do I describe the beginning.

I had a log fire going, the book on in me lap, and a wee drop of Jameson by my arm when there was a scratching on the door . . . I figured some stray dog.

I opened the door and no one there, then noticed a small envelope on the step, took it inside, reckoning it was another invite to some local event. Tore the flap and inside was a single sheet of paper with the words . . . *Semper Fi*

OK, so it knocked a stir out of me

I'm not going to argue the toss

But I'd been down this road

When I arrived in Ireland, before I got this cottage, I had to stay in Galway, in a hotel, no hardship there, but the city, it was like mini America . . . Gap, Banana Republic, MacDonalds, all the teenagers talking like hybrid rejects from The O.C.

And in the pubs, on tap, freaking Millers, Bud, Pabst . . . the fuck was going on?

And then I saw him, the blond kid, working the stick in a pub on quay St . . . the spit of Gerry and he smirked at me . . . like he knew . . . said

'You're a Yank . . . been there . . . *Dunne that . . .*'

Unnerved me, fuck, gave me a shot of the tremors but I was lucky, a local skel, a bottom of the pond dealer, hooked me up to my beloved speed and once I got in that place, I knew what to do

Scalped him

Yeah, see who *Dunne that*?
I have his blond hair in my trunk
And figured that was that
Now this
Who was fucking with me and why
The next Sat night, I'm in the pub and Dolan, the owner, smarmy schmuck, asks
'You met Gearoid?'
What?
I couldn't even pronounce it, one of those dumb Irish names that you need to be a German with a bad lisp to say, so I went
'Who?'
He smiles, indicates a group of young people drinking, yeah, bottles of Bud, Tequila chasers and I see the Brian Jones look alike, Dolan says
'That's him, he's got his own band . . . named Punk . . . he's hoping to get to America, you might give him a few pointers.'
I got the fuck out of there, leaving a full pint of Guinness on the counter.
I was back home, draining a double Jameson when Theresa came round, all concern, *Dolan* had told her I took a *turn* and she was fussing, like a freakign hen, the speed was hitting max in my blood and the Jameson was whispering to it, not whispering anything good. I asked
'That nephew of his, Garage . . . is it?'
She laughed, the dumbass Yank, mutilating the accent, and I tell you, I don't take mocking real good, she said

'Use the English form.'

My teeth were grinding, I could hear them and I near spat

'Gee, I would if you'd share it, is it like a secret or something?'

She shot me a look

Me . . .

Shoot me a look?

Was she fucking kidding, you don't give me looks, unless you're packing something more lethal than bad attitude, but then, she changed course, like women do, said

'Gerry, it's Gerry.'

I dropped my glass, Jameson leaking into the rug and she's fussing, searching for a cloth, I roared

'Leave the fucking thing, is that his name, are you jerking my chain?'

She put her hands on her hips, barked

'Don't swear at me mister, my late husband, God rest his soul, he never swore at me and I'm not going to let some . . .'

I cut her off, demanded

'Why he's here?'

She was thrown, asked

'What . . . he's on holiday, he has a band he . . .'

'I know about the fucking band, I asked you why he's here.'

She gathered up her coat and the groceries she'd brought for our meal, said

'Well, I know when I'm not wanted, I'll return when you soften your cough mister.'

After she was gone, I poured some Jameson, chanced another hit of speed, needed to think . . .

The kid in Galway, when I'd done him I'd been confused, because when I lifted his sleeve, there was no tattoo, none.

I went to my trunk, unlocked the heavy Yale on it and pushing aside the blond hair, I took out my knfie, the blade honed to wafer thin perfection, shouted out loud

'Let em come, I'm so fucking ready.'

Later, I chilled, thinking, I'd over reacted, new country and all, those spuds and the Guinness, that shit knocked you on yer ass.

So I calmed a bit, was even able to read some Yeats, selected a poem at random . . . *The Stolen Child*

Fuck, isn't that what the Irish love . . . that irony they go on about . . . I laughed out loud, laughed till the tears ran down my face, the knife sitting snugly in my lap.

Next few days were without incident, but I kept the knife in my jacket, I was easing down a notch but I was getting antsy, I was ready, they could send all the Brian Jones they liked, I'd take em all, see if I wouldn't

Changed pubs though

On the other end of the village, was a more modern place, I preferred the traditional one but what the hell, killers can't be choosers.

Sitting there over my pint, Bushmills as back, the Jameson was obviously not agreeing with me, a tiny hint of speed in me blood, reading the Irish Independent, lots of reports on Iraq, I skipped them.

Then a feature on a new movie about the life of Brian Jones, speculating that he'd been murdered.

A shadow fell across me, I looked up to see Dolan's nephew, sweeping the blond locks out of his eyes.

He was wearing faded flared jeans and a black sweat shirt with the logo

Harvard hurts

Like he'd fucking know?

He asked

'May I join you for a moment?'

His accent had that quasi American uplift, as if everything terminated in a question, if he asked me about The Mets, I'd pop him in the goddamned mouth. I said

'Why not.'

He slid onto the stool opposite, never taking his eyes off me, asked

'Get you a jar?'

'Least he hadn't called it a brewski . . . yet. His sleeves were rolled down and I couldn't see his arms, his left wrist had all those multicoloured bands they collect, the barman brought him over a bottle of Bud, packet of chips, or crisps as they call them here. No glass, he drank from the bottle, cool as the hippy choker round his neck. He raised the bottle, said

143

'Slainte.'

I raised my pint, said

'That too.'

His mouth had that half smirk going, as if the joke was known to everyone but me, I asked

'Help you with something?'

He drank noisily, I hate that, all gurgle and no finesse, he belched then

'Me and me band, we're going Stateside and I was wondering if you could hook us up with the names of some hotels in the Village, Like Greenwich Village, we're going to try for a gig at The Fillmore.'

Good luck

I said

'The internet, your best bet.'

Something dark flitted briefly across his face and he tossed his hair, said

'I thought you might know someone who, you know, would open some doors for us?'

He wanted to mind fuck, I'd gone rounds with the best of em and left em in the dumpster . . . so I could play . . . said

'Kid, my age, most people I know, they're dead.'

Didn't faze him, he signalled for another brew, said

'Ah, tis a pity but shure, never mind, t'was worth a shot.'

The speed hit a wave and before I knew it, I asked

'Show me your right arm'

'What?'

I kept my voice steady, said

'You're not deaf, you heard me.'

He stood up, gave me his tough eye, said

'Jaysus, you're not in it, you need to get a grip buddy.'

He was waving away the barman and the ordered drink, I said

'I'm not your buddy.'

He moved to the counter and joined some gaggle of girls, I could see them glancing over, laughing out loud

Man, jeering, that's all they've got, like that rates on my radar.

I finished my drink, made my way out and grabbed his arm, whispered to him

'Hair today, gone tomorrow.'

I stopped sleeping, I wanted to be ready lest someone leave something at my door, I slugged the Jameson, did some of the speed, read Yeats a lot but he'd stopped talking to me, the music was gone

Must have been a week after, I saw a poster for the band . . . Punk, last concert before the American tour

In the local hall.

The way I have it figured, I'll wait in the alley behind the venue, get him on his way out . . . No, better, follow him home and do the business

Then I'll get to examine his arm at leisure

The tattoo's going to be on there, isn't it?
I don't doubt that other blond punks will show
up but I'm real easy
The trunk has lots of room
Maybe I'll try another poet, you think?

PETER LOVESEY

NEEDLE MATCH

Murder was done on Court Eleven on the third day of Wimbledon, 1981. Fortunately for the All England Club, it wasn't anything obvious like a strangling or a shooting, but the result was the same for the victim, except that he suffered longer. It took three days for him to die. I can tell you exactly how it happened, because I was one of the ball boys for the match.

When I was thirteen I was taught to be invisible. But before you decide this isn't your kind of story let me promise you it isn't about magic. There's nothing spooky about me. And there was nothing spooky about my instructor, Brigadier Romilly. He was flesh and blood all right and so were the terrified kids who sat at his feet.

'You'll be invisible, every one of you, before I've finished with you,' he said in his parade-ground voice, and we believed him, we third-years from Merton Comprehensive.

A purple scar like a sabre-cut stretched downwards from the edge of the Brigadier's left eye, over his mouth to the point of his chin. He'd grown

147

a bristly ginger moustache over part of it, but we could easily see where the two ends joined. Rumour had it that his face had been slashed by a Mau Mau warrior's machete in the Kenyan terrorist war of the Fifties. We didn't know anything about the Mau Mau, except that the terrorist must have been crazy to tangle with the Brigadier – who grabbed him by the throat and strangled him.

'Don't ever get the idea that you're doing this to be seen. You'll be there, on court with Mr McEnroe and Mr Borg – if I think you're good enough – and no one will notice you, no one. When the game is in play you'll be as still as the net post, and as interesting. For Rule Two of the Laws of Tennis states that the court has certain permanent fixtures like the net and the net posts and the umpire's chair. And the list of permanent fixtures includes you, the ball boys, in your respective places. So you can tell your mothers and fathers and your favourite aunties not to bother to watch. If you're doing your job they won't even notice you.'

To think we'd volunteered for this. By a happy accident of geography ours was one of the schools chosen to provide the ball boys and ball girls for the Championships. 'It's a huge honour,' our headmaster had told us. 'You do it for the prestige of the school. You're on television. You meet the stars, hand them their towels, supply them with the balls, pour their drinks. You can be proud.'

The Brigadier disabused us of all that. 'If any

of you are looking for glory, leave at once. Go back to your stuffy classrooms. I don't want your sort in my squad. The people I want are functionaries, not glory-seekers. Do you understand? You will do your job, brilliantly, the way I show you. It's all about timing, self-control and, above all, being invisible.'

The victim was poisoned. Once the poison was in his system there was no antidote. Death was inevitable, and lingering.

So in the next three months we learned to be invisible. And it was damned hard work, I can tell you. I had no idea what it would lead to. You're thinking we murdered the Brigadier? No, he's a survivor. So far as I know, he's still alive and terrifying the staff in a retirement home.

I'm going to tell it as it happened, and we start on the November afternoon in 1980 when my best friend Eddie Pringle and I were on an hour's detention for writing something obscene on Blind Pugh's blackboard. Mr Pugh, poor soul, was our chemistry master. He wasn't really blind, but his sight wasn't the best. He wore thick glasses with prism lenses, and we little monsters took full advantage. Sometimes Nemesis arrived, in the shape of our headmaster, Mr Neames, breezing into the lab, supposedly for a word with Blind Pugh, but in reality to catch us red-handed playing poker behind bits of apparatus or rolling mercury along the bench-tops. Those who escaped with a detention were the lucky ones.

'I've had enough of this crap,' Eddie told me in the detention room. 'I'm up for a job as ball boy.'

'What do you mean – Wimbledon?' I said. 'That's not till next June.'

'They train you. It's every afternoon off school for six months – and legal. No more detentions. All you do is trot around the court picking up balls and chucking them to the players and you get to meet McEnroe and Connors and all those guys. Want to join me?'

It seemed the ideal escape plan, but of course we had to get permission from Nemesis to do it. Eddie and I turned ourselves into model pupils for the rest of term. No messing about. No detentions. Every homework task completed.

'In view of this improvement,' Nemesis informed us, 'I have decided to let you go on the training course.'

But when we met the Brigadier we found we'd tunnelled out of one prison into another. He terrified us. The regime was pitiless, the orders unrelenting.

'First you must learn how to be a permanent fixture. Stand straight, chest out, shoulders back, thumbs linked behind your back. Now hold it for five minutes. If anyone moves, I put the stopwatch back to zero again.'

Suddenly he threw a ball hard at Eddie and of course he ducked.

'Right,' the Brigadier announced, 'Pringle moved. The hand goes back to zero. You have to learn to be still, Pringle. Last year one of my boys was hit on the ear by a serve from Roscoe Tanner, over a hundred miles per hour, and he didn't flinch.'

We had a full week learning to be permanent fixtures, first standing at the rear of the court and then crouching like petrified sprinters at the sideline, easy targets for the Brigadier to shy at. A couple of the kids dropped out. We all had bruises.

'This is worse than school,' I told Eddie. 'We've got no freedom at all.'

'Right, he's a tyrant. Don't let him grind you down,' Eddie said.

In the second and third weeks we practised retrieving the balls, scampering back to the sidelines and rolling them along the ground to our colleagues or throwing them with one bounce to the Brigadier.

This was to be one of the great years of Wimbledon, with Borg, Connors and McEnroe at the peaks of their careers, challenging for the title. The rivalry would produce one match, a semifinal, that will be remembered for as long as tennis is played. And on an outside court, another, fiercer rivalry would be played out, with a fatal result. The players were not well known, but their backgrounds ensured a clash of ideologies. Jozsef Stanski, from Poland, was to meet Igor Voronin, a Soviet Russian, on Court Eleven, on the third day of the Championships.

Being an ignorant schoolboy at the time, I didn't appreciate how volatile it was, this match between two players from Eastern Europe. In the previous summer, 1980, the strike in the Gdansk shipyard, followed by widespread strikes throughout Poland, had forced the Communist government to allow independent trade unions. Solidarity – the trade union movement led by Lech Walesa – became a powerful, vocal organisation getting massive international attention. The Polish tennis star, Jozsef Stanski, was an outspoken supporter of Solidarity who criticised the state regime whenever he was interviewed.

The luck of the draw, as they say, had matched Stanski with Voronin, a diehard Soviet Communist, almost certainly a KGB agent. Later, it was alleged that Voronin was a state assassin.

Before all this, the training of the ball boys went on, a totalitarian regime of its own, always efficient, performed to numbers and timed on the stopwatch. There was usually a slogan to sum up whichever phase of ball boy lore we were mastering. 'Show before you throw, Richards, show before you throw, lad.'

No one dared to defy the Brigadier.

The early weeks were on indoor courts. In April, we got outside. We learned everything a ball boy could possibly need to know, how to hold three balls at once, collect a towel, offer a cold drink and dispose of the cup afterwards, stand in front of a player between games without making eye contact. The training didn't miss a trick.

At the end of the month we 'stood' for a club tournament at Queen's. It went well, I thought, until the Brigadier debriefed us. Debriefed? He tore strips off us for over an hour. We'd learnt nothing, he said. The Championships would be a disaster if we got within a mile of them. We were slow, we fumbled, stumbled and forgot to show before the throw. Worse, he saw a couple of us (Eddie and me, to be honest) exchange some words as we crouched either side of the net.

'If any ball boy under my direction so much as moves his lips ever again in the course of a match, I will come onto the court and seal his revolting mouth with packing tape.'

We believed him.

And we persevered. Miraculously the months went by and June arrived, and with it the Championships.

The Brigadier addressed us on the eve of the first day's play and to my amazement, he didn't put the fear of God into me. By his standards, it was a vote of confidence. 'You boys and girls have given me problems enough this year, but you're as ready as you ever will be, and I want you to know I have total confidence in you. When this great tournament is over and the best of you line up on the Centre Court to be presented to Her

Royal Highness before she meets the Champion, my pulse will beat faster and my heart will swell with pride, as will each of yours. And one of you, of course, will get a special award as best ball boy – or girl. That's the Championship that counts, you know. Never mind Mr Borg and Miss Navratilova. The real winner will be one of you. The decision will be mine, and you all start tomorrow as equals. In the second week I will draw up a short list. The pick of you, my elite squad, will stand in the finals. I will nominate the winner only when the tournament is over.'

I suppose it had been the severity of the build-up; to me those words were as thrilling and inspiring as King Henry's before the Battle of Agincourt. I wanted to be on Centre Court on that final day. I wanted to be best ball boy. I could see that all the others felt like me, and had the same gleam in their eyes.

I've never felt so nervous as I did at noon that first day, approaching the tall, creeper-covered walls of the All England Club, and passing inside and finding it was already busy with people on the terraces and promenades chatting loudly in accents that would have got you past any security guard in the world. Wimbledon twenty years ago was part of the social season, a blazer and tie occasion, entirely alien to a kid like me from a working class family.

My first match was on an outside court, thanks be to the Brigadier. Men's singles, between a tall

Californian and a wiry Frenchman. I marched on court with the other five ball boys and mysteriously my nerves ended the moment the umpire called 'Play.' We were so well-drilled that the training took over. My concentration was absolute. I knew precisely what I had to do. I was a small, invisible part of a well-oiled, perfectly tuned machine, the Rolls Royce of tennis tournaments. Six-three, six-three, six-three to the Californian, and we lined up and marched off again.

I stood in two more matches that first day, and they were equally straightforward in spite of some racquet abuse by one unhappy player whose service wouldn't go in. A ball boy is above all that. At home, exhausted, I slept better than I had for a week.

Day Two was Ladies' Day, when most of the women's first round matches were played. At the end of my second match I lined up for an ice-cream and heard a familiar voice. 'Got overheated in that last one, Richards?'

I turned to face the Brigadier, expecting a rollicking. I wasn't sure if ball boys in uniform were allowed to consume ice cream.

But the scar twitched into a grin. 'I watched you at work. You're doing a decent job, lad. Not invisible yet, but getting there. Keep it up and you might make Centre Court.'

I can tell you exactly what happened in the Stanski-Voronin match because I was one of the ball boys and my buddy Eddie Pringle was another, and has recently reminded me of it. Neither player was seeded. Stanski had won a five-setter in the first round against a little-known Englishman, and Voronin had been lucky enough to get a bye.

Court Eleven is hardly one of the show courts, and these two weren't well known players, but we still had plenty of swivelling heads following the action.

I'm sure some of the crowd understood that the players were at opposite extremes politically, but I doubt if anyone foresaw the terrible outcome of this clash. They may have noticed the coolness between the players, but that's one of the conventions of sport, particularly in a Grand Slam tournament. You shake hands at the end, but you psych yourself up to beat hell out of your rival first.

Back to the tennis. The first set went narrowly to Voronin, seven-five. I was so absorbed in my ball boy duties that the score almost passed me by. I retrieved the balls and passed them to the players when they needed them. Between games, I helped them to drinks and waited on them, just as we were programmed to do. I rather liked Stanski. His English wasn't up to much, but he made up for it with the occasional nod and even a hint of a smile.

Stanski won the next two sets, six-four, six-three.

Half the time I was at Voronin's end. Being

strictly neutral, I treated him with the same courtesy I gave his opponent, but I can't say he was as appreciative. You can tell a lot about players from the way they grab the towel from you or discard a ball they don't fancy serving. The Russian was a hard man, with vicious thoughts in his head.

He secured the next set in a tie-break and took the match to a fifth. The crowd was growing. People from other courts had heard something special was happening. Several long, exciting rallies drew gasps and shrieks.

Voronin had extraordinary eyes like wet pebbles, the irises as black as the pupils. I was drilled to look at him each time I offered him a ball, and his expression never changed. Once or twice when Stanski had some luck with a ball that bounced on the net, Voronin eyeballed him. Terrifying.

The final set exceeded everyone's expectations. Voronin broke Stanski's service in the first game with some amazing passing shots and then held his own in game two. In the third, Stanski served three double faults and missed a simple volley.

'Game to Voronin. Voronin leads by three games to love. Final set.'

When I offered Stanski the water he poured it over his head and covered his face with the towel.

Voronin started game four with an ace. Stanski blocked the next serve and it nicked the cord and just dropped over. He was treated to another eyeballing for that piece of impertinence. Voronin walked slowly back to the line, turned, glared and fired a big serve that was called out. The second was softer and Stanski risked a blinder, a mighty forehand, and succeeded – the first winner he'd made in the set. Fifteen-thirty. Voronin nodded towards my friend Eddie for balls, scowled at one and chucked it aside. Eddie gave him another. He served long. Then foot-faulted. This time the line judge received the eyeballing. Fifteen-forty.

Stanski jigged on his toes. He would never have a better opportunity of breaking back.

The serve from Voronin was cautions. The spin deceived Stanski and the ball flew high. Voronin stood under, waiting to pick it out of the sun and kill it. He connected, but heroically Stanski got the racquet in place at the far end and almost fell into the crowd doing it. The return looked a sitter for the Russian and he steered it cross-court with nonchalance. Somehow Stanski dashed to the right place again. The crowd roared its appreciation.

Voronin chipped the return with a dinky shot that barely cleared the net and brought Stanski sprinting from the back to launch himself into a dive. The ball had bounced and risen through another are and was inches from the turf when Stanski's racquet slid under it. Miraculously he found enough lift to sneak it over at a near-impossible angle. Voronin netted. Game to Stanski.

Now there was an anxious moment. Stanski's dive had taken him sliding out of court and heavily into the net-post, just a yard from where I was crouching in my set position. He was rubbing his right forearm, green from the skid across the grass, and everyone feared he'd broken a bone. After a delay of a few seconds the umpire asked if he needed medical attention. He shook his head.

Play resumed at three games to one, and it felt as if they'd played a full set already. The fascination of the game of tennis is that a single shot can turn a match. That diving winner of Stanski's was a prime example. He won the next game to love, serving brilliantly, though clearly anxious about his sore arm, which he massaged at every opportunity. Between games the umpire again asked if he needed assistance, but he shook his head.

Voronin was still a break up, and when play resumed after the change of ends he was first on court. He beckoned to me aggressively with his right hand, white with resin. I let him see he wouldn't intimidate me. I was a credit to the Brigadier, showing and throwing with the single bounce, straight to the player.

Stanski marched to the receiving end, twirling his racquet. Voronin hit the first serve too deep. The second spun in, shaved the line and was allowed. Fifteen-love. Stanski took the next two points with fine, looping returns. Then Voronin met a return of serve with a volley that failed to clear the net. Fifteen-forty. The mind-game was being won by Stanski. A feeble serve from the Russian allowed him to close the game.

Three all.

The critical moment was past. Stanski's confidence was high. He wiped his forehead with his wristband, tossed the ball up and served an ace that Bjorn Borg himself would have been incapable of reaching. From that moment, Voronin was doomed. Stanski was nerveless, accurate, domineering. He took the game to love. He dropped only one point in winning the next two. It was over. The crowd was in ecstasy. Voronin walked to the side without shaking hands, slung his racquets into his bag and left the court without waiting for his opponent – which is always regarded as bad form at Wimbledon. Some of the crowd booed him.

Stanski seemed to be taking longer than usual in packing up. He lingered by the net-post looking down, repeatedly dragging his foot across the worn patch of turf and raising dust. Then he bent and picked something up that to me looked like one of the needles my mother used on her sewing-machine. After staring at it for some time he showed it to the umpire, who had descended from his chair. At the same time he pointed to a scratch on his forearm. The umpire nodded indulgently and I heard him promise to speak to the groundsman.

I learned next day that Stanski was ill and had withdrawn from the tournament. It was a disappointment to everyone, because he had seemed to be on a roll and might have put out one of the seeds in a later round.

Two days after, the world of tennis was shocked to learn that Jozsef Stanski had died. He'd been admitted to St Thomas's complaining of weakness, vomiting and a high temperature. His pulse-rate was abnormally high and his lymph glands were swollen. There was an area of hardening under the scratch on his right forearm. In the night, his pulse rose to almost two hundred a minute and his temperature fell sharply. He was taken into intensive care and treated for septicaemia. Tests showed an exceptionally high count of white blood cells. Blood was appearing in his vomit and he was having difficulty in passing water, suggesting damage to the kidneys.

The next day an electrocardiogram indicated further critical problems, this time with the heart. Attempts were made to fit a pacemaker, but he died whilst under the anaesthetic. It was announced that a post-mortem would be held the following day.

I'm bound to admit that these medical details only came to my attention years later, through my interest in the case. At the time it happened, I was wholly taken up with my duties at Wimbledon, programmed by the Brigadier to let nothing distract me. We were soon into the second week and the crowds grew steadily, with most interest on the show courts.

Eddie and I were picked for the men's semi-finals and I had my first experience of the Centre Court in the greatest match ever played at

Wimbledon, between Bjorn Borg, the champion for the previous five years, and Jimmy Connors. Borg came back from two sets down, love-six and four-six, to win with a display of skill and guts that finally wore down the seemingly unstoppable Connors. I will go to my grave proud that I had a minor role in that epic.

I'm proud, also, that I was one of the ball boys in the final, though the match lacked passion and didn't quite live up to its promise. John McEnroe deserved his Championship, but we all felt Borg had fired his best shots in the semi.

Like Borg, I was forced to choke back some disappointment that afternoon. I'd secretly hoped to be named best ball boy, but a kid from another school was picked by the Brigadier. My pal Eddie (who wasn't on court for the final) put an arm around my shoulder when it was over. We told each other that the kid had to be a brown-noser and the Brigadier's nephew as well.

I may have heard something later on radio or television about the post-mortem on poor Jozsef Stanski. They concluded he died from blood-poisoning. Samples were sent for further analysis, but the lab couldn't trace the source. At the inquest, a pathologist mentioned the scratch on the arm and said some sharp point had dug quite deep into the flesh. The match umpire gave evidence and spoke of the needle Stanski had picked up. He described the small eye close to the point. Unfortunately the needle had not been seen since the day of the match. In summing up, the coroner said it would not be helpful to speculate about the needle. The match had been played in full view of a large crowd and there was no evidence of anyone attempting to cause Stanski's death.

Huge controversy surrounded the verdict. The international press made a lot of the incident, pointing out that as recently as 1978 a Bulgarian writer, Georgi Markov, a rebel against his Communist government, had been executed in a London street by a tiny poison pellet forced into his thigh, apparently by the tip of an umbrella. The poison used was ricin, a protein derived from the castor oil seed, deadly and in those days almost undetectable in the human bloodstream. He took four days to die, protesting that he was the victim of political assassination. Nobody except his wife took him seriously until after he died. The presence of the poison was only discovered because the pellet was still embedded in a piece of Markov's flesh sent for analysis. If ricin could be injected in a public street using an umbrella, was it so fanciful to suggest Jozsef Stanski was targeted by the KGB and poisoned at Wimbledon two years later?

In Poland, the first months of 1981 had been extremely tense. A new Prime Minister, General Jaruzelski, had taken over and a permanent committee was set up to liaise with Solidarity. Moscow was incensed by this outbreak of liberalism and summoned Jaruzelski and his team to the Kremlin. The Politburo made its anger known. Repression followed. Many trade union activists were beaten up.

The papers noted that Stanski's opponent Voronin had quit Britain by an Aeroflot plane the same evening he had lost. He was unavailable for comment, in spite of strenuous efforts by reporters. The Soviet crackdown on Solidarity was mentioned. It was widely suspected that the KGB had been monitoring Stanski for over a year. He was believed to be acting as a conduit to the free world for Walesa and his organisation. At the end of the year, martial law was imposed in Poland and the leaders of Solidarity were detained and union activity suspended.

Although nothing was announced officially, the press claimed Scotland Yard investigated the assassination theory and kept the file open.

Since the Cold War ended and the Soviet bloc disintegrated, it is hard to think oneself back into the oppression of those days, harder still to believe orders may have been given for one tennis player to execute another at the world's top tournament.

In the years since, I kept an open mind about the incident, troubled to think murder may have happened so close to me. In my mind's eye I can still see Stanski rubbing his arm and reaching for the water I poured.

Then, last April, I had a phone call from Eddie Pringle. I hadn't seen him in almost twenty years.

He was coming my way on a trip and wondered if we might meet for a drink.

To be truthful, I wasn't all that keen. I couldn't imagine we had much in common these days. Eddie seemed to sense my reluctance, because he went on to say, 'I wouldn't take up your time if it wasn't important – well, important to me, if not to you. I'm not on the cadge, by the way. I'm asking no favours except for one half-hour of your time.'

How could I refuse?

We arranged to meet in the bar of a local hotel. I told him I have a beard these days and what I would wear, just in case we didn't recognize each other.

I certainly wouldn't have known Eddie if he hadn't come up to me and spoken my name. He was gaunt, hairless and on two sticks.

'Sorry,' he said. 'Chemo. Didn't like to tell you on the phone in case I put you off.'

'I'm the one who should be sorry,' I said. 'Is the treatment doing any good?'

'Not really. I'll be lucky to see the year out. But I'm allowed to drink in moderation. What's yours?'

We found a table. He asked what line of work I'd gone into and I told him I was a journalist.

'Sport?'

'No. Showbiz. I know why you asked,' I said. 'That stint we did as ball boys would have been a useful grounding. No one ever believes I was on court with McEnroe and Borg, so I rarely mention it.'

'I made a big effort to forget,' Eddie said. 'The treatment we got from that Brigadier fellow was shameful.'

'No worse than any military training.'

'Yes, but we were young kids barely into our teens. At that age it amounted to brainwashing.'

'That's a bit strong, Eddie.'

'Think about it,' he said. 'He had us totally under his control. Destroyed any individuality we had. We thought about nothing else but chasing after tennis balls and handing them over in the approved style. It was the peak of everyone's ambition to be the best ball boy. You were as fixated as I was. Don't deny it.'

'True. It became my main ambition.'

'Obsession.'

'OK. Have it your way. Obsession.' I smiled, wanting to lighten the mood a bit.

'You were the hotshot ball boy,' he said. 'You deserved to win.'

'I doubt it. Anyway, I was too absorbed in it all to see how the other kids shaped up.'

'Believe me, you were the best. I couldn't match you for speed or stillness. The need to be invisible he was always on about.'

'I remember that.'

'I believed I was as good as anyone, except you.' Eddie took a long sip of beer and was silent for some time.

I waited. It was obvious some boyhood memory was troubling him.

He cleared his throat nervously. 'Something has been on my mind all these years. It's a burden I can't take with me when I go. I don't have long, and I want to clear my conscience. You remember the match between the Russian and the Pole?'

'Voronin and, er . . . ?'

'Stanski – the one who died. It should never have happened. You're the one who should have died.'

Staring at him, I played the last statement over in my head.

He said, 'You've got to remember the mental state we were in, totally committed to being best boy. It was crazy, but nothing else in the world mattered. I could tell you were better than I was, and you told me yourself that the Brigadier spoke to you after one of your matches on Ladies' Day.'

'Did I?' I said, amazed he still had such a clear recollection.

'He didn't say anything to me. It was obvious you were booked for the final. While you were on the squad, I stood no chance. It sounds like lunacy now, but I was so fired up I had to stop you.'

'How?'

'With poison.'

'Now come on, Eddie. You're not serious.'

But his tone insisted he was. 'If you remember, when we were in the first year, there was a sensational story in the papers about a man, a Bulgarian, who was murdered in London by a pellet the size of a pinhead that contained an almost unknown poison called ricin.'

'Georgi Markov.'

'Yes. We talked about it in chemistry with Blind Pugh. Remember?'

'Vaguely.'

'He said a gram of the stuff was enough to kill thirty-six thousand people and it attacked the red blood cells. It was obtained from the seeds or beans of the castor-oil plant, *ricinus communis*. They had to be ground up in a pestle and mortar because otherwise the hard seed-coat prevented absorption. Just a few seeds would be enough. Old Pugh told us all this in the belief that castor oil plants are tropical, but he was wrong. They've been grown in this country as border plants ever since Tudor times.'

'You're saying you got hold of some?'

'From a local seedsman, and no health warning. I'm sorry if all this sounds callous. I felt driven at the time. I plotted how to do it, using this.'

Eddie spread his palm and a small piece of metal lay across it. 'I picked it out of a litter bin after Stanski threw it away. This is the sewing machine needle he found. My murder weapon.'

I said with distaste, 'You were responsible for that?'

'It came from my mother's machine. I ground the needle to a really fine point and made a gelatine capsule containing the poison and filled the eye of the needle with it.'

'What were you going to do with it – stick it into my arm?'

'No. Remember how we were drilled to return to the same spot just behind the tramlines beside the umpire's chair? If you watch tennis, that place gets as worn as the serving area at the back of the court. The ballboys always return to the same spot. My plan was simple. Stick the needle into the turf with the sharp point upwards and you would kneel on it and inject the ricin into your bloodstream. I'm telling you this because I want the truth to come out before I die. I meant to kill you and it went wrong. Stanski dived at a difficult ball and his arm went straight down on the needle.'

'But he went on to win the match.'

'The effects take days to kick in, but there's no antidote. Even if I'd confessed at the time, they couldn't have saved him. It was unforgivable. I was obsessed and it's preyed on my mind ever since.'

'So all that stuff in the papers about Voronin being an assassin . . .'

'Was rubbish. It was me. If you want to go to the police,' he said, 'I don't mind confessing everything I've told you. I just want the truth to be known before I go. I'm told I have six months at most.'

I was silent, reflecting on what I'd heard, the conflicting motives that had driven a young boy to kill and a dying man to confess twenty years later.

'Or you could wait until after I've gone. You say you're a journalist. You could write it up and tell it in your own way.'

He left me to make up my own mind.

Eddie died in November.

And you are the first after me to get the full story.

RAY BANKS

REAL GONE

Afternoon slurs into evening. Tony is standing on the balcony, a tab in his hand, staring at the rolling Tyne, the figures in the distance crossing the Millennium Bridge, similar figures on the roof of the Baltic. Inside the flat, Cleo has her legs curled under her, watching a repeat of *Trisha* on the big-screen television. All humanity is there, from the pinch-minded biddies to the shrill and ignorant flabby families airing their grievances at prime time.

Cleo was a Bollywood beauty at seventeen. Eight months later now and her eyes are hollow and black. Her works are sitting out on the coffee table, tin foil moving slightly in the breeze. Tony feels a stab in his lungs, ditches the cigarette over the rail and walks into the living room.

'I'm gonna see Grundy,' he says.

Cleo doesn't say anything. He doesn't expect her to.

'I'm gonna sort this out, Cleo.'

The buzzer sounds and Tony tells Jacko he'll be right down. He grabs his Adidas bag from the

171

bedroom, stops in the doorway before he goes and takes one last look at Cleo.

Somebody'll take care of her.

The sounds of war are loud in Goose's lounge. He's a guy with a pot belly and one leg, sitting in a wheelchair and talking like he's kept the best eight ball for himself. He calls himself Goose because he says he lost the leg at Goose Green in '82. Anyone who's known him longer than a minute knows he lost the leg because he tried to mainline an artery. Nobody mentions it, though. Goose provides gear that's second-to-none. There are too few decent wholesalers in Tyne and Wear, and having a one-legged dealer means he doesn't step on the merchandise so much. That's the way Goose tells it, anyway.

So whoever spends their time with Goose, they have to sit there and hear the crazy bastard's stories from a war that didn't last three months. In the background, Goose keeps a tape of *Tumbledown* playing on the video, and he'll tell you all about the time he put his cock in a dead Argie's mouth and 'hang on a sec, I got a picture of it somewhere . . .'

'Goose,' says Tony. 'I seen it already.'

'I didn't come or nowt. I'm not sick.'

'Goose, leave it. You know I wouldn't push if time weren't a factor.'

'Nah, I appreciate that, Tone. I appreciate that. You always been up front.'

'Good, 'cause I got a favour to ask off of yez, Goose. Only one I'm gonna ask you, but it's a big one.'

Goose nods to himself, his bottom lip sticking out. 'I heard you had some trouble, like.'

'I ain't bringing the busies to your door, man.'

'I never said that.'

'It's what you're thinking. I got an old score to settle.'

'And this is the favour?'

'This is the favour.'

'Wey,' says Goose. 'You know me, son. You can ask us to do owt you want, long as the cash shouts loud enough to drown out me conscience.'

Tony smiles. 'I'm pretty sure you'll hear nowt but the folding of note, marra.'

Raw Earth is blasting their 1970 cut of 'Get Ready' as Tony slips into the Mazda. He puts Goose's package on his lap as he gets settled.

'Y'alright?' says Jacko.

'Aye.'

'It's sorted.'

'Aye.'

Tony listens to the music as they pull away from the kerb. It soothes, just like all good soul does. Tony's tried to get Jacko into this, but Jacko's thick as fuck, too hopped up on shite dance to appreciate a good horn section. He doesn't get the dirty-sweet soul of Solomon Burke or Lou Pride. Tony remembers the time he took Cleo to see Pride at The Cluny, up close and sweaty. A tiny stage, it was amazing that his band all managed to fit on it. Especially Pride himself. He wasn't in the Burke league of flabby bastards, but he was heaving around a lot of man that night.

Tony digs out a wrap, dips his thumb and raises it to his nostril. The ache in the back of his neck spikes to a full stab. He wipes his nose, offers the wrap to Jacko. Jacko shakes his head.

'You still sure about this, man?' say Jacko.

Tony looks at his driver, blinks. Jacko's got that face on, the same expression Jacko had the night they burned down Phillie's place on St James Boulevard. He's scared out of his mind. Tony wants to laugh. What the fuck does Jacko have to be scared about?

'Aye,' says Tony. 'I'm still sure about this.'

'Where you gonna go?'

'I can't tell you, you know that.' Tony fiddles with the seat, leans back. 'I don't tell you nowt, you can't tell any other fucker nowt.'

'I'm not gonna grass you up, Tone. Jesus fuckin' Christ, you don't trust us or something?'

'Trust's got nowt to do with it, marra. And I'm not saying you're a fuckin' grass. I'm saving you from yourself is all. You know nowt, you got nowt to grass if things get a bit fuckin' hairy. You know as well as I do, man, morality's circumstantial. You're not playing the martyr for me, no fuckin' way. It's nowt personal.'

174

'Sounds fuckin' personal.'
'Then get over it, Jack.'

Baby Hucy and The Babysitters, 'Listen to Me', cross-fading into 'Change Your Ways' by Willie Kendrick. Jacko throttles Kendrick as he pulls the Mazda into the NCP. They park up, get out, Tony lighting a Regal.

It's a short walk to Grundy's club. It's called Grundys. Kevin Grundy has no imagination. The crowd outside the club couldn't give a fuck what the place is called, though. Saturday night, and the check-shirt brigade is out in force. Tony reckons it looks like they're holding the World Ugly Contest right outside the club, but then this place isn't known for its beautiful people. Studio 54, it ain't.

Inside, they're playing a thumping bassline instead of music, making Tony's heart shake in his chest. Makes him think he's walking on loose stones as he crosses the dance floor, Jacko at his back. He wishes he'd thought to bring Errol. Big fucking Errol, the prize-fighter looking bastard, deep nasty eyes and shoulders as broad as his accent. But Errol was seen in bad company and Tony can't take the chance. Jacko's a streak of piss, he's a runner, but he's arrow-straight and has a talent for survival. Jacko can smell a bad situation like a Sikh's fart, and Tony's glad to have him as an early warning.

Muscle would be a bonus, though.

Right now the only muscle Tony trusts is the

one twitching in the back of his neck. He can't be relaxed in Grundy's club. The word is, Kevin Grundy's losing his mind one snort at a time. And one thing Tony's learned, you don't fuck around with a cokehead. Those fuckers know no mercy.

Right now, it's pure Martha Reeves and The Vandellas: '(Love Is Like A) Heatwave'. Sweat glistens on Tony's forehead, runs down and stings his eyes. The DJ mixes in that ubiquitous shite which brings the fat girls out to throw their arses around like the bird in the sweaty-crotch video. One fat girl makes a play for Jacko; he smiles and ducks out of the way, gets slapped by arm fat that'll be a bingo wing in about twenty years' time. The fat girl has an L plate on her lifted-and-separated chest. One glance at the gaggle of women following her onto the dance floor and the smell of a hen night suddenly fills the air like knock-off Estée Lauder. Over at the fluorescent glow of the bar, a gang of short-haired men swig bottled beer.

'This fuckin' place,' says Jacko. 'It's like Butlins on fuckin' mescaline.'

'Aye.'

'Grundy about tonight, you reckon?'

'I know a man who'll know,' says Tony, leading the way to the chill-out room.

Colin's the last lad who should be in a chill-out room. He breathes electricity, his hands flying about like a couple of methed-up doves when he talks. Which he does. A lot. His fingers brush at what little hair he has left on his head, wearing it away, making him look a good thirty years older than he is. He throws numbers in one of the glass and sandstone buildings down by the Quayside. Way he sees it, it's a slow death, but it lets him live at night.

Jacko taps his hands on his knees. Tony waits it out. Colin's been at the wraps since he finished work Friday night, it looks like. He's chewing Extra. The lad needs gum or else he'll chew the inside of his cheek to ribbons.

'Last week, right, last week, we had these gadgies in the office. And they were laying cables for the new network, right, these blokes, these electricians, and I was going to take a piss, right, I was going to the bogs, and I realise that one of these workmen blokes is gonna take a piss, too. And what happens? I hang back, know what I mean? I make out I'm going to the water cooler to get me a cup of water, make out like I'm dead fuckin' thirsty and that. And then I think to myself, what's the fuckin' point in losing me bottle like that? This cunt, he's no fuckin' hardcase, he's no tough lad, why'm I getting my bollocks all shrivelled 'cause of this cunt? So I go in the bathroom and he's in one of the cubicles and y'know, I can *hear him pissing*. Like he's one of them, you know them, the fuckers with the tiny cocks and he's not comfortable pissing at one of the pissers, like he has to sit down and take a piss like a fuckin' bird, right? So I get all boiling and that. And I kick the fuckin' cubicle door. Hard, so it slams right open and there's this gadgie and he's sitting with his trousers round his ankles and it's a good fuckin' job he's sitting down because I think he just shat himself. And I tell him – get this – I tell him. 'Nobody's gonna fuckin' believe you . . .' and I leave him. Can you believe that, man? Can you fuckin' believe that? I am *dangerous*. I am a fuckin' time bomb.'

You're a twat, thinks Tony. You're a twat and I haven't got time for this shite.

'Did you take your piss?' asks Jacko.

'Fuck's this?' says Colin. 'Fuck's the cheeky cunt?'

'Where's Kev the night, Colin?' says Tony.

'He's not in, man. It's Wednesday.'

'It's Saturday,' says Jacko.

'Fuckin' funny cunt, eh? I'd fuckin' batter you, son, I weren't so fuckin' dry,' yells Colin.

'It's Saturday.'

'Fuck do you know? If it's Saturday, he's about. If it's Wednesday, he's at home. Fuck you asking me for? I look like I know what's going on? Now you selling or what?'

'Not tonight, Col.'

'Fuck's the matter with you?'

'I got some business with Grundy.'

'That's *Mister* Grundy, fuckhead, alright? You ain't selling? Really? Fuck's the matter with you, you're not selling? You're always selling.'

Tony gets up. 'I'll have another scout around.'

The gents' toilet stinks like a Drew Barrymore movie. Jacko's at the bar. One brush with Colin and he said he needed a drink. Tony splashes cold water on his face, notices the heavy shake in his hands when he lowers them. He can't remember the last time he slept. Above the mirror, someone's scrawled TOON ARMY. The floor throbs under his feet; his head starts to thump in time. The chemicals in his blood start to thicken in his veins like slow-freezing water. Tony reaches into his pocket, does the rest of the wrap.

Blinks. Closes his eyes for a second.

Fuck this. Fuck this noise. Baby Huey: 'There's a thousand people out here, watching me . . .'

'Can you say Mighty, Mighty?'

He looks at his reflection in the mirror, feels for the package in his jacket.

If this works out, he tells himself, he'll be cool. He'll be fine. Just one step at a time.

Cleo watches Living TV. Movie of the week. Battered wives and alcoholic husbands. Tony wishes life was that simple. Wishes there was a twelve-step programme for what he has to do tonight. Christ, wishes there were ad breaks every fifteen minutes so he could grab a breather, a chance to think straight.

Tony swallows back acid phlegm, screws up the wrap and tosses it into the sink. The reason he stopped doing this shite in the first place, his mind caught in a runaway train of thought, turned in on itself, colliding.

The bang of the toilet door makes him turn. He's ready to deck Colin, the fucker.

179

But it's Jacko.

'Grundy's here,' he says. 'Says he'll talk to you out back when you're ready.'

Cleo and Grundy, that's how it used to be. Grundy with his ponytail and flapping lips sheened with perpetual spit. Grundy with his tacky club and delusions of grandeur, thinking that a fistful of cash and a couple of bent coppers would make him anything other than the pig-nosed prick he was. Cleo singing, 'Mr Big Stuff, you never gonna get my love . . .'

Kevin Grundy doesn't have an office anymore. He used to have one above the club decked out with a *Carlito's Way* vibe. Back then, he fancied himself a kingpin, a drug lord, Tony Montana with a ponytail. Tony remembers the first time they met, he said, 'You know why it's called a pony-tail, Kev?'

''Cause it looks like a pony's tail.'

'Nah, it's because when you lift it up, there's always a horse's arse underneath.'

Grundy's lips thinned. No imagination, no sense of humour.

Now Grundy's a silhouette down the end of the alley that runs behind the club. He's smoking a tab by a skip, flicking ash onto the ground. Doing business in an alley like he's ghetto. Tony recognises the big bastard next to him: Errol.

'Y'alright, Tone?' says Grundy.

'I been better, Kev.'

180

'Aye, looks like it. Who's your muscle?'

Jacko works his mouth.

'You buying, Kev?'

Grundy ignores him, says, 'How's that bird of yours?'

'Cleo's fine.'

'I heard things is all.'

'You got ears, you're gonna hear things. If you're not buying, I'll go, man. I just heard you was in the market.'

Grundy smiles; it looks like someone's taken a Stanley knife to his face. He dumps his tab. 'Aye, Tone, I'm buying. I'm just wondering why you're selling wholesale.'

'This is a one-off. Call it a favour for an old mate.'

'You think?'

'Aye, I think. You're not interested, I'll find someone who is.'

'Way I hear it, you're not doing much business these days.'

Tony can feel Jacko staring at him. Wondering how he's going to play this. Tony wonders if Jacko ever really knew what was going on. 'I'm doing fine, Kev. Business never been better.'

Errol shifts his feet; Tony glares at him. Any information Grundy's got, he's got it from Errol. But fuck it, this deal and Tony's out of here.

Tony hears movement behind him. He hefts Goose's package in his right hand. 'It's a solid weight, Kev. You got the cash?'

Grundy rubs at his nose. 'You know what, Tone? I don't think so. That's from Goose, right?'

Tony doesn't say anything.

'Well, thing is, Goose gave us a call. Telt us what was transpiring here. He's not happy about a bunch of fuckin' things. Mostly he's pissed off 'cause he's losing a valuable customer, but then there's the shite you got in your hand there. It's one thing to lose a customer, right? It's another thing when that customer tries to poison future trade.'

'I don't know what the fuck you're—'

More movement behind him, the scrape of a foot on concrete.

And then there's the smell of burnt hair in Tony's nostrils, the crackle of a stun gun, the flare against his cheek. And Tony's world flashes red, white and blue (how very fuckin' patriotic) before he loses his legs, hits the ground in a shaking heap.

'Man plans, and God laughs his balls off, Tony-son.'

Somewhere in the fog, Tony swears he can hear 'One Toke Over The Line', someone singing loud and off-key. That, and the growl of an engine.

The night before, Tony finds Cleo on the couch, her legs curled under her. The big-screen television is on, but it's just Teletext. Tony knows something's rotten.

When he tries to get Cleo's attention, he knows what it is.

And he spends the rest of the night with her in his arms. He weeps until his throat is dry.

He talks to her, tells her what he's going to do. Tells her he's giving up the life, tells her he's going to see Goose tomorrow, get him to cut a brick through with arsenic, bleach, fucking strychnine. Punt that brick onto the cunt that got her in the habit in the first place. At worst, let him stamp on it, sell it on and fuck his reputation by killing his customers. At best, and what Tony prays for, Grundy takes a shot himself, feels his veins burn up, his heart explode.

Then, pull a Keyser Soze, ride off into the sunset.

Live the happy ending.

'Antony David Hills . . .'

They used his Sunday name, his court name. And right then, he knew he was fucked. These were the busies Grundy liked to use. Grundy once said to him, 'I like using coppers, man. They always know where the really good fuckin' spots are, know what I mean?'

They've laid the foundation on the student and key worker accommodation, but there's a development down by City Road that's just started. Tony remembers watching the builders with Jacko, telling him that the students of Northumbria University would be gagging for a decent dealer.

'The world is ours,' he said.

Now Tony can't see anything but grey and black, his eyes swollen shut. The smell of fear and blood in the air, the ammonia stench of his own urine, burning his thigh.

I didn't cry. Least I didn't fuckin' cry.

Underneath him, a wooden pallet's holding him upright, his legs splayed out and twisted in front of him. He whistles when he breathes, air squeaking through the blood crusted around his nose and mouth. He thinks about how he tried not to scream, not to cry, playing the hardcase. The thought makes his face tighten, bringing a wave of pain from freshly opened cuts, a high screeching horn section to the bassline ache of his battered body.

He calls out for Jacko, but the name comes out cracked and low: '*Aggo?*' It kills him to speak, and he knows Jacko's not going to respond. Tony was conscious when the big bastard copper, the one with the stun gun and the girl's laugh, stamped his boot down hard on the back of Jacko's neck, heard that dull crack, a soft thump and smelled Jacko's bowels loosen.

But Tony's not dead. That's where they fucked up. Not so long ago, back when Tony Hills was king of the world, he wouldn't have allowed that to go by. Someone tries to kill you, someone tries to fuck up your business, you show no mercy. You put him in the ground. But these coppers didn't have the nous to finish the job. Which means he's in the clear, out of the city just as long as he heals.

I fuckin' tried, love. I fuckin' tried. At least I did that. Get them back for you. Jack it in, fuckin' throw the life to the wind, get the fuck out of Dodge.

Tony tries to pull himself off the pallet. The ringing in his ears stops, the sound of an engine outside.

'Fuckin' hell,' says a voice, punctuated with a high-pitched giggle. 'Would you look at that?'

The sound of a shovel scraped across concrete, coming closer.

Tony digs his fingers into the ground; it's cold to the touch. His cheeks warm and stinging. Pulling himself away from the voice. A fingernail snaps.

'What d'you want me to do?' says the voice.

I'm sorry, love. I'm so fuckin' sorry.

'Fuck d'you think? *Drop* the bastard . . .'

A breeze brushes Tony's face. Then a white flash and the world falls.

Man plans, and God laughs.

Aye, that'd be right.

AMY MYERS

THE PILGRIM

Perhaps it was merely a foolish whim to walk
the last mile or two to Canterbury. The idea
of driving into the city to find a parking place
didn't seem right on the path along which so many
pilgrims had passed before him. He wanted to
reflect, not to fight twenty-first century traffic. He
was over eighty now, but this was his penance, and
his own two legs must carry him to it.

Here at the bend of the eastern edge of
Harbledown Hill, pilgrims had caught their first
glimpse of Canterbury Cathedral, its steeple
crowned with a gilt angel. Here they would
dismount and fall on their knees to give thanks,
for within that cathedral lay their destination, the
shrine of St Thomas à Becket.

Murder and religion, he reflected. The passions
aroused by both had been linked in the day of
Archbishop Thomas as they had been ever since.
In the year of 1170 it had taken four knights to
strike down Thomas à Becket within his own
cathedral, and for the rest of their lives, so legend
said, they had wandered the world in penance and
misery after their terrible crime.

A night in Canterbury in World War II had changed his life too. He had been a young man in his early twenties when the murders were committed. He, unlike the other two, had lived on. Perhaps that in itself required a penance at the Martyrdom or the site behind the Cathedral altar where Becket's magnificent shrine had once rested. Then Thomas Cromwell had boasted that he would make Henry VIII the richest king of England there had ever been. The Pope's supremacy had been renounced, and Cromwell's men destroyed and looted even this most sacrosanct of memorials.

Before that time, the pilgrims would advance up the steps from the Martyrdom to the Trinity chapel, first to see the golden likeness of the Saint's head, and then to the shrine itself, guarded by iron railings through which only the sick were allowed to enter. The shrine would be invisible as they approached; it was concealed by a wooden canopy suspended from the roof by ropes. At the given moment, the canopy was drawn up, and the shrine itself blazed forth with all its glittering jewels and gold decoration. The largest jewel had been the Regale of France, given by King Louis VII. It was a huge carbuncle, a ruby said to be as large as a hen's egg, which glowed fiery red as the light caught it.

For sixty years the man had forced himself not to think about the night of Sunday 31 May 1942, but now he must do so. It had been sheer greed that brought murder to Canterbury. Did the whole story matter now that the jewel was gone for ever? Yes.

As the music of the great organ of Canterbury Cathedral soared around him, Lieutenant Robert Wayncroft wrestled with his conscience. On Friday after his grandfather's funeral the solicitors had given him the sealed envelope he had expected. His grandfather had been his sole close family relation, and so Robert had been permitted a brief compassionate leave to sort out his affairs. He had inherited the house on Lady Wootton's Green, and Chillingham Place, the Tudor ancestral home near Chilham, now in a sorry state of repair and requisitioned by the army. It was the letter that concerned him most, however, for it contained the details of the closely guarded secret that had been handed on from generation to generation of Wayncrofts: the whereabouts of the Regale of France.

'The blessing of God almighty . . .' The service was ending, but Robert remained in the cathedral, thinking about what he should do. With Canterbury under constant threat of air raids, the jewel could hardly be safe where it was. Only ill health had prevented his grandfather from moving it, as had happened before when the jewel seemed in danger – not least when Napoleon looked set to invade Kent. That much was clear. What was less clear was what should happen to it after he had found it. Try as he might, the insidious thought of the money that the huge ruby would fetch crept into his mind, and refused to leave. He could do so much with it when the war was over. He could even rebuild Chillingham Place; alternatively he could, his conscience told him, give the money to the church. Then he battled with more personal ways of spending the money. What was the point of the jewel being hidden away when if he sold it to a museum it might be displayed for all to see?

'Only to ensure the safety of the jewel is your duty, Robert, not its future,' his grandfather had made clear in his letter.

Yet this was wartime, Robert argued with God, and there was no sign of the war's ending. The time for old legends was past, this was the twentieth century, and the old faith would never again be restored to Canterbury Cathedral.

He stood up. It was time to leave. He would go to where the jewel lay hidden and take it to safety. That was the first priority.

He glanced around him as he moved out into the aisle, aware of the increased tension in the city streets even though it was still light. Most people would be at home, fearful of air raids in retaliation for last night's RAF bombing raid on Cologne. What better cathedral to aim for than Canterbury? Since April German policy had been to strike at the historic cities of England: so far, Exeter, Bath, Norwich and York. A target as tempting as

Canterbury could not be long delayed, and the sooner he fulfilled his mission the better.

Something made him stop. Would he, even now, be followed by someone watching in the dark recesses of the cathedral? He decided to make his way through the Cathedral precincts to the Broad Street exit, and he slipped out of a side door and down the steps to the remains of the old monastery. It was silent here, and despite the daylight, gloomy as he entered the so-called Dark Entry. He paused to listen for any footstep following him, and as he did so he remembered his grandfather telling him that there had been gruesome stories about the Dark Entry passageway even back as far as Henry VIII's reign.

'It was here, Robert, that your ancestor Sir Geoffrey Wayncroft met his death in trying to prevent the theft of the Regale by Cromwell's men.'

As a child Robert had been terrified by the place, imagining that any Wayncroft who walked here might meet a similar fate.

He pulled himself together. He was a soldier, trained to kill if necessary. What if someone *were* following him, someone who remembered his foolish talk on the beaches of Dunkirk two years earlier. The nightmare came back. He had been sitting with two other soldiers, but not from his battalion. They were in the lightly wounded category, waiting, it seemed endlessly, for ships that might with luck return them home across the

Channel to England. With the Luftwaffe screaming overhead, minutes ticked by like hours. Family secrets hadn't seemed so important then; lack of food, sleep and the need to communicate with anyone, made him loose-tongued.

'Ever heard of the Regale jewel? It was a huge carbuncle,' he heard himself saying.

'That's what you get on your bum, ain't it?' the private sniggered.

Robert had been furious and it made his tongue the looser. 'It was a ruby as huge as an egg. It hasn't been seen since the sixteenth century – and I'll tell you why. When my grandfather dies, I'll be the heir and know the secret of the hiding place. The Wayncrofts have been guarding it as a sacred duty until the Pope returns to Canterbury.'

'May that be soon, *mon ami*,' said the French lieutenant.

Robert had been too engrossed in the need to bolster his own importance. Now he glanced at the other two men, and saw naked greed on their faces: the Cockney and the Frenchman, Lieutenant Christophe Bonneur and Private Johnnie Wilson.

'And your name is Wayncroft?' asked Bonneur.

'You must have heard of the Wayncrofts of Chillingham Place.' Robert glided smoothly away from the topic of jewels. 'We had to move out, patriotic duty of course in wartime, but we'll go back when the war's over. The old pile's falling down though.' Even then he had thought it was a pity that the family hadn't put the jewel to better use.

To his horror, Christophe had replied casually: 'I've heard of this Regale, *mon ami*. It belongs to France, you know. It was our king Louis VII, who gave it to the shrine.'

Robert had tried to be equally casual. 'He tried very hard *not* to, you mean. He offered a mint of money to the Archbishop in compensation for loss of the jewel, and it was accepted, but the Regale had other ideas. The story is that it simply flew out of his hand and stuck like glue on to the shrine.'

'So our poor king lost money and jewel too,' Christophe laughed. 'That is evidence, is it not, that the jewel belongs to France, not once but twice. Yes?'

Johnnie Wilson, who had been listening quietly, now contributed to the conversation: 'How did you Wayncrofts get it then? Nicked it, did you?'

The nightmare had begun, a nightmare Robert had managed to suppress, until this evening. As he came out into Broad Street, every shadow seemed to hold a threat. It wasn't like him to be jumpy, he told himself, maybe he *was* being followed. He'd go back to the house at Lady Wootton's Green just in case, he decided, and come out later. No one would expect him to leave it so late. It would be safer then. Another hour or two would not matter.

The jewel had waited for over 400 years.

Sir Walter Barbary dismounted at Harbledown, for Canterbury was in sight. He had no penance to perform as pilgrims usually had, only a mission on behalf of his dying monarch. It was cold and raining, and he took refuge in the inn from the November chill, while he made his final decision on what he should do.

'Walter,' Queen Mary had rasped last evening. 'I know you to be a good Catholic and true to our faith, as you are to me. Would you do me one last service?'

He bowed his head. 'Your majesty.' It was well known that the Queen was near her end. She had been slipping in and out of consciousness, and it was rumoured she was dying of a broken heart. She had good cause; the child she longed for had never come, despite all her fierce endeavours she had not completely restored the Pope's supremacy over the English church, and now Calais, England's last foothold in France, was lost.

When he had been summoned to St James's he had guessed it was not merely to give him thanks. Queen Mary had something more in mind.

With an effort the Queen withdrew a shabby velvet pouch from among the cushions of her bed, and handed it to him. It was heavier than he had expected from its size and within seemed to be a large oval stone that felt cold even through the velvet.

'Do not stay to open it, Walter. We may be disturbed. Take this to Canterbury, for me, back to the place from which it was stolen by those rebelling against the true faith. Those who influenced my misguided father.'

Sir Walter did not proffer his own views on the part played by the late King Henry VIII in establishing the new church. It had been, as his daughter Mary knew full well, imposed on England to satisfy his own lusts with the sanctity of a so-called marriage to Anne Bullen – a marriage that had failed to produce the male heir he wanted.

'My father used it as a toy, a huge ring worn on his thumb,' Mary whispered, 'and when he tired of it, he gave it to me to wear in a golden collar. I have done so for his sake but it lies heavy on my conscience. I would have my soul at peace as I face God. When Cromwell's Royal Commission destroyed the shrine of the blessed St Thomas, they stole the Regale and it must be returned.'

'Your majesty,' Walter chose his words carefully, 'despite all you have done to restore England to the guidance of the Holy Father the Pope, the Cathedral might not yet be a fitting place for the Regale. Once more it might be treated as a toy.'

'You are a diplomat, Walter.' Queen Mary smiled with great effort. 'You mean if – *when* – my sister Elizabeth rules, she will bow to no Pope. Walter, you must ensure that the stone is kept safely in Canterbury until the true faith is established there once more.'

He had left for Canterbury immediately. This morning, as he left the inn, news had just arrived

194

that the Queen had died at dawn. By that time, thanks be to God, he was well set on the pilgrims' route to Canterbury. They would have sent to Hatfield for the new Queen and once she entered into London the hunt for the Regale would begin. If he knew Bess Tudor, who had a great liking for jewelled collars, she would waste little time. He must be gone, and gone for ever.

Walter decided to lead his horse for the last mile or two in order that Our Lady might grant him inspiration, for despite his halt at Harbledown, he still could not decide what to do with the jewel. As he neared Canterbury, he could hear the bells ringing – but for no Pope. He knew he could not hand over the jewel, nor keep it for himself, for this would go against his promise to Queen Mary, yet he would instantly be suspect when the jewel was missed. He had no choice. He must fulfil his mission, then ride for Dover and sail overseas for France.

He paused unrecognised at the Cathedral entrance, watching as the dignitaries of Canterbury came to give thanks for the new queen, whether they were sincere or not. One of them was Sir Edward Wayncroft, whom he knew well, and Walter gave thanks to Our Lady, for surely here was his answer. Sir Edward was of good Catholic family, staunch to the last. It had been his father who had been slain in the passageway trying to prevent the theft of the Regale by Cromwell's men. He would ask Sir Edward to guard the jewel until these rebels and their so-called new religion were swept away.

As twilight came, Robert retraced his steps to the Cathedral, on the grounds that on the remote chance that anyone was *still* following him, the assumption would be that the Regale was hidden there. His stalker – was he real or in his imagination? – might even be amongst those few bowed heads still in the cathedral at this late hour. Involuntarily he glanced over his shoulder. His grandfather's death had been announced in *The Times* as well as in the local newspapers. What if his avid-eyed companions on the beach at Dunkirk had remembered his chance words? He had seen neither of them since, but in theory they could be here, waiting for him to make his move to reclaim the jewel. Would one of those so earnestly praying suddenly rise up and strike him down, as Becket himself had been?

Robert took hold of himself. Of course they would not do so. Even if one of them were waiting for him, he could not be sure whether Robert had the letter, or when he would go in search of the jewel. In any case, he would need to follow Robert to where the jewel lay hidden. His imagination was getting out of control, Robert decided, but nevertheless he would take precautions. He would linger by the steps to the Murder Stone, then walk briskly down the north aisle to the main door – then *past* it. Instead he would stroll up the south aisle, and mount the steps leading to Trinity chapel where was the site of the shrine itself. Yes, that was fitting, since any pursuer would assume the Regale was hidden near there, and would pause there regardless of whether he could still see his quarry. By that time, Robert would have hurried down to the cloister door, and out in the night air.

He breathed it in thankfully as he walked into Burgate Street and then through Butchery Lane and on to the Parade. Robert felt safer now, if only because it was uncommonly light, even for the end of May. There would be no air raids tonight. A man whistled, nothing uncommon in that; a few people hurried towards their homes, that too was natural. A cat howled as he passed the Corn Exchange and came into St George's Street; the sound of Glenn Miller on a wireless drifted down through a blacked-out window.

Briskly, he walked in the twilight past a row of timber-framed buildings. There was a confectioner's, a tobacconist, all very normal – and yet his confidence began to ebb away. It was so very still in the half-light. On such a night he might even pass knights on their way to murder Thomas in the cathedral. The eerie atmosphere was only in his *mind*, Robert told himself, as he passed the grocery store of David Greig. There ahead of him was the tower of St George's church. He was nearly there. He crossed over Canterbury Lane, remembering its bakery shop and how he had loved as a boy to gorge himself on the Chelsea buns. Innocent pleasures in pre-war days, all gone. He sensed a moving shadow behind him; an innocent one perhaps, but it turned him from the church and into the White Lion pub next to it. He would have a pint of beer to steady himself.

'You're lucky, mate,' someone remarked. The bell for last orders had rung as Robert paid for his order.

'My lucky day.'

In Robert's pocket were his masked torch, gloves, a small hammer and chisel, all he should need for his mission. He drank his pint slowly, wondering whether the door might open and his pursuer enter. What would he do if that happened? Robert firmly quelled the flutters of his heart. No one came in, and Robert departed with his fellow drinkers. Then at last he walked through the Norman tower doorway into St George the Martyr's church.

St George's was an ancient church much extended in Victorian times, and Robert strolled all round it, not yet needing his torch. He strained for the slightest sound, alert to the smallest movement, for he could not begin until he was sure he was alone. Suppose those men had remembered, suppose someone in the solicitor's office had read the letter and resealed it. After all, the solicitor had access to the house and the seal was in his grandfather's desk. Robert steadied himself. This was the solitude and approaching darkness speaking, not common sense. Resolutely he walked to the old doorway that had once led to the belfry staircase. Now it was blocked up, and what better place to hide the jewel? Quickly he looked above the lintel, and for the place behind the plaster where the stonework had been loosened to insert the jewel and only lightly replaced. It was old mortar, and should give easily, the letter had told him.

Swallowing, he built up a small pile of hassocks to stand on, and identified where he must excavate.

Just as his chisel was poised to chip the plaster the silence was shattered. The familiar eerie wailing of the air raid siren was joined almost simultaneously with the shrill sound of Tug-Boat Annie, the local name for the Canterbury inner warning system. Usually this followed the siren alert to indicate that hostile aircraft were approaching the city; to have it come so hard on the siren's heels was ominous.

What to do? How could he leave now for an air-raid shelter? Feverishly Robert chipped away, almost sobbing with tension, expecting to hear the crash of bombs at any moment. Tug-Boat Annie's three blasts on the steam whistle would be repeated every fifteen minutes until danger was past.

He worked on as the light began to fade more quickly, but as Tug-Boat Annie sounded once more, he realised to his horror he'd made a mistake. He'd chipped off the wrong corner. Again he began his work, trying to control his trembling hands, and was rewarded after five minutes by the sound of the 'all-clear'. The original warning was a mistake, of course it was. No German bombers would be fool enough to come so early, on such a light evening.

It took him another two hours or more before at last sweating with fear and exertion, he managed to prise the stone concealing the pouch out. It fell to the floor with a crash, and the noise resounded throughout the church. He listened, heart in mouth, in case it might attract attention from outside, but there was nothing. Excited now, he put his hand in the hole and pulled out the prize for which he had worked so hard, the canvas pouch, for Sir Walter's velvet covering had been changed several times.

Robert's heart thudded painfully as he held it in the flickering light of his masked torch, for the light inside had now gone. Carefully he balanced the torch on the pile of hassocks and opened it. Within the canvas was another, silken pouch, through which he could feel the chill of a large stone. Was it fear or excitement that was keeping every nerve taut? Carefully he withdrew the silk covering.

The Regale was in his hand. He held it in the light of the torch and even in that dimness it glowed red, as fiery red as the pilgrims to Becket's shrine had reported long ago. Its beauty confused him, making him once more uncertain of what he would do with it, save that he must take it with him.

'*Bonjour, Robert!*'

For a moment the words did not register. The whisper came from nowhere: it was the voice of conscience, or the voice of St Thomas. But then, with a deadly chill sweeping over him, Robert realised it was human, and that the words were French.

He sensed, then half saw, a black figure in the darkness moving towards him. It was Nemesis, in the form of Christophe Bonneur.

'It's you,' Robert said flatly, some of the terror evaporating. An enemy, even in the darkness, is easier to deal with than the unknown. He began to laugh at the inevitability of fate. 'You remembered? Of course you would.'

'You have found my jewel for me, Robert. *Merci.*'

'*Yours?*' His hackles rose. 'What the devil do you mean?

'*Mais oui, cher ami.* I was intrigued by your so-interesting story on the beach at Dunkirk. All families have legends, my family too. It is said that an ancestor of mine was English but he came to France where he married a French girl and took her name for fear of enemies from England. It is said that Sir Walter left in Canterbury what he should have brought with him to return to the king, the famous Regale carbuncle.'

'It was given by your king to St Thomas's shrine.'

'Against his will, *mon ami*, and you told us in your interesting story that the Regale was returned to Canterbury on condition the true faith was restored. It never was and so is ours again by right.'

'It was given into the safe-keeping of my family.' Robert's mind was numb. Desperately he tried to size up his situation.

'*Non*, it is to be returned to its rightful owner.'

Robert regained the power of logical thought. 'And will you restore it to the crown of France?' he sneered.

Christophe laughed. 'There is no crown to receive it, and France is under German occupation. Never fear, I will keep the Regale until happier times. Would you return it to St Thomas if I left it with you?'

'That would be against my duty,' Robert prevaricated.

'But there is a Catholic church in Canterbury, a mere stone's throw away. Why not surrender the Regale to its priest?'

'What I do with it is my concern,' Robert snapped. The ruby seemed to glow warmly in his pocket where he had put it for safety, as if it were telling him that it too had a voice in this discussion. Perhaps it did, for in the sudden silence that fell, Robert heard the sound of aircraft. A long way off – no need for concern.

Or so he thought, until the siren alert wailed out, and once again Tug-Boat Annie's three blasts.

Through the windows the sudden light in the sky confirmed Canterbury was the target, as flares were dropped by German aircraft.

Christophe laughed as though nothing had happened. 'So you will not hand me the Regale – and I have no qualms in telling you, *mon frère*, that the public coffers of France will know nothing of either.'

'You speak,' Robert managed to say evenly, 'as if it were in your pocket, not mine.'

'It soon will be, my friend. Or shall we share it amicably?'

'Never.'

Christophe sighed. 'Your British SOE has given me excellent training in silent methods of killing. If you refuse to give it to me, I shall have practice as well as theory before they drop me into occupied France.'

Robert quickly debated his options. He was strong enough, and a trained soldier, but he was unarmed, save for his tools which would make uncertain weapons. If this Frenchie was right about his training, Robert would stand little chance against him, unless he could take him by surprise. He estimated they were about three yards apart, although it was hard to tell in the dark. If he could knock Christophe off balance he stood a chance of escaping with the Regale while the Frenchman recovered. The tower door was close, though not quite near enough to make a run for it without first distracting Christophe. But how to take him by surprise? Robert slid his hand into his pocket and realised there was only one way. It was a risky one, but with the aid of his torch it might be possible.

He inched the stone out of his pocket, making no sudden movement, and flung it straight at where Christophe's face must be.

He hit truer than he had dared hope, according to the Frenchman's howl of pain as the carbuncle took him full in the face. In a flash, Robert was at his feet, scrabbling on the floor for the stone as Christophe, blood streaming from his face, dropped to the floor to clutch at him.

'*A la mort*, Englishman,' he hissed.

Where was the Regale? Sobbing, Robert tried to tear off the clutching hands, and just as the first crash of bombs came in the distance, he saw the ruby. Christophe wrenched his hand away and stretched it out to where it lay. But another hand reached towards it, a hand whose owner had been hidden in the darkness listening. But it was Robert, having scrambled to his feet again, who grasped it first – until Christophe tripped him, sending him crashing to the floor again. Murderous hands round his neck made him loosen his hold on the stone.

'Ta very much. Thanks, mate.' There was a whisper, as the hands round his neck fell away, the words were almost drowned by the crash of bombs on Canterbury's ancient city. The explosions were almost overhead now.

Two of the men escaped, the other lay dead even before the bomb hit St George's church.

Private Johnnie Wilson paused briefly in Canterbury Lane. The heavy bombers were screaming overhead, and more and more arriving. Was anyone following him from the church? He looked back past the White Lion to the church. It was time to get the hell out of here and find a shelter, if no one was following him.

But there was. A moving shape lit by the flames in the sky was coming out of the doorway. He took to his heels, all thoughts of a shelter gone. He was nearly at Butchery Lane by the time the bombs demolished half of St George's Street behind him.

The blast knocked him to the ground and stunned him; he was choking on the dust when he came to. Tug-Boat Annie was sounding, there was the noise of bombs falling and the roar of more aircraft coming in. He picked himself up and stumbled onwards, with falling masonry and fires from the incendiaries all around him. There was a split second of eerie silence, and then he could hear screams.

Was he still being followed? If so, who by? The Englishman or the Frenchman? He'd seen the Frenchie at Canterbury station, and as he had read the report of Wayncroft's death in the local rag, Johnnie had guessed exactly what he was doing here.

Now he was in a hell like no artillery barrage he'd ever been through. He stayed right where he was in the middle of the road, as buildings crumbled like card houses. Where he was standing seemed relatively untouched, but St George's Street behind him was an inferno.

Johnnie lost all sense of time, listening only to the bomb explosions. Rose Lane area seemed to have copped it badly, and the whole city was lit up by flame, smoke and flares. Canterbury was disappearing. The road behind him was like the old pictures of Passchendaele. Where there had been pubs, shops and the old gateway to Whitefriars monastery were now only piles of rubble and smoke. He could hear the clang of fire engine bells, but no all clear yet. The barrage was still going on.

St George's church had been hit, but the tower was still standing, and its clock still sticking out like a yardarm. *And there was someone coming after him.* Automatically Johnnie took to his heels, his ears deafened by the blast. He couldn't even think about that stone in his pocket.

'You all right, mate?' An air raid warden caught his arm as he stumbled on.

'Yeah. I'll give you a hand,' Johnnie replied. But he didn't. He had a bit of a limp, a godalmighty bruise from a lump of stone or something, but nothing too bad. Even so, it was like running in a nightmare; his legs wouldn't move as quick as he wanted, and all the time his pursuer was gaining on him. Where should he go? Johnnie hesitated for a moment.

Then he knew the answer. Over there he could see the cathedral, still standing proud, lit up by flame. Bits of it must have been hit judging by the smoke, but the cathedral looked mainly intact. Johnnie was not a God-follower, but he knew now what he had to do. He had to get into that cathedral. It was like St Thomas was waiting for him.

People were coming out on to the streets, even though the all clear had not yet gone, emerging to see the ruins of their city, or their houses, and to help where they could, though the raid was not yet over. Johnnie staggered through the gateway to the cathedral grounds, glancing back to see if he were still being followed. He bloody well was, though by whom he couldn't tell. He had to get into that cathedral and quick. But they wouldn't let him.

The fire fighters and wardens stopped him, the officious twits. 'Not in there, mare,' said one smugly. 'Don't know if it's safe yet.'

Breathless, terrified, Johnnie remembered his battalion being brought to a service here, and that there was a door into the cloisters from the place where old Thomas à Becket met his Maker. He rushed round to the north side of the Cathedral, scrambling his way into the cloisters. No bombs here, and he ran for the door into the cathedral – only to find it shut. Sobbing with fear, he turned left, for there was no way back.

At the far end was another door, but in the corner of his eye he caught a glimpse of a man running to cut him off from this exit. Everywhere was noise and the smell of smoke, which was billowing out into the cloister. With relief he realised that what he'd taken to be a window was in fact the entrance to a passageway between two buildings.

Or had been two buildings. The one he passed was more or less intact but the further one, he saw as he reached the passageway was a pile of smoking, smouldering rubble behind the cloister wall. It had been a library by the looks of the charred paper and leather, but there was little left save part of the far wall.

He could hear his pursuer behind him as he stumbled over the debris that had spilled into the passageway. In seconds he would be upon him, and Johnnie realised this was going to be as near as he could get to St Thomas. He reached the end of the passageway, clambering over the piles of smouldering rubble into what had once been a Cathedral building.

He took the Regale from his pocket, and felt his pursuer's hot breath and then his hands round his neck – just as Tug-Boat Annie sounded once more. For a split second they both looked up – to see part of the remaining masonry of the wall by their side about to collapse upon them. With his free arm and last ounce of strength, Johnnie tore himself free and threw the Regale into the fiery rubble of the library.

'Here you are, Tom,' he shouted. 'If you can't have it, no one else is bleedin' going to.'

After sixty years there were no traces here now of that terrible night of the blitz in 1942. The tower, fully restored, was all that was left of St George's church, its clock still projecting from it as though to remind the passer-by that this church could not be defeated by time. Much of St George's had fallen in that night and what was left had been demolished save for this tower. A casualty had been found within it, so he had read: a soldier gone in there to pray. Apart from this tower there was nothing to recognise – or fear – in St George's Street or its church.

He had come to pay penance to St Thomas for the night that had changed his life for ever, a penance for being alive, when morally there was little difference between the three of them. He was a murderer, no doubt of that, though he'd had good reason. Yet the knights that had murdered Becket had believed that too, and they had ended their days reviled and hated by all men. Johnnie Wilson had given the ruby back to St Thomas just as he was pushed under that falling wall. He hadn't meant to kill him, he was just crazed out of his mind. And after all, Johnnie Wilson was a murderer. He had knifed a man to get the stone away from him.

Nevertheless Johnnie had redeemed himself. He had given the jewel back to St Thomas – and through his action redeemed his killer, so he was twice blessed. That final shout of Johnnie's had changed his life. He had devoted his life to the good of others. Just as the knights who murdered Becket went on pilgrimage to the Holy Land, he had taken aid and food wherever it was needed in the world, and when too old for that had returned to run a well-known charity.

It wasn't quite enough. He paid his entrance fee and walked into the Cathedral to the place of Becket's martyrdom.

There, to the great astonishment of the tourists around him, Robert Wayncroft fell to his knees in penitence.

NATASHA COOPER

THE STREET PARTY

T he crash of breaking glass made Maggie flinch. It always had ever since the Blitz.

'Don't worry, Mrs Cross,' said the woman from Number 23, 'it's only Phoebe dropping her tumbler. Look, Colin's picking up the bits.'

At the far end of the long table, with its red checked cloth and pretty flowers, one of Number 23's sons was reassuring five-year-old Phoebe from next door.

'He's only fourteen,' said Number 23 proudly. (Maggie couldn't remember any of the names of these young people who spent fortunes buying houses in her street.) 'But as tall as me already.'

'Yes,' Maggie said, wishing her eyesight was better. But she could tell he was taking trouble with the little girl.

'Have another sandwich,' Number 23 said, 'or a cake.'

Maggie took a small brown sandwich with smoked salmon in it. 'Thank you,' she said. 'This is nice. We never had parties like this in the old days. Not even when the war ended.'

211

'You must have been here longer than anyone else. When did you first come?'

'I was born in your house. My dad was a coal heaver.' Maggie tried not to smile at the thought. 'But it wasn't grand like you've made it with the conservatory and all that. I moved in to 46 when I married Alf.'

'Isn't that wonderful?' said Number 23. She wasn't nearly as snooty as she seemed at first. 'But it makes what happened to you even worse. I was so glad when I saw you safely back from your sister's and out and about in the street again. And even more when I heard you were coming today.'

'I wouldn't have missed it for the world,' Maggie said. 'You've all been so good to me since Hallowe'en.'

A faint blush spread in Number 23's cheeks. She must have been remembering the days when they'd all talked about 'Mad Maggie' and the 'old witch in Number 46, who never weeds her front garden'. Funny how being so frightened could make you a heroine, Maggie thought.

'I wasn't sure I could ever come back,' she said. 'Not till you all sent that card to my sister's and invited me to the party.'

'We were so shocked by what happened to you. Those louts could've burned the house down.'

'I know.' Maggie always tried not to think about it. For weeks after Hallowe'en, she hadn't been able to sleep, and she'd spent her days hiding behind her curtains in case they came back. She'd always hated Hallowe'en and the trick-or-treating children. But it had never been as bad as last year. She shivered now, in spite of the sun and the kindness all around her.

First she'd had raw eggs thrown by a group of teenage girls who thought she hadn't given them enough, so she didn't answer the door to the next lot. They put flour through her letterbox to punish her, and it turned the eggs into a terrible mess. The arthritis was so bad she couldn't bend down to clean it up. Not wanting more flour, she did answer the door the third time and saw two big figures in horror masks. One of them looked as if he'd drawn a bat on his hand. It was only when she peered more closely that Maggie saw it was just a birthmark.

She was angry by then, so she told them what Hallowe'en really meant and how they should be praying for the souls of the dead, not scaring old ladies and demanding money with menaces. Then she shut the door on them and their greediness. Someone filled up her teacup and asked if she needed another cushion.

'No thank you, dear,' she said, glad of the respite from her memories. 'I'm very comfortable.'

If she shut her eyes, she could still hear the hiss from outside the door as the trick-or-treaters lit their firework, and the bang as it fell on to her mat, shooting out sparks and flames. If it hadn't been for her heavy winter coat, hanging ready on the peg by the door, she'd never have been able to put them out. Number 23 was right: she could have burned to death.

'You've been so brave,' she said now.

Suddenly Maggie remembered her name. 'It's kind of you to say so, Sarah,' she said. 'And I'm having a lovely time today.'

One of the young men from the far end of the street had a guitar and was playing a folk song Maggie recognised. She began to hum in tune. Lots of the others joined in.

Everyone was smiling at her. They'd welcomed her like royalty and made her feel safe again. Tonight she could go to bed happy.

'I think you made those awful boys from the council flats really ashamed of themselves,' Sarah said when the song ended. They've never given any trouble since. We all owe you so much, Mrs Cross.'

'Thank you, dear. I'm getting a bit tired now. And the sun's very bright. I'd like to go home.'

'Shall I come with you? Just to make sure you don't fall?'

'Don't you move. I'm sure your Colin would help me, and he's already on his feet.' She beckoned.

A minute later the boy was standing beside her, smiling gravely, and asking if she wanted him to help her off her chair.

'No, thank you. Just to walk with me over the potholes in case I trip.'

'Of course, Mrs Cross.' He kept a steady hand

under her elbow, then waited patiently while she looked for her door-key at the bottom of her big bag. When she'd opened the door, he smiled, showing off his brilliant white teeth. 'Will you be all right now?' 'Yes. I want to give you something.'

'No, no, please,' he said. 'It was nothing.'

'It's advice. There's no point disguising yourself with a mask at Hallowe'en if you let everybody see that birthmark on your right hand.'

'I . . . Mrs Cross, you . . . I . . .' Now his face was bright red, and there were tears welling in his eyes. 'What are you going to do?' 'I'm not sure, yet.' She found herself smiling at him, no longer scared of any memories. 'It's funny how seeing other people frightened makes you feel strong, isn't it, Colin?'

BARBARA CLEVERLY

A THREATENED SPECIES

An Ellie Hardwick, Architect, Mystery

I knew I shouldn't be doing this. It was against all the firm's safety rules to enter a deserted church, at dusk, alone.

I was due to inspect the place the next day anyway, in the morning sunshine and the comforting presence of Ben Crabtree, the country of Suffolk's best ancient buildings contractor. So why couldn't I wait? Why was I creeping, ankle-deep in rotting wilton, along the aisle, jumping at every owl hoot and mouse rustle, torch in one hand, mobile phone in the other and the firm's hard hat on my head?

I'm a romantic, I suppose, and I love old buildings in all their different moods. I'd come to catch what might well be the grace notes of the splendour of All Souls, adrift in the fields outside the village of Crowden. It would be my five-year survey tomorrow that would sign the death warrant for this once-lovely building. It had been disused for years and the grants for money, never generous enough, had finally run out. The fabric

216

was considered dangerous and it was inevitable that the bulldozers would roll. The only people vocal in its support were the Bat Group.

'But the pipistrelles!' they shrieked. 'They're a protected species! Their habitat must not be demolished!'

'I've nothing against bats but I'd like to slap a closing order on their support groups!' I'd said to my boss when he handed me the church file with a warning. 'The Barmy Bat Army! That chairman of theirs! Lady What's 'Er Name . . .'

'Frampton,' supplied Charles. 'Lucinda Frampton.'

'Yes. Well, the lady gave me a very bad time over Mendlesett Church last year. I don't fancy another encounter just yet.'

'Oh, I don't know,' said Charles vaguely. 'I suppose the bats are worth saving. Never seen it myself but they do say the twilight flights of bats out of the church tower is one of sights of Suffolk. They were still firmly in place when the last quinquennial inspection was done. Byam did it. Now *he* seemed to get on all right with the lovely Lucinda.' Charles rolled his eyes in a meaningful way. 'They spent quite some time observing the habits of our leather-winged friends in remote church towers all over the country, I seem to remember.'

'Byam? Byam who? Or should I say who Byam?'

'Ah . . . He left a couple of years before you arrived. Byam Somersham. Good architect . . . but . . . Anyway, he left the country soon after this bit of work. Went to Spain . . . or was it Portugal?'

I'd been passing on the main road on the way home from a job in Norfolk and had suddenly caught sight of the tower of All Souls silhouetted against a darkening blood-red sky, streaked with saffron. One of those vivid late-summer sunsets we get just after harvesting. I couldn't resist. 'I'll just poke my head inside,' I told myself, turning into the driveway to the church. 'Might be in time to witness the twilight flight of the pipistrelles.' I watched the shadows lengthen under the stand of ancient oaks which gathered protectively, still wearing their dark leaf canopy, around the secluded stones but no bats flew out to greet me.

And here I was, giving into temptation and enjoying the guilty frisson of going against all common sense and Charles's firm rules. I paused to sit on the back row of pews to say a silent prayer for the building as I always did and then went on down the aisle, sorrowful for the poor condition of the fabric, the boarded-up windows, the cracked masonry, the water stains running down the plastered walls.

And then I heard it. A trickle of sound at first, growing louder and more insistent: the chirping, twittering, agitated noise that bats make when they're about to take off. I decided to find out where they were roosting. If I was quick enough, I might actually see them emerge from their holes in the rafters or window dressings. I hurried silently back down the nave to the bell tower. The door was swinging open. Checking the state of the staircase with my torch, I was relieved to see that this bit of fabric at least had been replaced since the Middle Ages. It was of stout steel. Not pretty, but a tug and a kick convinced me it was firm. I began to climb. I planned to go as far as the first floor but no further than that. Too risky. Up on the platform, the noise of the bats was louder. Would the light of my torch disturb them? I shone it anyway over the floor. Stout oak floorboards, complete, and no holes down which I might stick a foot. There were hundreds of bats tuning up in the woodwork all around me and, I guessed in the very top floor above my head, thousands more. Not too late, then.

I shone the torch upwards from my feet. No staircase to the top floor. A very old oak ladder reached upwards to the trapdoor giving access to the bell tower. I ran the beam along it to check its condition. There was no chance I would climb that tonight but if it was obviously rickety I would ask Ben to bring a ladder with him tomorrow and impress him with my forethought.

Looking up, I became aware of a darker shadow amongst the shadows of the raftered roof. As I watched, it moved gently with a sudden gust of wind through a broken pane.

I leaned against the ladder to steady myself, unable to look away.

Above my head a huge black shape was suspended, life-sized, vampire-like. A stiff cape flapped in another gust. With a mew of ear audible even over the noise of the bats, I held my torch in both hands, lighting up the horror dangling above my head. Life-sized, yes, because this thing had once been human and alive. Legs and feet hung from the cloak, arms reached upwards, truncated, caught under the heavy trapdoor. I forced myself to light the face. This was no pallid, bloodstained Dracula mask of horror films but – no less terrifying to me – I saw leathery features which might have lain, undiscovered for millennia, in an Egyptian sarcophagus or been hauled, as brown as the envelope earth, from the depths of a peat bog.

I gulped and, as people do when frightened out of their wits, I said something very silly, just to hear the human sound of my own voice. 'Byam? Byam Somersham? Could that possibly be you?'

At that moment, with a rush and a high-pitched whirring, the whole population of bats poured from holes in every part of the tower. They surged into the air, zipping and diving past me and I flapped at them in panic, groping my way back to head of the stairs. I was grateful to hear the clang of my boots on steel treats as I scrambled down. I ran out to my Golf and, still shaking, dialled up a number on my mobile phone.

'Inspector Jennings? I wonder if you remember me? It's Ellie Hardwick here. I'm at All Souls' Church near Crowden and something awful's happened!'

Richard Jennings of the Eastern Counties CID

groaned. 'I'm just going off duty and I don't think I want hear this. What *is* it with you and churches? Oh, go on, then . . .'

He listened silently as I burbled on, ending dramatically with, '. . . Inspector . . . it's every architect's nightmare – getting themselves caught up in one of those trapdoors! In a deserted church . . . no one to hear you scream . . . your phone's in your pocket and you can't get to it . . .' And, with an increasing hysteria I didn't like to hear: 'And you know no one's going to come near the building for another five years! It's Byam, isn't it? Byam Somersham?'

'Calm down and I'll get straight out to you,' said Jennings. 'Don't move from your car! Have you got a flask of coffee in there? Good. Keep some for me. Ten minutes.'

Cocooned in the lights of my car with an up-beat jazz album playing and the windows fogging over with coffee fumes, I managed to get my teeth to unclench and my hands to stop trembling by the time the police car drew up. The Inspector was by himself. He slid into the passenger seat, a large, masculine presence, took my cup from me and drained my coffee. He listened again to my story, nodding quietly.

Finally, 'I've been on the phone with head-quarters on the way here,' he said. 'Spoke to someone in Missing Persons. Your bloke Somersham was reported to them nearly five years ago. By his wife. But then she had to withdraw the notice because he turned up in Spain.' He paused for a moment, thoughtful. 'His car was found abandoned near Stansted airport. And he sent her a postcard on her birthday from Barcelona. He's sent one every year since he went off. CID checked. Date stamped in Spain. Certified husband's handwriting. A constable was actually on hand at the letter box to intercept one on delivery. At the lady's request. So that was that. No case. We'll have to look further. Floating cloak, you say, on the body? Ecclesiastical gear? What's the odds that a vicar's gone missing lately, wearing one of those what do you call-ems?'

'Surplice? No, it's much shorter than that. Like . . . an old-fashioned policeman's cape . . .'

'Eh? Good Lord!' said Jennings.

The Inspector's torch was more powerful than mine but I stayed as close to him as I could without inviting comment.

'You don't have to do this, you know,' he said when we reached the ladder. 'Leave it to me.'

'I'm coming with you,' I said and began to climb after him. 'Don't worry. I won't touch anything I haven't already touched.'

We stood together gazing in silence at the corpse. The brighter light of the police torch revealed further horrors. Now I saw that the dead face was even more appalling than I'd guessed from my first startled look. It didn't have the dreamy, at-rest quality of a bog-burial or a Pharaoh: the eyes had been picked out long ago by the carrion crows that haunted the fields around and accusing black holes were trained down on us; the shoulders were stained with trailing white patches of pigeon droppings. It had the macabre force of medieval execution, the look of a body left to rot away on a gibbet.

And that was odd, I thought.

And not the only odd detail. 'Look at his shoes,' I whispered. 'Under all that dust those are smart shoes, practically unworn. He didn't walk three miles in those. He drove here. So, if this Byam, who took his car to the airport and why didn't they come forward when he disappeared?' I shuddered at the implication.

Jennings put an arm protectively around my shoulders and I didn't shrug it away. I'd noticed that, in spite of his strength, the arm was quivering. I think he was glad of my company.

Half an hour later several urgent phone calls had produced a squad of professionals and I had lost the Inspector to the well-oiled police machine as it took over, reducing the gothic horror of the setting to an arc-lamp-illuminated, plastic-taped, sanitised crime scene.

He paused by my car to say, 'You can go home now, Ellie, and I'll take your statement in the morning. Probably no more than a grisly accident we think but I'll call by your office at – say – nine? You'll have to put off your survey for while, of course. Oh, your first guess was right, by the way.

His hard hat's abandoned in the upper tower . . . wallet in his pocket had his driving licence and cards in it . . . It *was* Byam Somersham.'

By the time Ben Crabtree arrived to pick me up at the office I'd spent an hour studying the Crowden file. Richard Jennings had given me his automatic 'just leave it to the experts' speech but I was hardly listening. And in this field I counted myself an expert anyway. Ben hurried in, stunned and excited in equal measures by the brief outline I'd given him on the phone. After a few a few minutes of, 'Corst, blast! Who'd ever a thought it? So the old devil got his comeuppance! That trap's lined with ten pound lead, did you know that, Ellie? Accident waiting to happen! Poor old sod, though . . . awful way to go . . .' we settled down, file open on the desk, coffee mugs at elbow, to a gossipy discussion of the dead architect and his work. Strangely, Ben had most to say about the man himself.

His broad honest Suffolk face clouded and he looked at my shiftily. 'Don't want to speak ill of the dead but . . . he were right lot of no good, yon chap, Ellie. Fair architect – no denying *that* – but no good to the firm or any firm for that matter. We all said it when he went off – "Good riddance!"'

'That's a bit harsh, Ben? Why do you say that? Oh, come on, you can't leave it there!'

'Not to be trusted with the . . . er . . . female clients, shall I say?' he finally confided.

'Really! Attractive man was he?'

'Oh, yes, I'll say. Even *I* could see it!'

This was quite an admission from the aggressively masculine Ben. And as far as he was prepared to go. Suffolk people are nothing if not discreet and unjudgemental and I was going to hear no more gossip from Ben.

Not so with Charles though. Hurrying through the office at that moment, he hesitated, picking up his bag. 'Attractive, you say? Byam? Good looking bloke but it was his manner more than anything. He'd look at a woman – very long eyelashes he had, I remember – as if she was the only woman in the world and, do you know, at that moment he very likely thought so . . . And he could make 'em laugh. He'd have made *you* laugh, Ellie. You'd be surprised how many female clients suddenly decided to splash out on an extension so long as *he* was the architect in charge! I must say – he certainly brought the work in!'

Charles carried on, oblivious of our disapproval, 'Vain bloke though! Lord, how the man fancied himself! Snappy dresser and always wore a suit to work. But that cloak! Used to whisk about in it something sickening! He thought it made him dashing – and the trouble is – it damned well did! While the rest of us were muddling about on mucky sites in plastic Andy-Pandy suits for protection, he'd be swishing about looking like some sort of superhero. The blokes on site used to laugh but the women loved it because he could carry it off! Anyway, whatever he did, it worked.'

He looked thoughtful for a moment and added, 'No . . . they don't make them like that anymore.'

'Sounds like a species we can well do without,' I said crisply. 'He had a wife hereabouts, didn't he?'

'Catherine. Poor Catherine. Lovely Catherine. Still lives in the village. No one could understand why she put up with him and his goings-on. But she always maintained he'd come back. Showed everyone postcards she got from him in Spain every year. "It's just a question of time," she says. "He's working out there. He'll be back when he's made his reputation." Not that she couldn't have done well for herself, either. She'd had a bloke in the background for years. Gentleman-farmer type. Scott. Have you heard of him?'

I nodded. Handsome, middle-aged and perpetually broke, Tony Scott was quite a figure in the village. A single man since his divorce, he was rumoured to be paying out large alimony bills. I'd never connected him with the artistic Catherine Somersham with her eyes always dreamily on the middle distance. I'd seen her at village street fairs, I'd even bought one of her paintings, but had never met her.

Charles went off with a cheery, 'Say hello to the Plod for me . . . Sorry I can't stay, but it's you they want to see, Ellie.'

Ben and I turned to the quinquennial survey

226

typed and filed and I raised a question that had occurred to me even while gazing at the leathery corpse. 'Look, I don't know much about the state of dead bodies and no doubt the pathologist will have answers but, Ben, how do you think it could have been preserved like that for five years? Didn't putrefaction occur? You were the appointed builder at the time, I see, can you remember what the weather was like that summer?'

Ben's jaw dropped and he began to stir excitedly. 'That were hot. Days and days of heat. Best harvest for years, they say. And the autumn, the same. Do you think he might have been . . . well . . . kippered? Swinging about up there like an Orford smokie?'

'Could be. We'll ask Jennings when he arrives. But something else puzzled me, Ben . . . I'd have expected the body to have . . . um . . . fallen apart . . . been eaten by insects. Wouldn't you?'

Ben considered for a moment. 'Look on page one, there should be something about pre-existing conditions . . . there – look.'

His splayed thumb indicated a paragraph and I read, '. . . extensive anti-infestation treatment carried out on all woodwork . . . insecticidal fluids . . .' Mmm . . . Heavy duty stuff. And the tower was sprayed. Small space – Byam prudently says he put the inspection off for a couple of days to allow the fumes to dissipate. I see. Are you thinking that any winged creatures that might have been interested in a body would have been knocked cold by the treatment?'

'It's possible, I'd have thought.'

There was a screech of gravel outside and Jennings strode into his office. He looked refreshed this morning and as brisk and bright as I remembered. He'd never met Ben before and I introduced the men, explaining the builder's role in the Byam Somersham saga.

'. . . So, accidental death is what it seems to have been. A cracked skull caused instant death. He didn't suffer, Ellie,' the Inspector was concerned to tell me. 'It looks as though he was coming down from the upper bell tower (though what the hell he was doing up there when the survey job was complete, I've no idea), missed his footing on the ladder and dropped the trap he was holding up over his head. It crashed down – did you known it was lead-lined? – of course you did – sorry. It bashed in the back and top of his head . . . here . . .' He picked up a file and demonstrated on Ben's head. 'Killed him at once and trapped his arms which were still extended over the lip of the hole.'

'We were wondering why the body didn't disintegrate and drop?' I said tentatively. 'In fact we've had some ideas.'

'To start with the most obvious thing – his suit was of very good quality, a light summer fabric but strong enough to sustain the weight of his body until . . . well, until we found it. To go on – we think putrefaction didn't occur because of the exceptional weather . . .'

'All those hot harvest days and it was well ventilated up there. Not one of those louvred windows is intact. "Kippered" is what Ben's saying.'

'Right. Yes. Well done.' He fished about in his briefcase and produced an email print-out. 'Forensic entomologists – that's grub experts to you – are a bit puzzled though,' he said. 'This is just a preliminary statement – work could take days – but they're not able to find a great deal . . .'

'Ah. We think we can help you there!' Ben and I exchanged smug looks.

After Ben left, Jennings 'you'd better call me Richard', stayed on for a second cup of coffee. There was an uneasiness about him and I sensed that he still had questions. He didn't know whether to grill me in his role of interrogator or chat to me as a helpful assistant so I made it easy for him by launching into a few questions of my own.

'What was he doing up there when the report was finished and had been handed in for typing? Look here. Charles is very old-fashioned and doesn't yet quite trust modern technology. Oh, it's all on computer but he keeps the original dictated tapes just in case. Someone told him a bolt of lightning can have a dire effect on your hard-drive, since when it's been belt and braces.' I showed him a plastic bag which had been filed next to the document. I took out the small Dictaphone cassette it contained. 'I've checked it and you should perhaps have this but it's nothing more than the architect's survey. This is what may be important.' I peeled the small pink post-it note from the back of the cassette. 'It says "Bats! A.S. Ch. 8 p.m." He'd forgotten to inspect the bat accommodation. No reference to it in the body of the report. I think he probably went back as an afterthought to check up on the colony.'

'A.S.?'

'All Souls, the name of the church.'

'Of course, I'd better take those. Yes, thanks, Ellie. This all begins to fall into place. Except . . .'

'Those postcards to his wife? He can't have sent them. Who did? Is Catherine lying? What's going on?'

Jennings looked uncomfortable. 'I called on the widow last night and broke the news. She seemed distressed and horrified, I'd say. She stuck to her story about the cards . . . she keeps them in a row on her mantelpiece . . . And, as the authenticity was corroborated by the police – what can I say? It's all a bit awkward.'

Carefully, I said, 'I was thinking that, on behalf of the firm, I'd go along to see Catherine and express our condolences. A bunch of flowers, perhaps . . . What do you think, Richard?'

He grinned. 'I think that would be a good idea, Ellie. She teaches art at the local college. You'll probably find you have a lot in common.'

He turned to me as he left, his hand on the doorknob. 'Oh, if you get into a girlie chat with

230

her, you might ask how's she's going to spend the two hundred grand.'

'The two hundred grand?'

'Life insurance policy. She'd kept up the payments on her husband's life.' He paused and added thoughtfully, 'I always think it should be called a "death insurance policy", don't you?'

Catherine Somersham's greeting when she answered the door to the Old Mill House (conversion by Byam, I guessed) was warm. She even knew my name. I stood uncertainly on the doorstep, almost hidden by a generous armful of white arum lilies.

'Come in! It is Ellie Hardwick, isn't it? You work with Charles? I'm just making some tea, will you have one? I won't say "Oh, you shouldn't have,"' she said gracefully, taking the lilies, 'because these are my favourites! Flowers *are* a sort of consolation, you know. And consolation is, even after five years, much needed.'

While she went to put them in water I cast an eye around the living room and began to relax. I find anything minimal bleak and soulless and this room was the very opposite of minimal. It defied any label – I doubt Catherine was the kind of woman who cared about style – and she would probably have laughed if I'd suggested 'bohemian-chic'. It looked as though she had just collected into the room everything she admired or found comfortable. White sofas covered in coarse linen, wooden floors with Scandinavian rugs scattered over, books spilling over from shelves no longer equal to the task of housing them, white walls and everywhere, paintings, not all her own.

The conversation was surprisingly easy and led on from my genuine and enthusiastic comments on the painting I'd bought at the previous year's village art festival. She invited me to look at the other pictures on the walls and, while on my feet, I took the opportunity of strolling to the fireplace and admiring a bronze turn-of-the-century figure of a little dancer on the mantelpiece.

'No! It can't be a Degas, I know that! But it's the next best thing!'

'It's my great-grandmother.'

'She sculpted this?'

'Oh, no, sorry! She was the model. My great-grandfather did it,' she smiled. I replaced it carefully, then hastily began picking up the pile of postcards my manoeuvrings had scattered.

'Oh, dear!' I said in tones of mock horror. 'I wouldn't have taken you for an admirer of modern architecture . . . Spanish is it? . . . Yes, these two are in Barcelona – a couple of Gaudi's best . . . then the Guggenheim Museum? The Sant Jordi Sports Palace? Not my favourite!'

'Nor mine,' she said easily. 'You can look at them if you want to. They're postcards Byam wrote.' She chewed her bottom lip for a moment, started to say something, sighed and then took the plunge. 'Ellie, I don't know what to do! Oh, do you mind my laying this on you? You'll wonder what on earth you've walked into!'

I made encouraging noises and she went on haltingly, 'I've been fooling the police and now they know it. That nice Inspector who came last night saw straight through the rubbish I was telling him. I'm not a good liar and I think he's pretty smart. What on earth can I say to them? I think they might be going to arrest me.'

'It's never a bad idea to tell the truth. That Inspector you saw . . . Jennings? . . . he's half-way human. He would listen. I could give you his number if you like. Er . . . if it would help to rehearse it, see how it comes out, I'd gladly listen.'

I put on my receptive face. Not difficult as I was eager to hear and she responded by launching into her story.

'Five years ago when Byam disappeared I was left in limbo. Not a word. No note. He'd told me he was due some leave and he was going off for a few days by himself.' She glanced at me, her expression one of mixed defiance and shame. 'He did that occasionally. It was a price I paid . . . not happily but with a certain resignation, I suppose. But this time, none of the local ladies he'd had an affair with had gone missing in a companionable way.'

I looked at her, startled by her cold rationality.

Misinterpreting this she said hastily. 'Oh, *you* weren't . . . surely you . . . ?

'I never met the man,' I said firmly, 'I've only been working in the village three years.'

She took a photograph from a table and handed it to me. 'Meet him now,' she said quietly.

Even from the photograph the quality of the man leapt out. Not classically handsome, I thought, but I'd have turned in the street to look at him and speculate. Humorous, clever and interested is what he looked. It made last night's horror even more of an obscenity.

She took the photograph from me and sat holding it in her lap while she continued. 'Shortly after he went off I had a very good reason to insist that he was still alive at least. I didn't want to be a widow and I didn't want to get a divorce. Two years before, we'd had a holiday in Spain and he'd bought and written out some postcards to friends and family and, as usual, he handed them to me to do the donkeywork – "Here, Cath, you'll remember the addresses. You can finish these off." Well, I rebelled. I didn't bother. They just came back home with us in the luggage. When I wanted to prove he was still alive, I remembered them. I took five or six of them over to a place I know in Spain and paid the hotel manager to post to them to me on a given date, one a year. I put each of them in a typed envelope. The police believed me because – well, why wouldn't they? I was saying what they wanted to hear. They must have been expecting me to try to prove he was *dead* because of the life insurance

234

policy. But I needed my husband *alive*. For personal reasons.'

I was about to encourage her to enlarge on this when a Range Rover tore down the drive and parked in front of the house. A florid-faced man got out and hurried straight in. I noted with distaste that he had a bottle of champagne in the capacious pocket of his waxed jacket.

'Cathy! Cathy! Have you seen the news? Accidental death is what they're saying. Oh, who's this? Didn't realise you had company.' He looked around in a stagy way for my car.

'I walked. I work in the village.'

Catherine performed the introductions. 'My neighbour, Tony Scott.'

He stood glaring at me, willing me to leave. He was too large for the room, he'd left muddy prints on the shining floor, he smelled of diesel and he frightened me.

'Pleased to have met you Mr Scott,' I lied with a sweet smile, 'but I must dash. Oh! Before I go! Nearly forgot, Catherine! The name of that new hairdresser . . . I like to support local initiatives, don't you?' I confided as I scribbled. 'Ask for Ricardo at Hairtique,' and added his mobile number.

Catherine smiled and nodded. 'Quite right, Ellie. Thank you for coming. I'll take your advice,' she said.

'It's so obvious why she's been deceiving people like that,' I said to Richard over a pint in the Angel that night. 'That Scott won't take no for an answer. She's been doing a Penelope.'

'A what?'

'Odysseus's wife! Repelling suitors by insisting her old man's still alive. Just taking an awfully long time to get back from the Trojan War. Penelope promised to marry one of the brigands who were after her fortune as soon as she'd finished a bit of weaving she was doing. But at night she used to creep down and unpick what she'd done in the day time. Delaying tactics! Spun it out for years! Catherine's house must be worth a bob or two and now you tell me she's due to get a large sum from the insurance company. Tony's well known to be a bit short of cash . . . well – there you are. He's been putting pressure on her. Won't take no for an answer. You know the type. He's worried, Richard. He's a ball of pent-up violence. You're not to go near him.' I stopped abruptly and bit my lip.

'I'll be sure to keep my styling scissors ready in my back pocket,' he grinned.

'You'll just have to forgive her. All she's done is waste police time, isn't it?'

'I'll forgive your new friend if you'll do something for me,' he said mysteriously. 'Would you mind presenting yourself back at the scene tomorrow morning? Something I want to check on.'

'Never had the Law at my feet before.' I almost giggled with nerves at the sight of Richard's body, face down, on the dusty floor of the tower.

'Get on with it, Ellie,' he grumbled. 'My helmet's conveniently over there in the corner, you've coshed me on the head with one of those planks that litter the floor. I'm dead. Now pull me towards the trapdoor.'

'Ankles or knees, Richard?'

'Take your pick.'

I tugged him by the ankles and to my surprise his body moved easily with the grains of the boards to the hatch. Gingerly I climbed halfway down the ladder and pulled him after me. When I'd got him balanced with the weight of his upper body still bearing on the lip of the hole, steadying him firmly against the oak structure, I reached up and grasped the handle on the flap of the trapdoor which I'd propped open with a piece of planking on either side.

'I could do it Richard!' I gasped. 'If I push out one of the props and then the other, tugging you as it gives way, you're a dead man! Would be if you weren't already!'

He surged back to life and carefully moved the door out of reach.

'It could be done!' he said with satisfaction. 'And if *you* can do it, a 5' 4" female, anyone can. Let's get out of here, shall we?'

We went out into the sunshine and I flapped a hand at his jacket front, covered in dust and worse. He looked at it with interest.

'Probably splinters of oak floor boarding in there as well,' he said. 'Just like the ones we found down the front of Byam's cloak. We know he'd arranged a meeting up here with someone. Had he lured some female up here with romantic intent? "Come up and experience the twilight flight with me?" he purred. He studied his jacket. 'Nice roll in the pigeon droppings? Amatory activity witnessed by a million swooping bats? Not the place *I'd* choose for an assignation.'

'Wouldn't work for me either,' I agreed. 'Have you thought, Richard, someone could have lured Byam here? He (could be she) set up a meeting, gets someone to drop him off here, climbs the tower and kills him, leaves him dangling. He takes the keys from Byam's pocket – or perhaps they'd just been from there to anywhere in the county. With everyone's eyes on Spain, no one's going to look in a deserted church lost among the cornfields. He'd finished the job anyway and, according to his schedule, was supposed to be going on holiday.'

'The killer knew that the body would be found sooner or later but you could reasonably expect a body exposed like that to be judged a nasty accident as – for the moment – it *is*,' said Richard. 'And to show your faith in his survival and your innocence, you keep up the payments on his insurance policy and by waiting patiently – you know he'll be discovered in five years at the outside – you come into a tidy sum of money – and five years' rebate probably. They're in it together! Catherine and Scott.'

'Hold on! I'm not so sure,' I objected. I was remembering the way Catherine had held her husband's photograph. Protectively. Lovingly. 'We're missing something here. Take me back to the office will you, Richard? There may be something in Byam's work records that throws up some information. Let's find out what else our local Don Giovanni was busy with.'

Charles was out on a job when we got back and we settled down with the dusty ledger from five years earlier which recorded the hours spent by each architect on each of his jobs. I pointed out Byam's record. It seemed he had quite a full programme. Ongoing repairs at five churches besides the quinquennial on All Souls. He had, typically, spent half a day at each, usually mornings. His afternoons had been spent on domestic projects: he'd been working on extensions to two private houses. In the record, one was named as 'Moat Farm Extns.' The other 'The Limes Extns.' Both were common names hereabouts.

'Out-of-county contractors, I see, on both so no use asking Ben for his insights,' said Richard.

I remembered the cutting comment Charles had made about the ladies who ordered extensions and I wondered. I shared my suspicions with Richard.

'Names,' he said. 'How do we correlate these jobs with names of clients?'

'We look in the back. That's where Liz wrote down the accounts and payments before it all went on computer.'

We tracked down the two extension jobs and looked at the names of the clients.

'But isn't this . . . ?' Richard started to say, recognising one of them. 'Oh, Good Lord! You don't imagine . . . ? Surely not . . . ?'

I stared at the page for a moment, taking in the meaning of the scene we had uncovered and, in an unthinking gesture of appalled rejection, I slammed the ledger shut.

'We can't leave it there,' said Richard. 'However much you might want to. But at the moment, all we've got is the suspicion of a scenario that could possibly have led to murder. It's not much. How can we find out more without committing ourselves?'

'I think I know how. Look at the dates. The work was started a year before Byam died. This lady was spinning it out? 'While you're here, Byam, you might as well look at . . .' We get a lot of that. Can you imagine? It would have been under way by Christmas six years ago. I'll get the album.'

Every year Charles threw a party in mid-December for staff and clients and anyone who'd been involved with the firm in the past year. He enjoyed going around photographing the junketing and faithfully stuck his shots in an album. It was well thumbed. I leafed back to the Christmas in question. Byam's last. Faces, familiar and unfamiliar, smiled happily or drunkenly at the camera.

'Look at this one, Ellie,' Richard murmured. 'Says it all really, don't you think?'

Byam was standing with his arm around a dark and flamboyantly good-looking woman. He was grinning at the photographer and waving a glass around. The woman was paying no attention to the man behind the camera; she only had eyes for Byam. I was a stranger to both of them but the relationship was clear. It seemed to be clear also to the man standing to the right of the pair, some feet away. He was not smiling. Head lowered, he was showing all the aggression and pent-up anger of a tormented bull. An anger directed straight at the unconcerned Byam.

Richard put a hand down the centre of the photograph, covering up the partying crowd in the background and concealing all but the two main players. The effect was astonishing. Revealed was a crime about to happen. 'Murderer and victim, would you say? I think Byam extended himself a little too far on this occasion,' said Richard. 'Husband sees wife the victim of a serial cuckolder . . . perhaps she's threatened to leave him and go off with the glamorous architect . . . so what does he do? Makes an appointment with the scallywag in a remote place and engineers his disappearance.'

'It didn't work, you know,' I added slowly. 'All in vain. The lady left her husband anyway, shortly after. He lives by himself.'

'A tragedy for all of them then. Makes you want

to just slam the trapdoor back and cover the whole thing over,' said Richard surprisingly.

We sat together in silence, each assessing the evidence, hunting for a flaw, neither of us ready to take the next step. 'Oh, who's this?' said Richard, annoyed. 'Someone's just drawn up in a van. You've got a visitor.'

'It's Ben. You met him yesterday morning. I'm sure he can shed some light on this.' I said. 'Want me to leave?'

'You just stay put!'

Ben came striding in with his usual sunny confidence and stopped as he took in the books and the album open in front of us. Richard rose to his feet.

'Ah! The Christmas party book,' Ben said and he sat down in Richard's vacated chair to look at the photographs. 'You'll have figured it out then?' he added prosaically. His calloused forefinger gently traced the face of the dark-haired girl. 'You never met her, Ellie. Rachel. She was always too good for me. I knew that.' He swallowed and growled, 'She deserved better, but not him. No, never *him*! I couldn't stand by and watch her break her heart over that no-good poser. If he'd loved her back I don't think I'd have bothered.'

Richard stood uncertainly by. He seemed to be waiting for me to say something.

'You rang and arranged to meet him at the tower, Ben? Mentioning some problem with the bats?' I suggested. 'The contractor,' I explained for

Richard's benefit. 'Just about the only person in the world the architect would have agreed to see at that late hour at the end of a job. You got one of your blokes to drop you off and after you'd . . . afterwards . . . you drove off in Byam's car.'

'Story came out that he'd gone off to Spain. Broke my Rachel's heart. She didn't blame me. Why would she? – I never let on. But she pined for him. Never laughed again. Not like that.' He looked again with pain at the photograph. 'Nothing I could do. Seemed I'd killed her as well, in a way. She packed her bags and went off.'

Seeing Richard's shoulders tense he added wryly, 'Oh, nothing sinister! You'll find her at her mother's in Stowmarket. Well, shall we go, then? I always expected it would come out. But I reckoned I had five years. Five years to try to get her back. No chance now.'

He turned to me, tears glazing his eyes. 'Wouldn't be sorry to hear that damned church had been demolished. Was looking forward to swinging a half-town ball at it myself! Let me know, Ellie, would you, when you've done the deed?'

SIMON AVERY & IAN FAULKNER

LOST IN DARKNESS

'No change,' Neil said. A redundant statement. He smiled to himself ruefully.
Charlton nodded. Placed a hand on one
of Aimee's. Squeezed. He looked to the heart
monitor, and back down the corridor to the
crowded wards, to the windows full of darkness
and rain. To Aimee's brother and his lover. Felt
his eyes burning. Looked away again before he
gave way beneath the weight of it all.

'Time for coffee,' Neil said with too much forced
levity in his voice.

'Leave me here,' Charlton said. 'You go.'

Neil was shaking his head. 'Coffee and a smoke
then. On me.'

'No. I'll stay here.'

'*Up.*'

Charlton felt his fist close. Blood rushing in his
head. He closed his eyes.

A darkness waited for him there, one he was
reluctant to admit. It was the dark of rage, of
wanting retribution for what was done, the dark
that was pacing him day and night wherever he
went. It refused to be outrun, outdistanced; it

waited for him to wake in the morning, it hindered his sleep at night.

He got up.

'It's my fault,' Charlton said as he closed his hands around the cup. 'My fault.'

'Bollocks,' Neil said quickly, too quickly. John looked up from scratching at the Formica surface on the table. Smiled. 'Bollocks,' Neil said again, quietly this time. 'This has *nothing* to do with you. You can't protect people twenty-four seven. This shit just happens. It's a fucking harsh thing to sit with but it's true. There's no point in feeling guilty. It's not going to help her, and you know it.'

'Why your fault?' John enquired quietly.

Charlton could feel his jaw clenching. Tension rising in him. *Christ, he had no fucking control any more.* 'A white woman with a black man?'

'Oh, bull*shit*. It was just some—'

John raised a hand. Placed it over Neil's to placate him. There were families glancing up whenever Neil raised his voice. They only wanted this to be a haven from the problems *out there*. Just somewhere to drink their coffee and smoke their cigarettes; to stare out of the window at their own darkness looking back at them.

Neil saw all of this in John's eyes, Charlton realised. It was the kind of closeness that came with time and intimacy. Had he shared that with Aimee? He couldn't decide. Her absence kept making him remember her differently, made him soften the edges perhaps. But it was nothing they'd not have been able to iron out, given time. Just the residue of past relationships, old wounds and recriminations that she hadn't felt able to speak about. All he'd got were the scars they left on her, both actual and otherwise; the rough edges that he'd not been given the time or opportunity to smooth away.

Rage again. Boiling in him. Every time it was a struggle to keep it down. He'd known from the get go that once he and Aimee had developed into an item that certain types of people would have a problem with the idea. Even members of his own family. The only answer he felt was just to *get on with it*; fuck everyone else. Living your life according to other people's expectations was no life at all. But now he wasn't so sure. He had no idea if this was guilt or something else. Just a feeling for the sake of feeling.

Charlton hung his head and smoothed a hand across his brow. He had to stay calm. He couldn't afford to explode. His emotions were a roller coaster crashing from uncontrolled rage to uncontrolled grief. He needed to retain some semblance of control.

Intellectually he knew Neil was telling him the truth. There was no proof the attack had been anything other than some sick fucks getting their kicks at Aimee's expense. But his heart and gut told him different. His chest cavity was filled with broken glass and each beat of his heart ground the ache in deeper; compounded the fear and guilt.

He *was* to blame. No matter how he looked at it, it was his fucking fault. He'd promised to protect Aimee, sworn he'd never allow her to be hurt again.

He had failed. And worse, he had lied.

The noise of the chair slamming over on the tiles cut the room's murmured conversations off like a gunshot. Charlton felt frowns and hostile scowls lash his back as he pushed through the swing doors and fled down the corridor. He ignored them. He could feel the darkness growing inside him; alienating him from everyone. He didn't know how to stop it or if he even *wanted* to.

The rain splashed over him as he escaped the confines of the hospital. Above him the evening blossom of fireworks lit the sky. He ran through the hospital car park, the falling water blinding him. He needed distance in order to think. And used the movement in order not to.

When Charlton stopped and came back to himself he was standing on the lawn in front of Aimee's flat, blankly staring at the darkened windows. His clothes were soaked through. He was cold and wet, but his head was clear. The fury that had driven him from the hospital had momentarily abated, sunk once more into the depths. Charlton slumped, sagging, suddenly weary without the adrenaline rush of his rage. Wide-eyed he stared at the sky. *Shit,* he thought, *what've I done?* He shook his head, despondent, finding no easy answer in the heavens. He shivered and looked back at the flat before him. The blocky edifice was dark, the windows along the face darker still. It was late. Time he went home. He needed sleep.

He raised his eyes one last time to the third floor window that was Aimee's bedroom and flinched, starting at the sudden blaze of light. The window was no longer a blind pool of shadow. It shone with warmth and colour. 'Aimee?' he asked, his voice little more than a sigh. Charlton frowned. *What the—? Was someone in Aimee's flat?* Anger flared, flooding his brain with hot molten fury. *Someone was in Aimee's fucking flat!*

With a bang, Charlton flung open the glass outer door and, before the noise had cleared from the stairway, pounded up the two short flights. At Aimee's front door he pulled her spare keys from his sodden jeans and scraped them over the metal lock plate, haste making his fingers clumsy. He twisted and pushed simultaneously, crashing into the hallway, the door banging against the wall and tearing the keys from his hand. Charlton bulled into the unlit living area, a snarl plastered across his face. A growl rumbled in his throat. God help whosoever was in the flat, because Charlton wouldn't – he couldn't help himself. If there was someone fucking with Aimee's stuff, he'd kill them. So help him God, he'd fucking kill them!

The bedroom door was ajar. Light filtered through the gap. Movement. A shadow. Charlton crossed the distance and kicked open the door. 'Right, you fuckers!' he screamed, spittle flying from his lips. Hands fisted and ready.

No one. The room was unoccupied, just as it should be.

Charlton spun around and searched the remaining rooms, slapping the walls to light the flat, switches digging into his palms. Living room. Bathroom. Kitchenette. There was no one. The only presence he felt was the fading ghost of Aimee.

The scent of her perfume lingered in the bedroom, floating up from pillow and sheets, wafting from her wardrobe when he threw open the door. On the bedside cabinet Harry Potter lay discarded, unfinished, her place marked with a slip of paper. Cosmetics were haphazardly scattered on bathroom shelves, a crumpled tissue forgotten on the vanity unit beneath. Silken, spun gold threads were caught between the bristles of her brush. A cushion sagged and shaped by wear in the living room. Aimee's outline imprinted upon the sofa from countless evenings sat before the television. The jewelled shell of a CD lay discarded on the hi-fi, hinting at her last mood. A cup stained with stale dregs of tea on the end table.

Like a marionette with cut strings Charlton folded down onto the sofa. Visions of Aimee flashing through his memory like slides through a projector. Each remembrance more painful than the last, until grief broke in him and he cradled his head in his hands, his chest hitching as the sobs tore him apart.

He couldn't stop here. It was too painful. Aimee's absence was too palpable. And he knew from bitter experience that his own flat would be little better.

Everywhere he looked he saw Aimee.

The projector clicked in his head. The slideshow changed. The pictures cast upon the screen were no longer the Aimee that was. No longer the tall and willowy Aimee with the long blonde hair that seemed to shine from within; with the robin's-egg blue eyes that changed with her mood, one-minute pale green, the next lightest blue. No longer the beautiful, trembling, loving, hopeful woman he had fallen for. Now the slideshow was all the ravaged and broken Aimee. Raped and beaten so brutally her skin had turned the colour of rotten fruit. Bones broken. Skin torn, stripped, grazed and cut in a million places. New, far worse scars layered on top of the old, faded, almost forgotten ones. His beautiful Aimee lost in the darkness of a coma. Lost in a darkness that would be with her even after the drugs were washed from her system.

His own darkness welled up from within Charlton and swamped him. Like a wave it rushed through him, smothering the pain, banking the hate. It was a darkness that demanded.

Thrusting himself up from the sofa, Charlton left the flat. He slammed the door behind him and headed down the stairs. Feeling sorry for himself did no one any good. The motherfuckers that had blinded Aimee, that had cut out her tongue and punctured her eardrums, that had carved signals of hate upon her chest, they would all pay. Three times three. An eye for a fucking eye.

He wanted to know how Neil stayed so fucking calm. He was her brother for God's sake. Neil should be out there hunting those scumbags down with him.

He's got John to think about. Charlton stopped. He was breathing hard. The chill air and the steadily increasing rain cooled him down. Had Neil been right? Did shit just happen? Was it really nothing to do with him? Or had his philosophy of *fuck 'em, who cares, it's our life* been to blame? Was he really *so* blameless? No. It had to be his fault. *If she'd been going out with a white bloke this would never have happened.*

Round and round. Up and down. Charlton felt like he was going mad. he needed to sort his fucking head out. He needed some place to chill.

Pulling his mobile from his jacket, Charlton dialled up Neil and John's number. Ear pressed to the thin plastic he listened to the phone trill, counting the number of rings. Was it too late? Perhaps he shouldn't call—

'It's me, Charlton. I . . .' He didn't know what

251

to say. What the hell was he doing ringing these guys? They had enough on their plate without mollycoddling him.

'You OK?' John asked the silence. Wide-awake now. 'CK, you there? You OK?'

In the background Neil asked a question. The words were muffled, lost across the distances, but the concern was clear as a bell. Charlton felt his throat threatening to close around his voice and hurriedly choked out his request. 'Can I crash at your place? I . . .' He couldn't finish.

'Sure. What's happened? Are you OK?' John asked.

Charlton couldn't answer, his throat was too tight; it clicked whenever he swallowed, too dry to work. No moisture left. He heard John's voice, tinny in the background. He heard the phone exchanged. 'Charlton, it's Neil. What's up? Are you OK?'

'I'm fine. I just can't . . . I just need a place to stay. For tonight?'

'Where are you? You OK to get here?' Neil asked. Then without pause, 'Look, get a cab. I'll cover the cost, OK? It's not a problem. We'll see you in a bit, yeah?'

There was no hesitancy in Neil's voice. Like Aimee, his door was always open. It made Charlton's chest tighten. 'Thanks, Neil. I'm . . . Well, I'm sorry about this evening, you know, at the hospital? I didn't mean to go storming off like some—'

'It's forgotten,' Neil interjected, cutting Charlton off. 'Just come home. OK? Just come home.'

They'd made up the spare bed for him by the time he arrived. Neil and John sat him down, trying to work the edges out of him. But he was having none of it. He couldn't decide why this was; he felt as if he were outside of himself, incapable of any kind of stillness. There was no placating him. But he could suddenly see with cold clarity the distance between good and bad. It seemed that there were no greys left in the world. *Pick a side.* His head was fucked.

'Have a drink,' Neil was saying, disappearing into the kitchen. 'There's some Vodka some-where . . .'

'Just *sit* for a while,' John said. He sat on the table opposite Charlton; his eyes set with concern, frustration at not being able to get through. 'This is not doing anyone any good.'

'I thought I saw someone,' Charlton said as Neil reappeared with half a bottle of Smirnoff, and some glasses, which he placed in between the three of them. 'In Aimee's place.'

'Aimee's?' Neil said, a note of concern rising in his voice.

'But it was empty,' Charlton said disconsolately. 'No one fucking there. Ridiculous. I'm seeing things now.'

Neil had emptied the Vodka into the tumblers. 'We're all at our wits' end, mate. Drink up, eh?

To Aimee?' He raised his glass and an eyebrow, hoping for affirmation from the others.

He didn't think he'd sleep but when he put his head down in the dark, shivering despite the radiators creaking with warmth throughout Neil and John's flat, he succumbed quickly. In the dream Aimee called to him and, without any conscious volition, Charlton found himself following. She led him barefoot into the city, her hair flying into her face and hiding her eyes whenever she glanced back Charlton to beckon him on, urging him to keep up as he stumbled and tripped in somnambulistic haste, unable to close the distance between them.

The city surrounded Charlton, vacant but for the birds flooding the sky. They arced across his vision, seemingly trapped in a perpetual loop. Like a moment spliced together that never ended. He had followed Aimee once before and knew what came next.

Tears ran down his face as Aimee pressed herself in and out of the shadows cast by the cathedral and back into darkness through the gates out onto Colmore Row.

She guided him across the road, past the empty façades that housed an office and a bank, and turned to wait at the mouth of the deserted alleyway, the piece of the loop where her three attackers stood, ready to enact, without remorse or regret, scenes that would haunt him time and

254

time again. Aimee stepped into the alley and her eyes dragged Charlton in with her, forcing him to bear witness to the atrocities her attackers performed, seeking out his eyes at all times as he watched helplessly, unable to look away, recording the detail of their crimes to ensure punishment was just.

Ben MacKay dodged a solitary car, the Queensway slick under his Adidas as he crossed the road, Hurst Street at his back. The chill wind cut through the cheap denim of his jacket, prickling and puckering his flesh like a fear he felt at the flat. He'd just had to get out; score something to get him through the night, let him sleep without the nightmare. There was no way he could spend another minute in that flea-infested shit hole the council had stuck him with, not without a little smack or blow to take the edge off. The bloody place freaked him out. Ever since Lewis had got done in, the walls had seemed too thin. He could hear the old farts next door whispering about him, their voices scratching and scraping at his mind, making him paranoid. He kept seeing shadows at the edge of his vision, no matter how many lights he left burning; fleeting movement that made his heart race and the breath snag in his throat.

Last night he dreamt about the girl they'd done and woke up screaming like a baby. He'd been convinced she stood in the room with him, looming over his prone body as he thrashed in his sweat soaked bed. They'd only meant to scare her, have a bit of fun. Teach her a lesson for shacking up with a nig-nog. It just got out of hand, that's all, and now he couldn't sleep for thinking what they'd done. He'd spent the rest of the night in his living room, curled up on the threadbare and sagging sofa, eyes burned raw by the hundred-watt glare of the ceiling light. He would not admit it to Webb, or anyone else for that matter, but he was scared. Shit scared. His nerves were frayed, close to breaking; lack of sleep and too much shit taking their toll. He'd not been able to relax for over a week now. Way too jumpy. He felt hunted. Haunted.

Stepping onto the pavement Mack increased his pace, nervously glancing behind him as he turned the corner onto Hill Street, past what used to be the Albany Hotel. He thought he'd heard the slap of footsteps lapping at his own, but the dim sodium revealed nothing more sinister than little and shadow. Another car rounded the traffic island, a taxi taking some late night revellers home, the starry headlights flashing through the drizzle and hurting his eyes.

Mack faced forward, shaking his head as he hurried along. He really had to get a grip. Webb would beat the crap out of him if he ever let on he was freaked this bad. Webb didn't approve of Mack's habit at the best of times. Sure, he had a reason for needing a fix, what with the girl and then Lewis being killed and all. Not that there

256

was any link. The pigs reckoned Lewis had just fucked with the wrong people. He'd always been a psycho. Still, Webb would kick his arse if he found out about Mack being so shit scared he needed a little something just to turn out the lights.

A bent and discarded Coke can rang out on the pavement, clattering at his heels, and making him jump just as he stepped off the curb at St George's House to cross Station Street. 'Shit!' he cried out, suddenly breathless and panting. He swung around, his heart beating in his throat. But the street was empty of life.

Must have been the wind, he thought, stepping out of the road and crossing to the edge of the pavement, craning his neck in an attempt to see back around the Albany's corner. Nothing. There was no one in sight.

Mack swallowed, his throat suddenly dry. He wrapped his arms around himself, holding tight. He glanced across the road at The Crown, wishing the bar was open. He could've really done with a drink right about now: a couple of pints of lager, maybe a whiskey chaser to warm him up. Anything to calm him down. He knew he couldn't carry on like this. The strain of holding it all together was too much. He was literally jumping at shadows. Holding back tears, Mack threw a last glance over his shoulder at the way he'd come, then turned and shuffled on up Hill Street.

Fuck this shit, he thought. He couldn't let anyone

see him acting like this: like a big girl's blouse. He hawked and spat into the gutter, straightening up from the hunched posture he'd adopted, disgusted with being such a fucking poof. He had to pull himself together.

Pausing to light a Benson's, his hand cupped around the lighter's flame to shield it from the rain, Mack once more heard pursuing footsteps and his shakily reconstructed mask of arrogant belligerence crumbled. He spun around, the unlit fag dropping from his lip, a scream locked tight into his suddenly hitching chest. Eyes wide, pupils dilated, he scanned the street. There was no one. The street was still deserted.

Shaking uncontrollably, his breath coming in shallow gasps, rasping icily through his teeth, Mack backed up. This time he was certain he had heard the click-clack of heels from behind. He *hadn't* imagined it. Not this time. Someone was definitely following him. *Fucking* with him. His jacket scraped along the rough brickwork on his right, the noise startling him and making him cry out as he stumbled along.

Please leave me alone, he silently pleaded, terror bubbling just beneath the surface, pushing icy beads of sweat from his pores. *Just leave me the fuck alo—*

Mack felt a hand slide across his mouth, blocking his airway. Then an arm snaked around his throat and dragged him backward into the recess of an old abandoned emergency exit. He felt the first

258

blow strike his head and his legs crumpled. His vision wavered, black motes flapping at the periphery like crows. Pain exploded through his face as it smashed into the concrete. Lightning flashes of agony went off his skull. Blood poured from his nose, choking him. He could feel a flap of skin hanging down from his forehead and imagined the cold gleam of bone glinting through the rain.

Gagging, Mack spat out a tooth and attempted to raise his arms. If he could get to his feet, fight back, he might have a chance. A kick cracked his ribs and knocked him down. Pain lanced through him, bright and sharp. It hurt to breathe. He couldn't move. Another hard punch, a cheekbone shattered. His head whipped sideways, tearing his scalp on the rough brickwork. Blood swam across his eyes. Another blow. And another. And another. Mack twitched and whimpered amidst the stink of piss. A kick lifted him. Another caught his head. Blinding agony as his eye disgorged from the socket like a bloody oyster. The rain of blows registering less and less as darkness clawed at his senses. The last thing Mack felt was the crunch of his spine, then death claimed him and he felt no more.

When he woke Charlton felt the hard surface beneath him. Not the bed he'd fallen asleep in. Panic rose inside him as he felt something flutter against his face. A leaf. He sprung to his feet as if stung. He was in the square surrounding St Philip's Cathedral.

The phone roused him. He reached into his jacket pocket. Stared at it for a moment, not really registering the caller on the display. Distracted. The leaves were still blowing around him. The sound of early morning traffic sluicing through the rain. His clothes were sodden and stained. 'Neil,' he said. Nothing else. His mind was a blank.

The generosity had finally gone from Neil's voice. 'Where the fuck are you?'

Charlton closed his eyes. He was too tired for this. 'Town. When did I leave?'

There was a moment while Neil gathered himself. He was a man unused to bursts of temper. 'I didn't realised you *had*, you daft bastard. Came in this morning and you'd gone.'

'Too much to drink, I daresay,' Charlton said. He felt adrift. That distance again. Getting wider. Like looking at the remains of the world through the wrong end of a telescope.

'Two measures of Smirnoff?' Neil said. 'Not fucking likely.'

'Neil—'

'*Listen*. There's only so far you can go until you start alienating people,' Neil said, his voice quieter now, more controlled. 'And the rope is *fraying*, my friend. Don't let this change who you are.'

There were sirens somewhere in the city. A cacophony of them. Neil's voice was diminishing. Charlton stood, felt the wind leafing through him.

260

Ambulances. Police too. Something big. He couldn't think about that when all it did was remind him of Aimee. It was nothing to do with him. Forget it.

'Look, I'm *sorry*, alright. Neil? I need to sort this out myself. I'm fucked over this,' he admitted. But the line had gone quiet as the sirens diminished. Neil?'

'Charlton,' Neil said. 'I'll call you back, alright?'

Charlton couldn't decide what he could hear in Neil's voice. 'What?' What is it?' he asked.

There was a pause. Then Neil said: 'The police are here.'

They had all three of them in separate interview rooms by afternoon. Left them alone with the grilled window high above head height, the screwed down table; the uniform green paintwork; the tape recorders; both video and audio.

Charlton couldn't move. There was a weight inside him now that wouldn't be dislodged. *Bring it on*, he thought, *I don't give a shit*. What, after all, was there left to lose? He could hear the bustle of activity in the police station above him, in adjoining rooms. He wondered if they were interviewing them all in turn: John first, then Neil, then himself. Comparing answers, trying to find a chink in the armour. But their armour was *innocence*, surely to Christ. They couldn't pin anything on them if there was no guilt to be found. That kind of bullshit only happened in TV, in cinema.

261

By the time the investigating officer arrived with a young female DC, Charlton was asleep, spark out, his head on the table. However inhospitable this room was, it was a sight more comfortable than a park bench. He felt female hands rousing him and he started awake suddenly, the blood roaring in his ears. 'Rough night, Mr Keen?' the DI asked. The necessary stiffness in the man's voice instantly raised Charlton's hackles. He felt the chair complain and give as he leaned back into it. No good. Too many kinks to work out.

'*Every* night is a rough night at the moment.'

'I daresay. DC Allen, would you mind terribly getting Mr Keen here a cup of our delightful coffee?' To Charlton he said without a trace of humour in his voice. 'Black, I take it?'

Charlton felt a sudden rush of vertigo. Had to shake away the feeling that this old man who looked too much like Ernie Wise, but with a cross to bear, was not trying to goad him, to get him as edgy as possible before the interview began.

DC Allen turned on her heels and the DI watched her go, his eyes trailing from her shoes to her black tights to her rear end. Charlton watched him watching. Old school policing. Perfect. He felt heat in his extremities. Adrenaline pumping.

With the formalities dispensed with and the tape recorder set, the DI introduced himself as John Rose. Charlton stared from the file between them to the man's hard expressionless face. He tried to will a vacancy into his eyes. Clasped his hands between his knees. Heard *Bring me Sunshine* in his head, but it didn't help.

'First I'd like to know your whereabouts last night, Mr Keen. Could you give me an outline of your movements from the beginning of the previous evening after you left the hospital?'

The DC returned with a polystyrene cup of coffee. Set it down in front of Charlton and seated herself beside Rose. Her face was as blank as Charlton was willing his to be. He touched the cup. Watched the coffee steam. Could feel their eyes on his face.

'I found myself at Aimee's flat after I left the hospital—'

'*Found* yourself?' Rose interrupted. 'Had you not intended to return there? Do you often find yourself simply stumbling from one location to the next?'

Charlton found himself sighing through his nose. His jaw clenching. *You smug cunt.* 'I was disorientated.' Confused.' Charlton paused. 'Perhaps unconsciously it felt like the safest place to go.' If he expected any sympathy, neither of the faces on the opposite side of the table offered any. He suddenly felt afraid of where this might be going.

'Did you let yourself into Ms Williams' flat?'

Charlton saw the third floor window, awash with light. He saw himself rushing up the stairs, fumbling with the keys to Aimee's flat, bursting into each room in turn, finding nothing. No one. Just the ghost of Aimee's presence in her things, the way her life used to be lived. 'Yes,' he said. 'I thought perhaps someone might be inside.'

'Who? An intruder?'

'I don't know. Whoever attacked Aimee perhaps.'

'But there was no one?'

'No.'

'Just you.'

'Yes,' Charlton said, and fixed Rose with his eyes, hearing the implication in the man's tone. The DI stared him back down. There was an extraordinary stillness in Rose's eyes that left Charlton cold. There was no wedding ring on his finger, he noticed, for reasons he couldn't dwell on. This was a man who lived for the job, was changed incrementally by it over the years. The thought chilled Charlton. *Changing. Don't let this change you.*

Rose wanted to know, was he there long? What time did he leave? What did he do next? How would he describe his state of mind at the time? Charlton tried to keep a lid on the anger rising inside him. *Just answer the questions*, he thought. *They have nothing on you.* 'And afterwards,' Rose continued after referring to his notes, 'after you'd returned to Ms Williams' brother's home, what did you do?'

'We had a drink. The three of us.'

'Mr Williams, his *partner* Mr Saunders, and yourself?'

264

Charlton ignored Rose's tone when he said *partner*. 'Yes. The three of us.'

Rose snorted. Sat forward. 'Hardly the time to be drinking socially was it Mr Keen?'

Charlton gripped the hard plastic of the chair. 'I think it was *exactly* the time to be drinking socially. Neil thought it'd ease all of our nerves.'

'So you were saying your nerves were frayed. You were at your wits' end?'

'*Yes*,' Charlton said, adding quickly, 'but not the way you're implying. My girlfriend was beaten within an inch of her life, and even though the culprit is still out there, you see fit to waste your time badgering innocent people.'

'No need to get agitated, Mr Keen,' the DC piped up, her eyes wary. Her body was tensed, as if she expected Charlton to lunge at Rose. Perhaps it happened a lot. 'We aren't implying anything,' she added. 'We're simply trying to ascertain a clear picture of the last few days.'

Charlton sat back but Rose wasn't finished. 'But you hadn't been there long before you left again, had you Mr Keen? Where did you go upon departing?'

Charlton began to speak but then hesitated. Where *had* he gone? All he remembered was the dream of Aimee, guiding him to the scene of the crime, to watch helplessly as the loop continued. Unable to avert his gaze. A *dream*. So. What to say? The words felt wrong. Felt like a lie before he had them on his tongue and out. 'Walking. I walked into the city. I felt trapped indoors. I had to be out and about.'

He felt Rose's eyes searching his face. He tried to maintain eye contact but the lie wouldn't let him. But if Rose was aware of the deception, then his next question betrayed nothing. 'And you woke *where* exactly this morning, Mr Keen?'

'St Philip's Cathedral,' Charlton said, glad momentarily to be certain of something. He'd told Neil the same thing this morning and Neil would have said as much in his interview.

'On a bench,' Rose said. 'And you don't remember how you got there?'

'I must have been tired. No buses home, so I slept there.'

'No money for a taxi home?'

'I'd had a drink. I was tired. I wasn't thinking clearly,' Charlton said, exasperated.

Rose raised his eyebrows. Exchanged glances with DC Allen while Charlton sipped at his coffee. 'So you couldn't accurately describe your whereabouts from the hours of, say, four a.m. to six a.m.?'

Charlton sighed. 'No. Probably not.'

'And we wouldn't find incriminating evidence on your clothes, now would we, Mr Keen?'

But before Charlton could reply, Rose changed tack suddenly. Turned over a loose leaf of paper in his file on the table between them. 'Do you know this man?' He pushed a black and white photograph towards Charlton.

The face in the arrest picture rang no bells. He looked like an addict. A druggie. Hollowed out. Cheekbones you could cut yourself on. Hair unwashed and ragged, starting to fall out. Eyes that looked used.

Charlton shook his head, saw Rose watching his reaction to the face. 'No. Never saw him before in my life.' Shook his head again. 'Sorry,' he said heavily.

'What about this man?' A second picture. Skinhead, stubble growing in like grain on the photo. Hard eyes.

'No.'

Rose retrieved the pictures and closed the file on them. He looked disappointed. Then he yawned. Rubbed at his neck. There was an uncomfortable lull. The DC was not about to open her mouth again so the silence lingered. Rose tapped at the file, seemingly lost in thought. Charlton pulled at the edges of the cup, concentrating solely on his nails and the polystyrene sliding beneath them.

'One final question,' Rose said finally, his face troubled. He placed a palm flat on the file, then looked challengingly at Charlton.

Charlton waited, his hand frozen on the cup.

Afterwards, the walls couldn't contain him. He paced his flat like a wounded animal. Picked objects up and looked at them, hardly recognising them: the dish that held the seashells that Aimee had collected one wet morning in Bournemouth before he woke; the dog-eared John Updike paperback that he'd begun weeks ago and that had gone untouched since Aimee's attack; the plates on the drainer from the last meal they'd shared together; the pictures of them at Neil and John's last party, both of them too pissed to conceal their affections so late in the evening. How could an *event* reduce a life so? How could the loss of one person be enough to diminish the spark of another?

Charlton felt the familiar swirl of vertigo pluck at him. Pulling him off centre. The darkness rising. He felt sick. Nauseated. White noise hissed through his head. Deafening. Was this letting go?

Carl Webb. That name felt like a scar on his mind.

Questions were demanding answers he was unable to provide. He wanted to scream at the injustice of it all, to weep it all away. His sinuses burned from all the unshed tears evaporated by the anger raging inside. His gut was seething cauldron of bubbling hate for a man he didn't even know.

Carl Webb. How could he not have known about Carl Webb?

That was a question. That was *the* question. The *one final question*, and it had almost undone Charlton. Over and over it replayed in his head. The interview. The questions. Rose's innuendos and insinuations, poorly concealed barbs ripping at Charlton's mind, scarring it, permanently etching a name into the creases and fold, burning a single name into his psyche like a brand; the acid marking him for life.

'One final question,' Rose had said. 'One final question,' daring Charlton to rise to the bait. Waiting him out. 'One final question. Do you know a *gentleman* by the name of Carl Webb?'

The name had meant nothing. Charlton had resignedly shaken his head, just wanting it to be over. 'No,' he said.

'No?' Rose asked. 'I am surprised.' Rose had looked anything but as he'd stared at Charlton. 'Strange, that,' he continued after a beat, 'because I've been led to believe Ms Williams knew *him* quite well. *Intimately*, in fact. It also seems Mr Webb used to knock Ms Williams about. Not know anything about that either, do you, Mr Keen? Not something you like as well, now is it?'

The jet engine roar of Charlton's rage drowned the remainder of the interview out. Charlton had no idea how he managed to stop himself flying apart and answer Rose's questions that, no, he didn't know any Carl Webb, and, *no*, it wasn't something he liked. *How fucking dare he?!*

The thought of what Rose had been implying made Charlton's blood boil. Rose was nothing more than a dirty old bastard. He *knew* nothing. Probably thought Aimee got what she deserved for going out with a darkie. The racist fuck!

Why hadn't Aimee told him about Webb? Why protect the fucking scumbag? All Charlton had

269

known was her last boyfriend had hurt her. Hit her. He didn't know the bastard had put Aimee in the fucking hospital. She should have told him. What did she think he'd do? Didn't she trust him? Didn't she . . .

No. That wasn't it. It was just too painful. Bad memories. Aimee always said the past was history and the present was what counted. She'd just wanted to forget, move on, Charlton knew that. But why the fuck didn't she tell him? Why hadn't *Neil* told him? He must have known about—

Neil! The phone creaked in Charlton's fist as he pressed the receiver to his ear, listening to it ring at the other end of the line. *Where the hell are they? Come on. Answer the phone. Answer the damn phone.*

'Hello?'

'Neil. It's Charlton—'

'Where'd you run off to, you daft bastard?' Neil asked, cutting Charlton off before he could start. 'We need to talk.'

'Too fucking right we do. Why didn't you tell me?'

'Tell you what? When? Look, we need to—'

'About fucking Carl Webb,' Charlton shouted, ignoring Neil's confusion and concern. 'About Aimee.'

'Charlton. Listen, calm down.' Charlton could hear the strain in Neil's voice. 'We need to talk about the police. About Rose.'

'I don't care about Rose. I want to know about—'

'For fuck's sake,' Neil exploded. 'They're trying to fit you up. They think you—'

'Carl Webb.' Charlton snarled the name, once more overriding Neil. Nothing else mattered. He had to know.

There was a moment of silence on the line as Neil reined in his fraying temper. 'He's a Nazi prick, mate,' Neil finally answered, voice quiet. 'You *know* this. This is old ground, for Christ's sake. Forget him. You've got more important things to worry about.'

'He did it, didn't he?' Charlton said, numbly. His voice so soft Neil almost didn't catch it.

'What? Charlton? Charlton?'

The phone dropped from Charlton's suddenly nerveless fingers and clattered on the glass tabletop. Forgotten, Neil's voice was a distant, insectile buzzing from the handset's speaker. Charlton pulled the residential directory from the shelf beneath the telephone table and opened it. Finding the address he sought he moved woodenly down the short hall to the front door. Behind his eyes it all played out for him, the projector in his head clicked from one slide to another, fitting the pieces together. It all made a horrible kind of senser. Carl Webb, Aimee's Naziex, left behind for a black man; the swastika carved into Aimee's chest, raw and bloody; the motiveless, meaningless attack; the police, Rose's questions. Everything made sense.

With the front door to his flat open, Charlton paused in the doorway, his mind still reeling from the shock of discovery. He swayed. He couldn't seem to catch his breath. His balance was off. He seemed to be vibrating, suppressed energy shaking him from head to toe. Something in him wanted to let go, relinquish his hold and just float away, give in to the darkness.

The flat was down a side street off the Hagley Road. It sat above a dingy, rundown newsagent's. The shop's roughcast exterior flaked and stained. The unwashed display windows were dark and sightless, begrimed with dirt from the road. Discarded sweet wrappers, cigarette packs and torn front pages, forgotten already, huddled in the shop's doorway to escape the chill wind. A gated stairway at the side, lock broken, bulbs smashed, led up to Webb's flat.

The steep steps were litter choked and filthy as Charlton edged up them. Someone had smeared dog shit over Webb's walls and broken glass crunched under his boots. The claustrophobic space crowded him, suffocating, damp and reeking. In the gloom Charlton could just make out the tags and obscene cartoons that decorated the walls beyond the stain of shit. All around him were neon-coloured swirls of abuse, crowned at the summit of the staircase by a badly spray-painted swastika. Clearly Webb was already a marked man.

The darkness that had paced Charlton from the first moment he had heard what had happened to Aimee, finally, fully caught up with him. His mind went blank.

Charlton raced across the small landing that opened out before him, the space only fractionally wider than the staircase preceding it. He couldn't discern any light from inside. Charlton closed his hand around the corroded knob and twisted, but the door was locked. He banged on it. 'Hey!' he shouted, pounding on the wood with his fist. 'Open the door, you piece of shit!'

From inside he heard muffled thuds, the sound of a rat in a cage. 'Leave me alone you cunt! Just fucking leave me alone!'

Charlton hesitated. Did Webb know he was coming? He could hear fear in the man's voice. He sounded like a man who'd been under siege for days.

'Webb! You let me the fuck in or I swear I'll kick this fucking door down!'

'Fuck off! You've had your pound of flesh already. Isn't that good enough for you? You're a fucking maniac, you are!'

That was *enough*. He'd had his fill of people treating him like they *knew* him. How could they when he scarcely recognised himself these days? Charlton stepped back and rammed his shoulder into the door. It gave a little, the wood creaking under the impact, but refused to open. He raised his foot and kicked out. Wood cracked. He kicked again. And again. The wood splintered at the fifth blow, the cheap lock ripping free of the frame. The door slammed open and Charlton rushed into the flat, into the darkness.

The police found him on his knees in the living room, hunched over the body. Blood on his hands, on the carpet, on the walls. They took him outside, pushed him roughly into the back of the squad car. He pressed his forehead against the metal grille, until one of the officers told him to sit back. There was a vacancy burrowing itself into his gut, and absence of feeling. He heard the officers murmuring, could see the lights flickering in the street as a crowd of onlookers gathered. Staring at them he felt divorced from it all. *Us and them.*

He thought of being returned to the interview room and of Rose, and closed his eyes. Just darkness. Floating in darkness. *This* was how it felt to cross the threshold.

As the crowd parted to let the car pull away he felt the spark of something inside, and realised it was Aimee, standing in her flat, lying beside him, leading him through the city, and into Webb's flat. He'd carried her like a burden and like a light at the end of some impossibly long tunnel. A spark. Flickering in the darkness. He willed it to go out.

'How long do you wait?' *How many times do you ask yourself?*

'I don't know, love. You'll just know when it's time.'

'It's just such a huge decision. How do you decide?'

John didn't know of course; how could he? How could anyone?

Finally they talked themselves there. They'd stayed up all night, drinking cheap Australian wine, then had sex that Neil felt symbolised everything and nothing. Hung over and unshaven the following morning, he and John had brushed hands in the waiting room, stared at the vacant faces, then squinted at the sunlight that lanced through the doctor's office. Voiced the decision that Neil felt might change him forever. He'd felt rooted to the chair, as if gravity was forcing him down. Tying him to the Earth for his troubles.

There were forms to be signed and dated. Too many. John was a constant presence beside him; the rock that Neil swam to, clung to. When it was done, the day suddenly grew overcast and the doctor's office felt impossibly small. Neil closed a hand over his face while the doctor stepped outside.

That afternoon they turned off the machines almost ceremonially. It felt like closing a book that Neil wasn't yet done with. The room felt weighted down with silence. Neil buried his face in John's hair and wondered what there was to feel next, what there would be to feel in a week, a month, a year. He realised he was holding his breath on behalf of Aimee. But he couldn't let go.

He spoke to Charlton the following day on the phone. The conversation was terse, the silences intractable. How could he *know* this man any more?

'She was always there,' Charlton said. 'In the flat. In the street. In Webb's room. Always there.' He sounded inconsolable.

'She's gone now,' Neil said. 'At peace, I suppose.'

But wherever Charlton had gone, Neil couldn't follow. Had it happened to John, would he feel differently? Who knew? Charlton wasn't still denying he'd known anything about Carl Webb before the attack. But witnesses had placed him at Webb's flat *days* before. It only went to show how deeply losing Aimee had affected Charlton. Perhaps he had always been a coiled spring, violence waiting to happen. Had Aimee been his only comfort? His control?

He spoke about leaving, about floating into darkness, and with every word, Neil only felt more lost. Rooted to the spot. He was glad to be done with the call.

The day they sentenced Charlton for the murders of Darren Lewis, Benjamin MacKay and Carl Adam Webb, they flew to Italy for a week. John had surprised him with the tickets. Promised him sex, sun and culture but not necessarily in that order. And somewhere miles above the ground, Neil looked out at the clouds and realised that he was still holding his breath. Aimee's breath.

He breathed out.

JUDITH CUTLER

BURYING THE PAST

'It'll be simple,' Mary urged me. 'What better legacy can I leave you than escape from that man?'

It's hard to resist the deathbed wishes of a dearly loved older sister, particularly when they echo your own deep felt urges. I mulled them over as I sat in the dispiriting little cell that was all the NHS could afford for its psychotherapists, watching the doctor dig out my notes. A fairly thick file now. My previous therapist had had the decency to mug up on my problems beforehand. I found this physical reminder of all I'd said – or, more accurately, not said – particularly unnerving. I was supposed to be here for a free and frank dialogue, so I told him so.

'Exactly! That's why I'm doing it: just to get you to communicate with me.' His anxious eyes shone in his thin face: he always looked so concerned for me, though he might simply have been worrying about the effect on his life of his student debts. 'Unless and until you bring out into the open the terrible thing that happened to you, I can't possibly help you.'

'It didn't *happen* to me,' I said. 'Everyone says it was *done* to me. Quite different. And I can't survive if I think about it. It's one thing to be denied the prospect of ever having a normal sexual relationship, let alone having all my hopes of children completely destroyed. It's quite another to talk about my feelings towards the man who—' I stopped.

'Please. Try to go on.'

I shook my head firmly.

'The ostrich rechnique never works,' he pleaded.

If that was true, it was a pity. Because that was precisely what I wanted to do: bury my head in the sand and not come up, even for breath. Ever.

My sister's suggestion was a modified version of this. She wanted me to take her place. Oh, not literally. Not in her sick bed in the hospice. Though I would have done if I could. At thirty-six, she had so much to live for; I, though two years her junior, had so very, very little now. Outside, the early daffodils and narcissi planted to cheer people in her situation bobbed in the pale sun. I doubt if she could even see them by now. She, who'd always loved her garden, her organic vegetable plot, even her compost heap, as if they were children, was denied even that solace.

'It won't take much to change the name on the death certificate from Mary to Margaret. Not with Dr Terry's handwriting. It's lucky we had such unimaginative parents, isn't it?' A rictus contracted her face. I knew it was meant for a smile. 'So then

279

you're officially dead. You testify to a solicitor that you want to change your name by deed poll – oh, some whim of mine – and you sell your house and move into mine. You become me, miraculously in remission. You're pale and thin enough these days, goodness knows, to look as if you've been very ill. Come on, we've pretended to be each other often enough in the past. None of our boyfriends could ever tell our voices apart on the phone. But the moment you can, you sell my house. And move again. Cover your tracks. I want to make sure that both Margaret and Mary Lovett have completely disappeared from face of the earth. Maybe he'll send a friend to heaven to look there – and seek him in the other place himself! Oh, Margaret, do you remember the last time we saw *Hamlet* together . . .'

We talked actors and acting till I thought she'd drifted back into what passed for sleep those days. But suddenly her hand fluttered on to my wrist, her urgent grasp surprisingly fierce. 'Remember what he said in court. As they took him down.'

I shook my head.

'Oh, Margaret – surely you remember the expression on his face. He meant it. He'll hunt you down as soon as he's out.'

No, it was all mercifully hidden, behind that nice thick curtain of amnesia.

'In that case, you'll just have to trust me,' she said. 'And next time you come, bring your

National Trust booklet and a road map. We'll decide we're you're going to move to. It'll be ever such fun.'

Whatever else I might or might not do, I couldn't deny her such a simple pleasure, when she had so few others left. I obeyed.

I thought she'd abandoned her weird notion because for the next few days we talked not about where I might move to, but simply about the places we'd been. Bleak East Anglia for Felbrigg and Blickling; the affluent South for Bodiam and Sissinghurst; the West Country of our family holidays for Lanhydrock and Cotehele. But there were some places she'd never managed to reach, and her face would cloud as she drowsed off.

One day, just after I'd left her and was at home making a lonely cup of tea, the hospice called me. Mary had lapsed into a coma and was not expected to live. Leaving the tea where it was, I got into the still warm car.

Her doctor was writing notes as I rushed into reception. How anyone could ever decipher such a scrawl goodness knew. He caught me looking at it and flushed with embarrassed amusement. 'I know. One day I'll learn proper calligraphy. Now, Margaret, your sister was very worried about something. She got very agitated. So I promised to give you a message. It didn't mean anything to me. It may not to you.'

Bother messages. I wanted to be with her as long as she breathed.

He called after me, 'We've given her the maximum medication. You'll find her very quiet and peaceful now. There's not long to go.'

I darted into her room. The doctor had been right. It was only a short vigil. She who'd been such a fighter seemed glad to give up now.

As I was leaving, to my shame more exhausted than upset, the doctor stopped me. 'You never asked me what the message was. She said, "Start at Dunstanburgh.' That's all. 'Start at Dunstanburgh.'"

I shook my head. No, it didn't make any sense at all. After Mary's death, nothing did. Zombie-like, I simply carried out her last requests.

Lovely as Northumberland was, it was too bleak for me, and I felt my Midlands accent made me much too noticeable. But I stuck it out in my rented cottage, getting work temping as and when I could: we'd both got secretarial qualifications. Meanwhile, the house I'd actually bought near Oxford was getting more and more valuable as prices in the M4 Corridor ballooned. The solitary existence enabled me to grow into my new identity and to develop a side of Mary I'd never really appreciated – her green fingers. If she could turn a tip into a garden so could I. But she'd never had to contend with the late frosts and icy winds from the North Sea. My neighbours tutted with sympathy at the skeletal little remains of herbs and lavenders I'd so optimistically planted, and recommended hardier species for next year. But there wouldn't be a next year. I'd do as Mary had told me – a quick flit. One autumn day I was there, the next I was battling with an early blizzard down the A1 (M).

Not to Oxford, though. I'd sold that house at such a profit I managed to afford a bijou flat in that most anonymous of places, London's Docklands. I'd make my balconies – yes, I had two, one west, one south facing – testaments to the joys of container gardening. There wouldn't have been time for more, quite honestly, as I'd landed a full-time job in the City, earning silly money for looking efficient and being thin, two things I did quite well. Officially I was PA to some man in red braces. In fact, I spent most of my time sobering him up. Without ever even sailing near the wind of insider trading, I learned enough about shares to acquire a portfolio, bits and pieces of which I was constantly selling; in six months I'd made enough from my job, my shares and the rocketing values of the flat to be glad to escape from the pigeons which turned my little gardens from Eden into a grey and white patchwork. Maybe I should have kept the flat – the views up and across the Thames to Greenwich were an unfailing delight to a provincial woman like me – but I could see that slowly but inexorably the property boom was slowing. So I bought two places, one near Carcassonne, the other in Cheshire. Mary would have loved Little Moreton

Hall and Erddig, but would probably have turned her nose up at the industrial wonders of Quarry Bank Mill. Mary? I mean, my late sister Margaret, of course.

The West Midlands; the East Midlands. Each time I moved I made a bit more profit, enough to try the Cotswolds again. There was so much to see there I stayed long enough to become a mature student at Oxford Brooks University, and become a qualified teacher. A new job and then a promotion took me to schools in different locations – Herefordshire and Hampshire. And then I moved into Dorset, where we'd always planned to see Max Gate and Verities, as headmistress of a village school. On paper the village was called Wheelbarrow Town. In fact it was a disorganised jumble of cottages sprawling along a common on one side and deep fertile valley the other, and no one ever called it anything except Wilberton.

However hard they had to work these days, teachers earned a decent salary, and I was able to outbid affluent city types wanting a holiday home for three weeks a year. I wanted my neglected Georgian rectory, just beyond the village boundary, for far more than that. I wanted it to live in for ever and ever, enough to sell the cottage in France to raise the funds to buy it and restore the roof and the garden walls.

Secure in my latest existence, and comfortable in the weight and odd grey hairs of a woman in her mid-forties, at last I could allow myself to become part of the community I'd settled in. I joined things like the gardening society, tried hard to ring church bells and started a music club, hiring a minibus to take us into Bournemouth for symphony concerts. My school, once a run-down building with outside lavatories and depressed staff, benefited from an anonymous donation (the remains of the Carcassonne fund, of course) which built a new main block with not just lavatories but a computer room and a gym. Soon parents were queuing up to enrol their children. The Secretary of State for Education came down in person to congratulate us on our academic and sporting success. We were headline news on not just local but national TV.

The strange thing was that the happier I became, the more I started to get mysterious dreams. Nothing more than frightening fragments at first. I'd wake sweating with fear, impelled to check all my windows were locked. In the cold light of day I cursed myself for a fool, but nonetheless got my intruder alarm system upgraded. The young man installing it looked bemused – there was nothing of any value in the house.

'No,' I smiled. 'All my gold is in the garden. Look.' I pointed to the sea of daffodils in the orchard. I might have been waving to my sister.

For the first time I felt able to try my hand at truly organic vegetables. Friends from the gardening society had got me started on a compost heap as

285

soon as I moved in. There was enough room in the garden for a couple of modern converters, too, the sort you turn regularly to oxygenate the humus. Now they advised me on how to plant my cabbages and beans. Double digging and lots of lime for the former, they said. As for the latter, I'd long suspected there was more to it than simply popping beans into pots and transplanting them so they'd grow up rickety poles. I was right: I had to dig a deep trench – at least eighteen inches was the kindliest recommendation, though some insisted on nearer three feet – and fill the bottom with rich compost. Then I was to put in a layer of crumpled newspaper, then a layer of bonemeal and finally more compost. I was to soak the lot thoroughly before replacing the earth. I may have pulled a face but I knew I had to do it: this crop wasn't for me, Marion Lovage, but for a woman I'd loved years ago called Mary Lovett. Poor Mary. I might once have become her, but now I seemed to be outgrowing her. There were certainly many days when I was simply too busy at school to think of her. And she'd certainly not had the ambition that had driven me to find this sort of identity.

Or the reason that lay behind my moves. My nightmares lasted longer each time. Any time now I'd recall the incident that had set all this in train.

By now my screams woke me. I went so far as to get my GP to make me an appointment with a psychotherapist. The NHS being what it was, it would be weeks before he could see me.

While I waited, I immersed myself in work, both for the school and in the garden. A bright day in the Easter holidays told me the time had come. This was the day of the trench. Then I'd lime the cabbage patch.

Because the ground had long since lain fallow, one of my gardener friends had lent me a pickaxe, but I soon set it aside in the long grass. A few minutes with the spade showed that I was working friable loam. It probably didn't need all the enrichment I'd provided, but once I'd set my hand to the plough, as it were, there was no turning back. The trench grew with reassuring speed, deeper, wider, longer. When I'd refilled it and all the soil had settled, I'd make a strong wooden frame like my neighbours', one lasting for many years and many crops of beans all as long as your arm. Yes, it was hard work. But I was very fit after a winter of digging and barrowing and enjoyed every minute. I was sweating hard in the noonday sun when I heard the footsteps on the gravel path. It was that sound that finally broke all my nightmares. I was back in that quiet suburban cemetery, taking a shortcut on a warm summer's night because the last bus had broken down and it would be quicker to walk home than to wait for the replacement. The footsteps had been swift. In my silly summer shoes I couldn't run, but toppled headlong on to a Victorian grave.

Sacred to the memory of Thomas Parkinson, JP
Born 1815
Taken to the bosom of our Lord, 1877
And to his dearly beloved wife,
Anna, 1820–1840,
And his second wife,
Elizabeth Jane,
Mother of
Herbert, both taken to a better place in 1842
IN THEE WE TRUST

Goodness knew how many times I read it, learning it by heart, as you can see, much as I doubted the sentiment, anything to take my mind off what that man was doing to me. And then he flung me over on to my back, and started all over again. That was his mistake. He let me see his face. And his tattoos. And his cold, hard eyes.

His eyes were still hard but burning hot as he turned in court as they went to take him down – life, for aggravated rape – and pointed to me. 'I'll be even with you for this. When I get out I'll finish the job. I'll kill you.'

The face before me now had aged as much as mine had, but where mine was tanned and healthy, his was pale, with the sort of pallor that brought Mary to my mind. Prison pallor. His eyes were cold again. His tattoos moved as the muscles under them shifted: he was taking a firmer grip on his weapon of choice, an empty bottle. Then it had been beer, now it was wine. He said nothing.

He didn't need to. Fuddled as he might be with the wine, his intention was all too obvious.

As before, I screamed. As before, he laughed. This time he added, 'You can holler all you like. Place in the wilds like this – who's to hear?'

'The neighbours –' I blustered.

'No neighbours for miles, are there? And you don't suppose I exactly advertised my presence. I've got a nice little alibi already set up. So you might as well face it. I'm going to finish what I started all those years ago before you had me sent down.'

The headmistress in me spoke. 'I don't know who you are or what you're talking about. And how can you have a perfect alibi?'

He snorted with laughter. 'That stately home down the road—'

'Yes. Verities—'

'I got one of those timed tickets. Went in with the second party. Slipped out. No one will admit to having missed me – too bloody proud of their security.'

'Your family – friends—'

'You're joking!'

Yes, he looked as if he'd been sleeping rough.

'How did you find me?' I took a step back.

'Easy: you were on the bloody box, weren't you?'

With every word he'd inched nearer. And I inched further back. But not straight back. I drifted sideways, towards the grass. Resigned, I said, 'Let's get it over with then, shall we?'

★   ★   ★

The bean row looked remarkably professional. I could be proud of myself. It ran true and straight, with strong posts at each end supporting well-seasoned branches for the young plants to climb. George, the gardening club friend who'd lent me the pickaxe, awarded me ten out of ten when he came to collect his property.

He raised an eye when I presented him with a new one. I'd bought it at the same time as I'd bought a new load of lime.

'It wasn't quite up to the job of breaking up those old greenhouse foundations,' I laughed, pointing at the mess of brick ends. Had I really checked if I'd got all the hair and bloodstains from the original one? And, in case I hadn't, taken it with me to a head-teachers' conference in Derbyshire, and en route dropped the pieces in a landfill site? Surely I must have dreamt it. And why had I needed more lime? What had I spread the first lot on, if not on the garden? It wasn't the sort of thing you spread in bean trenches, not unless you wanted something to rot down quickly.

'You'd need a contractor for that,' George protested. 'I know you women claim you can do everything, but you have to draw the line somewhere.'

He was right. I did. I knew I'd have to stop all this racketing around the country, and put down roots at last. I had to stay here for as long as I lived. Probably I was relieved, but after so many years on the move, I might get itchy feet, and what then? No, I couldn't trust anyone else to look after my house and garden, that was sure, and I certainly couldn't put it on the market, ever. Not in my lifetime.

My decision made, I phoned the doctor to cancel the psychotherapy appointment. I'd managed to resolve my problems, I said. Finally. I'd faced the cause of my fears, just like it said in the self-help books, and dealt with it.

I didn't add that there was one matter I couldn't resolve. I couldn't ever fancy any of the beans. I might have buried the past, but eating it was another matter.

PETER TURNBULL

PUNCTURE POINT

Monday 3rd January

I t was cold, very cold, pleasantly, reassuringly cold, for this was January of the year, still within the twelve days of Christmas and was, as normally so, cold, as cold as the man could wish it to be, as cold as he recalled it being in his childhood. It was the period of snow and ice and biting easterlies, of the weather that folk would complain about. But in the last few years the winters had been mild, too mild, unhealthily mild, more like a prolonged autumn than a proper winter. No good, hard, prolonged frost which killed off all the sickly fauna and flora, and occasionally, tragically a few aged and sickly humans as well, but then, the man thought, that was the nature of winter, it was how things should be in this part of the world, and this winter was like the winter of old. Not as long lasting perhaps, but the cold snap had lasted for a few days now, ice formed on ponds, householders worried about burst pipes, black ice caused car accidents, the air was cold to breathe for the first time in a very long time. The man walked with his dog on Askham Bogs, the ground beneath his feet was reassuringly frozen underfoot. His dog, as all dogs are, was unhappy in the heat, but this weather suited him admirably, and the man himself, wrapped up against the cold, felt a sense of reassurance as he surveyed the frost, Christmas card-like scene, for this is exactly, exactly how it should be in Yorkshire during the winter. It was in Askham Bogs that the man, the dog walker, met another man who did not complain about the weather. The second man was dead.

The dog walker first saw the man when he was still some distance away, his heart thumped in his chest at the sight, a pit seemed to open in his stomach with such suddenness that it felt like he had been punched. Hard. For the second man was certainly dead, even from that distance, he was dead, ill clad for the weather and lying face down. It was, then, still only eight a.m. and the dog walker thought he knew what had happened, a youth, out partying, for this was the season to be merry, had taken too much alcohol, decided to walk home, become hypothermic and had begun to wander in a daze, finally collapsing to sleep his last sleep in the midst of lonely Askham Bogs. The dog walker turned to the other man for life may not yet be extinct, his dog too seemed to sense the urgency and trotted beside his owner. But the urgency was wasted. Upon closer inspection, the man lying on the cold, cold ground beneath a cold blue sky, was dead. Clad only in a shirt and denims and the sort of shoes joggers wear, he was clearly deceased, his arm already rising in rigor. He was youthful, the man saw a pleasant looking blond-haired youth of about twenty summers. A life cut short, tragically short. The man plunged his hand into his pocket and took out his mobile phone and noticed his dog's reaction with interest: the dog, knowing death, curled up on the ground some distance from the body but looking at it intently. The man phoned the three nines '. . . very dead, I'd say,' he said. 'Life is not threatened . . . not any more.'

The man pocketed his mobile and, calling his dog, he walked away from the body towards Tadcaster Road to await the police vehicle, and the ambulance. He was standing on the pavement of Tadcaster Road when the police vehicle arrived, followed by the ambulance. They would have been dispatched separately but had clearly 'met' each other on the traffic free, pre-rush hour roads.

'Oh, he's dead alright.' The man said to the youthful looking constable and the equally youthful looking ambulance crew, both female. 'I'm a doctor in general practice . . . life is extinct . . . you can't see him from here, but that direction,' he indicated a route about 90° from the road, 'follow your nose, you'll see him . . . fine looking young man. At least he was.'

'Happens every winter,' the constable said with

a cynicism which the man thought was beyond the constable's years. 'A youth, male or female, gets a skinful of alcohol, a walk home turns out to be not the walk they planned. I knew there'd be a death in this cold snap . . . just knew it.'

'Strange place to walk . . .'

'Sorry, sir? What do you mean?' The constable took out his notebook. 'Can I have your name by the way?'

'Clark, Jeremy, Dr . . .' He gave an address in the nearby Bishopthorpe estate.

'What do I mean? Well, like you I assumed this to be a tragedy, a young man with too much alcohol gets disorientated, but look where he is . . . he is wearing only denims and a shirt . . . you'll see that when you view the body. Where did he come from and where was he going that he might end up in Askham Bogs?'

'That's a point, sir.'

'It was freezing last night. If he left the nearest houses, which are where I live, he would have succumbed to the cold long before he reached the centre of the bogs, he probably wouldn't even have left the house in such an ill-clad manner.'

'Ah . . .' The constable gazed towards the bogs, trees clad in a white frost, hoarfrost on the grass, a blue sky above.

'Just a thought,' Dr Clark said, 'but it may be prudent to treat this death as suspicious until you know otherwise.'

The constable reached for his collar-mounted

radio, he pressed the send button. 'PC 347 to control.'

'Control receiving,' the radio crackled.

'Location . . . opposite Askham Bogs on Tadcaster Road, ambulance crew already in attendance . . . death confirmed by member of the public who is medically qualified . . . death may be suspicious CID attendance requested.'

'Control . . . understood . . . out.'

'Well, I will leave it with you.' Dr Clark shook his dog's lead. 'We must be off. My surgery starts at eight a.m.'

George Hennessey looked down at the youth as the SOCO camera flashed. Like the dog walker who had found the body, Hennessey was struck by the boy's youthfulness and his good looks. Not a person who would have any difficulty in attracting the girls, he thought, but he was now stiff with death. Soon his parents will be weeping. Dr Mann, turban-headed, smartly dressed, approached Hennessey.

'Life is pronounced extinct at 08.34, Chief Inspector,' Mann said.

'08.34.' Hennessey noted the time in his notebook. 'I'm sorry to have to drag you out here so early when a medical man has already pronounced death but procedures have to be followed.'

'That's perfectly alright, Chief Inspector,' the police surgeon smiled. 'It is my job, I am honoured to do it.'

'Thank you,' Hennessey smiled.

'I can find no evidence to suggest the death is suspicious from a medical point of view,' Dr Mann said, 'no injuries, for example, but I do take the point that it's a long way and a strange way to have walked by himself, especially so ill-clad.'

'Noted,' Hennessey replied.

'But whatever, he can be removed to York City Hospital for the post-mortem if you feel one ought to be performed.'

'I'd be happier,' Hennessey said softly. 'Both yourself and the gentleman who found him are medical men, both of you are of the opinion that this is a long way for him to come by himself from the nearest house. I'd be happier to have a thorough examination of this young corpse.'

The Scene of Crime Officer's camera flashed again.

'The body is that of a well nourished male of approximately twenty years of age.' Dr Louise D'Acre spoke for the benefit of a microphone which was attached to an aluminium angle-poise arm which in turn was attached to the ceiling of the pathology laboratory directly above the dissecting table. The body of the youth lay face up on the table with a standard white towel placed over his coyly termed 'private parts'. 'There is no sign of outward injury . . . but I think you are right to be suspicious of this death, Chief Inspector.'

297

'Oh?' Hennessey, observing for the police, stood at the edge of the laboratory.

'Yes . . . you see this area of darkened skin, here down his left side?'

'Yes . . .'

'That is hypostasis, it's caused by blood settling according to gravity. It meant he was placed on his left side at death or shortly after and remained in the position for at least twelve hours. It takes that length of time for blood to solidify after the heart has stopped beating. Now . . . if the young man was found laying face down, as I believe he was . . .'

'He was.'

'Well, in that case it means he died elsewhere and was moved after his death.'

'That is suspicious.' Hennessey raised an eyebrow and glanced at Paul Fry, the mortuary attendant who returned the glance with a smile and a shrug of his shoulders. Hennessey had time for Paul Fry, he had always found the short, rotund mortuary attendant to be a man of warmth and good humour, unlike many, nay, most, other mortuary attendants that Hennessey had met. He had often wondered whether such dour men are drawn to the job because it has some macabre appeal for them or whether the job makes them sour, cynical, and humourless. But here is Paul Fry, who radiates like sunlight in this room of death and tragedy. 'That and the fact he was so ill-clad for the weather.'

'Any identification?'

'No . . . nothing in his pockets . . . a till receipt . . . and a credit card receipt slip which we can trace him from, if it is his, but no wallet or similar. The till receipt is from a supermarket . . . seems to have bought food and cleaning materials . . . the sort of shopping a young man who lived alone would buy, so we don't think he lives at home.'

'I see . . . I think you're right to think that. A young man who buys cleaning materials is a young man who lives alone.'

'We'll see,' Hennessey smiled.

'Oh, take it from me,' Louise D'Acre also smiled, but avoided eye contact.

'He has a small callous on his right middle finger, a classic writer's callous . . . a lump where the pen lodges. He was right-handed and writes with a pen as much as or in preference to a word processor.'

'A student?'

'Possibly . . . but whatever, he used a pen a great deal. Now this is interesting . . .' Dr D'Acre peered at the right shoulder of the dead youth.

'What have you found?'

'Come and see . . .'

Hennessey, dressed in the same green coveralls as D'Acre and Paul Fry, walked slowly to the dissecting table.

'There,' Dr D'Acre said. 'You see that?'

'It's like a small mole.'

'It's a puncture point. It's caused by being injected quite roughly with a hypodermic needle, jabbed more than injected . . . and without the benefit of an antiseptic wipe beforehand. Druggies are covered with them but this is the only one . . . high up on the right shoulder . . . and the callous on his right middle finger tells us he was right-handed . . . it suggests . . . strongly so, that he was injected rather than injected himself. Even if he was ambidextrous, he would have difficulty injecting himself there with his left hand . . . even with a small syringe.'

'I can see that . . .' Hennessey mimicked the motion of injecting himself on his upper right shoulder. 'He'd be more likely to put the thing into his forearm, as drug takers do.'

'Mr Fry,' Dr D'Acre turned to the mortuary attendant, 'can you get a photograph of this please. Place a ruler beside it, we'll need a scale.' Dr D'Acre and Hennessey stepped back to allow Paul Fry access to the right shoulder. 'It's recent too,' D'Acre said as the camera flashed, 'very recent, twenty-four hours . . . possibly less. I'll trawl for traces of poison, see what we find . . . with a corpse as recent as this, traces of light toxins will still be in the bloodstream and long bones.' She thanked Paul Fry as he stepped away, having taken three close-up photographs of the puncture point. She took a scalpel and placed in on the stomach of the deceased as Hennessey returned to the edge of the room.

'I won't disturb the face . . .' She explained, 'He will have relatives who will doubtless be asked to identify him . . . but if you can't trace the relatives, I will remove the jaw . . . and take a cast of his lower dentures. He can be identified by dental records, if you can find his dentist.'

'Understood,' Hennessey said, though he knew the procedure well, having used it many times. If the police believe they know the identity of a deceased and can find out who his or her dentist was, then dental records will confirm or refute their suspicions. Very useful in the event of much decomposed or completely skeletal remains being found.

Dr D'Acre drew the scalpel over the stomach, dividing the flesh with three incisions in the shape of an inverted 'Y'. It was Hennessey believed, called a 'standard mid line incision'.

'Curiouser and curiouser,' Dr D'Acre said.

'What have you found?'

'Well he had no food for at least 48 hours before he died. And he looks well nourished and the supermarket receipt indicates that he was eating.'

'Strange . . .'

'Well, that's your department, not mine, but I would have to say he was kept against his will and then filled full of something. He died laying on his left side and was carried out to where he was found. I'll send samples of blood and tissue to the forensic laboratory at Wetherby . . . you'll get the results tomorrow.'

Afternoon, Monday 3rd January

'Sounds like Charlie.' The young woman in the red T-shirt which advertised an alcoholic soft drink, a so-called 'alcopop' pondered the description given to her by Detective Sergeant Yellich.

'Charlie?' Yellich glanced along the bar, the three other young women all wore the same style figure-hugging T-shirt. That brand of 'alco pop' was clearly being promoted.

'Charlie Pimlott.' The woman pulled a pint for a customer who limped up to the bar as if she knew which drink he wanted. 'He comes in here a lot . . . near daily . . . hasn't been in for the last day or two.'

'You give cash back, love?'

'Yes, up to fifty pounds . . . customers prefer to use the bar than go to a cash dispenser, they charge a fee, a pub doesn't. If they ask for fifty pounds they get fifty. If they draw out fifty pounds from a machine a further five pounds is debited from their account. The fifty pounds is credited to the pub's account and they receive the cash. They use it to buy drink.'

'I see . . . Charles Pimlot does that?'

'Yes, a lot.'

'What can you tell me about him?'

'Charlie . . . not much really.'

Yellich glanced around him. The Elm Tree was a dark dive, patronised by some very 'iffy' looking customers. It was still early, many seats were still vacant.

'He came in during happy hour, from three p.m. to seven . . . fifty pence off selected beers. Couldn't have much cash . . . only drank cheap beer. At seven p.m. when the price went up to normal, he'd turn and find the exit. Gabrielle is the one to ask.'

'Gabrielle?'

'Girl over there . . .' The barmaid nodded towards a worryingly thin looking woman with dark, greying hair who stood alone at the bar in front of a pint of lager. 'They were mates.'

Yellich thanked the barmaid and sidled along the bar and stood next to the woman identified as 'Gabrielle'. He showed his ID. 'I'd like to ask you a few questions.'

'About?' Gabrielle had a soft voice. She wore a long, dark blue skirt and layers of dark coloured clothing above her waist. She emitted an air of low esteem bordering on depression, so thought Yellich.

'A young man called Charles Pimlott?'

'Charlie? Not seen him for a day or two.'

'What is he to you?'

'Friends. Drinking friends. I'm a lot older than he is . . . there was nothing between us.'

'You are?'

'Gabrielle Ingham.' She raised her glass to her

lips and drank deeply, like a man. 'I do this during happy hour and then go home for a vodka or two . . . or three . . . I get through a bottle a day.' She fumbled for a cigarette and lit it with a bright orange disposable lighter. 'So what has Charlie done to make the police interested in him?'

'Nothing. He's dead.'

Gabrielle Ingham's knees buckled slightly, she clutched the bar and steadied herself. Yellich took her elbow but she shrugged him off.

'So you knew him?' Yellich continued after a pause.

'Aye . . . he lived with me once . . . I mean he rented a room off me, gave me a bit of rent.'

'Did he work?'

'Employed? No . . . but work, yes.' Gabrielle Ingham drew deeply on the nail. 'He wanted to be a writer . . . of fiction . . . was at university reading law, said it was too tame, wanted to write . . . what did he say? "Tell it like it is fiction" . . . "life as it is on the streets" . . . that sort of thing . . . that's how I got to know him. He started to come into the Elm . . . I mean, you can see what a dive it is, full of alcoholics like me . . . ex cons . . . some real ducking and diving going on . . . some students who live in rented houses rather than in halls of residence . . . Charlie came in here looking for 'copy' as he called it.' Gabrielle Ingham's voice was not just soft, but almost musical. Yellich thought that words tumbled from her mouth in a melodious manner.

304

He thought that near derelict as she appeared to be, she had clearly been in receipt of an education and had fallen from grace to become a barfly at the Elm, and had probably fallen a considerable distance.

'I warned him . . . but did he listen?'

'Warned him?'

'He was asking questions of the wrong people . . . this pub may be for lowlifes like me, but there's contacts to be had if you want them. The Elm is a conduit to some very dangerous people.'

Conduit. Again Yellich had the impression that Gabrielle Ingham had had an education and had fallen a long way from somewhere to have fetched up in The Elm.

'There are some dangerous people in this small city. He was wanting to talk to them for his book. What was it he said he wanted? Copy . . . that was it.' She took another drink of her lager, gulping it like a sailor would. 'I mean, you don't do that . . . not to these guys . . . these guys are seriously heavy.'

Yellich groaned. The naivety of youth, as with the youngster who went to Northern Ireland to try to make sense of the 'troubles' for himself so he could better understand them, went hitch-hiking round the province . . . eventually got into the wrong car and was later found by the roadside with a bullet in his head. Not only did he do that, but he did that when in possession of an

English accent. Fatal. 'Do you know to whom he was talking?'

Gabrielle Ingham shook her head, vigorously.

'Is it dangerous for you to talk?'

'Yes. They know you're a cop . . . I could get a kicking if they think I'm giving you information . . . not from anyone here . . . but word will get to where word will get to . . . a lot of tourists visit York . . . they never see this side of the railway line.'

'You've had an education, I think?' Yellich couldn't resist the question.

'I'm a nurse . . . a staff nurse . . . well, I have the qualifications . . . right now I am unemployed, on sickness benefit . . . long term. I won't work again. I sold my house and pay rent now . . . released a lot of money for this,' she tapped the side of her beer glass, 'and these.' She tapped the packet of cigarettes. 'I'm on the way out, 45 years old, so I want to make it as smooth as possible. Tuberculosis,' she said matter of factly. 'Used to be called consumption . . . seems a more accurate name to me . . . folk would visit spas to take 'the cure' knowing there was no cure . . . just remission now and again.'

Yellich nodded sympathetically. He had heard that the disease had re-emerged in the late twentieth century and had taken a toehold by the beginning of the 21st century. Not yet of epidemic proportions, but a toehold nonetheless. 'What specifically was Charlie Pimlott asking about?'

'The drug culture . . . the heroin trade. I mean, you don't ask questions of those people.'

'I see.'

'Where can I reach you?'

'Micklegate Bar Police Station. Do you have information?'

'Might do. I have done little of use in my life, and if I am to be planted soon, I think I'd like to do at least one good thing. And Charles was a nice lad . . . he didn't deserve to be murdered so young, even if he did invite it by his stupidity.'

'If it is Charlie. No positive ID yet.'

'Well his family live in the south, in the outer London area, somewhere in the Home Counties . . . the university will have his home address.'

'Where did he live?'

'Above the greengrocers on the corner of this street. There is a small flat above the shop, they rent it out. Charlie took the tenancy a few weeks ago . . . immersing himself in the street to get authentic detail for his book. So if I do have information, who do I ask for?'

'Yellich, DS Yellich.'

'I'll remember that name. We'll have to meet some place, can't meet here and I can't be seen walking into the police station . . . I'll be a watched woman for a few weeks now. I don't want my face carved or my ribs kicked to pieces. And that's the least I can expect.'

'Understood.'

Yellich left 'The Elm' and walked down the street, pulling his collar up as protection against the chill easterly. A slight drizzle fell. The street was typical Holgate . . . narrow, lined with soot blackened terraces, where washing would be strung across the street on a good drying day . . . not as Gabrielle Ingham said, the York the tourists visit. Yellich came to the greengrocers. He entered it. The greengrocer was a healthy looking man who seemed to love fresh vegetables. His younger female assistant also looked healthy amid the carrots and potatoes and the mushrooms. Yellich had the impression that they were an item, not just proprietor and assistant, but man and wife . . . lovers at the very least.

'How can I help you, sir?' the man smiled.

'By letting me look at the flat I understand you let out, the one above the shop.'

'Police?'

'Yes.' Yellich showed his ID.

'If the lad's in trouble, I know nothing of it. I told him I want no drugs, I don't even let the room to smokers, but he seemed alright.'

'He's not in any trouble. If he is who we think he is, he's dead.'

The man jolted . . . glanced at the young woman, who gasped. Then he recovered his composure. 'I'll get the spare key.' He left the counter and returned a few minutes later with two keys strung onto a Volkswagen key fob. 'The entrance is at the rear of the shop . . . round the corner, down the alley . . . metal staircase . . . careful of the staircase; it's slippery in the wet.'

'Chaos. Violence. Something happened here,' Yellich said to himself as he stepped across the threshold, not requiring the keys because the door of the flat was lying ajar. Inside the flat was a scene of destruction, of smashed furniture, of upturned tables and lamp stands. Yellich reached into his pocket and took out his mobile. He phoned DCI Hennessey. 'Better get here, boss. If this is the youth's flat, his name was Charles Pimlott and he didn't go without a struggle.'

'He definitely didn't, did he?' Hennessey looked round the small bedsit. The signs of struggle were everywhere as if what fight had taken place in the flat had spilled into every corner of every room, bed on its side in the bedroom, plates smashed in the small kitchen. A photograph on the mantelpiece showed a picture of a young man and woman side by side somewhere in the sun. The young man in the photograph was clearly the same young man who had been found earlier that day lying face down in the frost in Askham Bogs. A name on a Social Security card, also on the mantelpiece was that of Charles Pimlott. 'His home address will be here somewhere. I'll contact his parents when I find it.'

'Believed to come from the south,' Yellich said. 'I'll search for it once SOCO have finished.' A camera flashed. A second SOCO officer dusted for prints with a small squirrel hair brush. 'There are no witnesses that I can find. Had a chat with the greengrocer who lets the flat . . . all he could say is that it must have happened one evening or one Sunday day time. He lives elsewhere in the city and doesn't check on the flat, calls just once a week for his rent. The post was behind the door . . . the earliest post mark was four days ago, 31st December . . . no delivery on New Year's day . . . so it happened sometime before New Year's day, if he received something in the post each day.'

'Big "if", Yellich,' Hennessey growled. 'I don't think we'll pin the time of this attack by the post.'

'No, boss . . . just musing. Found someone in the local pub. I think she has information . . . but she's frightened. But she also seems angry about something. I'll be surprised if she doesn't contact us, Gabrielle Ingham, by name.'

Morning, Tuesday 4th January

It never got easier. It was the walk with the next of kin, the clutching, trembling hope against hope attitude, the drawing back of the curtian, the wailing, the sobbing as the person lying behind the glass, dressed in bandages and by some trick of light and shade, looking as if they are floating peacefully in space, is recognised as their own. In this particular case, Yellich found it easier than most, but it was still hard. The Pimlotts revealed

310

themselves to be of the English middle class, there was a brief gasp, a slight sob, but beyond that, their emotions were contained.

'It is our son,' Mr Pimlott said.

Yellich nodded and the curtain was drawn shut.

'How did he die?' Mr Pimlott had a trim moustache, suit, he carried an overcoat and trilby.

'We believe he was murdered.' Yellich spoke softly.

'How?' Mrs Pimlott turned to him, she was sombrely dressed in a blue two piece.

'He was injected with heroin. We found out just this morning . . . the toxicology report revealed a massive amount in his system.'

'But he was such a clean living boy . . .' Mrs Pimlott's words trailed off.

'There is no indication that he was a user,' Yellich said. 'The indication is that he was injected against his will. Did he tell you anything at all about what he was doing?'

'No . . . he gave up his university course. I wanted him to follow me into the law . . . but he left . . . he was doing something, he had a project he was working on but he didn't tell us what.'

'It was as if he was going to surprise us with some achievement.' Mrs Pimlott's voice was shaky. 'Can we go back to the hotel, dear?'

'Yes.' Mr Pimlott squeezed his wife's hand. He turned to Yellich. 'We drove up yesterday evening, booked into an hotel . . . as you can imagine we didn't get a great deal of sleep. We'll have a nap

311

and then drive home. You don't need us for anything else?'

'No . . . thank you.'

Yellich walked the walls of the medieval city back to Micklegate Bar Police Station. He signed in and checked his pigeonhole. There was a message from Gabrielle Ingham. She had phoned requesting him to meet her at the Rose and Crown pub in Selby (opposite the Abbey) read the note. Yellich looked at the constable at the enquiry desk whose initials were on the note. 'How did she sound . . . drunk?'

'No, sir. Well, if anything, she was frightened. She phoned from the railway station, I heard the public address system in the background. That's York Station . . . I know Selby . . . there isn't a P.A. system at the station there. Train information is by way of a television screen.'

'Good for you,' Yellich smiled. 'It's that sort of observation and local knowledge that gets results. I'll go and meet her.'

Yellich walked to his office and recorded in the file on Charlie Pimlott that his identity had now been confirmed by his parents. He then drove out of York across flat landscape the short twenty minute drive to Selby. He parked his car in the railway station car park in the shadow of the Abbey and located the Rose and Crown. It was, he found, quite different to the Elm . . . carpets . . . a soft, quiet hotel-like atmosphere, bar staff in smart

312

uniform of white shirts and black waistcoats. Gabrielle Ingham, dressed in the same long skirt she had worn the day previous and in the same black jacket, sat at a table in the corner. She smoked a cigarette, a pint of beer, half consumed, stood in front of her. She smiled at Yellich who sat next to her.

'I wasn't followed,' she said. 'I wouldn't be here if I was followed, they don't rate me much anyway. I'm a slush . . . not a real threat.'

'They?'

'Baruch's boys.'

'You're not involved with them!'

'Not me . . . I'm just a soak, a bar fly, but I see things . . . Baruch's moving into Holgate.'

'Bit downmarket for him . . . from what we know, he supplies cocaine to the county set and ecstasy to the clubbers. I've never seen him.'

'No one has. They say his house is like the Tower of London . . . wire . . . guards . . . dogs . . . he's a frightened man. He's moving heroin into Holgate.'

'Really?'

'He's selling it to the youth. Remember the pub yesterday?'

'Yes.'

'Did you see two guys at the end of the bar . . . one with a beard, the other clean shaven?'

'Didn't notice them.'

'Well, they're always there . . . Sydney Jarvis and Henry Cooke. They were *the* villains in Holgate, selling cannabis and some duty free tobacco, playing at it really. Anyway, recently they were told that they were now working for Baruch . . . and they were moving heroin. They're out of their depths, they are scared. I mean, I am scared, but not like they must be.'

'So, what happened?'

'What exactly, I don't know . . . but Charlie Pimlott was asking questions, like I told you . . . this didn't come from me, right? I won't make a statement or give evidence.'

'OK.'

'But you should talk to Cooke and Jarvis. I overhead something . . . they had something to do with Charlie's murder . . . on Baruch's orders.'

'Understood.'

'That's all you're getting from me . . . and don't follow me out.' Gabrielle Ingham stood. 'I may not have been followed, but Baruch's people are everywhere . . . seriously, everywhere.'

Both men looked nervous. Very nervous indeed. When they were placed in separate cells at Micklegate Bar Police Station, they looked even more nervous.

'We can hold you for twelve hours without charging you,' Hennessey said to Cooke. 'I'll come back and see you in ten hours time . . . so wait here and decide what you want to do . . . just you and your thoughts. You work for yourself or you work against yourself. We'll listen to you if you want to talk to us before your mate. I'm now going to see him and say the same thing to him. Remember, Baruch will know you've been lifted by now.' Hennessey left the cell and the door was clanged shut.

Tuesday evening

'If I tell you, I'm dead.'

'If you don't tell us you're dead. Baruch won't take any risks, he'll have you silenced anyway. You and your mate both.'

'He's not that much of a mate.' Henry Cooke stroked his beard nervously.

'Well, he may well drop you in it. We haven't talked to him yet.'

'I never wanted it to go this far.'

'No one ever does.'

'But you don't mess with Baruch . . . never seen him, but if he gives the word, someone dies . . . he hides away . . . if he goes out he's chauffeur-driven in a car with tinted glass. He can see out but you can't see in.'

'We know. We've wanted Mr Baruch for a long time.'

'But I've seen him.'

'Do you want a lawyer present?'

'No, this is off the record, the less people that know what I am saying, the better.'

'It can't stay off the record.'

'You won't get Jarvis to testify, Baruch's got something to hold over him . . . he's got family in

315

Holgate. One word from Baruch and they'll all disappear. But I haven't . . . Baruch's got nothing to hold over me.'

'Keep talking.'

'I want witness protection . . . new name . . . new identity.'

'Only if you are a witness, if you murdered him or were part of the crime, you won't qualify . . . and you have to stand up in court and testify.'

'Baruch murdered the boy.'

'Go on.'

'He heard the boy was asking questions . . . he had him brought to his house, Baruch is totally paranoid. Anyway, me and Jarvis were told to come to Baruch's house out in the Vale of York . . . the boy was there . . . he'd been starved of food for three days to make him talk. Baruch was certain the boy knew all about his operation, but the boy knew nothing. When we got there, he was tied to a chair . . . a wooden upright chair . . . putting his fingerprints all over it. Like he was leaving you guys a present.'

'Really?' Hennessey turned to Yellich who raised his eyebrows.

'Then Baruch produced a syringe . . . and said to me and Jarvis "this is what I do if I don't like someone" and jabbed it into the boy's arm. Then we were driven away. Didn't know what happened to the boy until yesterday.'

'Better get out there,' Hennessey said. 'Go in force . . . if we can lift Charlie Pimlott's fingerprints from the chair . . . with the statement, that will convict him. He's slipped up.'

'Only if he hasn't sent in the cleaners.' Yellich stood, 'We'd better move quickly.'

Ten months later Hennessey and Yellich sat in silence as a scarlet clad judge sentenced Thomas Alfred Baruch, aged 33, to life imprisonment for the murder of Charlie Pimlott, and twelve years imprisonment for the possession of a quantity of cocaine with intent to supply. Both sentences to run concurrently.

After giving evidence at the trial at York Crown Court, Henry Cooke was ushered away in a police vehicle to begin a new life in a new location with a new identity. He lived from then on with the knowledge that from his prison cell Thomas Baruch had put a one million pound price tag on his head.

GILLIAN LINSCOTT

A BLESSING OF FROGS

A scream quivered out from Lady's rooms upstairs, followed by soft thumps of bare feet running. My Master sighed.

'Sounds as if they've found another one. Or a dozen.'

Eyes didn't glance away from the man on the stone-flagged floor.

'It's a strange business, investigating a man's murder in a world full of frogs,' he said.

There were two of them in the hot white room, Master and Eyes. Or three, if you counted Baker, who was dead on his back on the floor with a knife in his chest. Or four, if you counted myself, who is not usually counted. Or several dozen if you counted the frogs, which was not easy to do since Master was striding up and down all the time, making them scatter from under his feet. As I watched, one of them hopped onto Baker's forehead, blinked a few times and hopped off again.

'Where do they all come from?' Master said.

He was more disturbed than I'd ever seen him, forehead beaded with sweat, voice unsteady.

'From the river,' I could have told him. 'From a thick bubble of water with a black dot inside.'

But I said nothing, because I must not speak to the Master or to anybody else above me (which is very nearly everybody in the world) without being spoken to first. I could have told him too that the bakery – with only a few dozen frogs – was nowhere near as full of them as the rest of the house because they loved shade and coolness. They were clustered so thickly under the palm trees in the courtyard that they looked like the trees' own shadows made flesh. Every now and then, as Master paced and Eyes looked down at the body with his hands beside his back, more screams would drift in from the kitchens, the laundry rooms, the granary, the storerooms. Brooms were thumping and swishing in the background as the overseers tried to make the slaves stem the tide, but it was like attempting to hold back the Nile itself.

'I believe the priests are working on it,' said Eyes, still looking down at the body of Baker.

Eyes seemed unworried by the frogs. I liked him for that. Eyes was an important man. Probably I should never breathe the air in the same room with a man so important. In fact, I was trying to breathe as little and as shallowly as possible, so as not to take up any air he might need and show lack of respect. I always did that if I happened to be with Master, who is Pharaoh's Bread Steward,

319

and from the way Master behaved I knew Eyes outranked him by several steps. Eyes was not as imposing as Master to look at, being thin and lower than average height, but there was a great stillness about him.

'How was the body discovered?' he asked.

His voice was deep for a small man's and smooth as water just before it plunges over a cataract. Master nodded towards me.

'Woodboy found him.'

'When?'

'He'd just come back with the wood, soon after sunrise. He informed the guard, who sent word up to me. Naturally, I sent a messenger running to Pharaoh's household at once, but unhappily . . .'

Master stopped and his face went red.

'It was some time before anybody would take any notice of the messenger, on account of the frogs,' Eyes said, politely passing over the fact that Master might have come within a breath of criticising Pharaoh's household. 'Does the boy always come with the wood at the same time?'

'Yes. Woodboy's duty is to bring bundles of wood up from the river and put them to dry in the sun, ready to fire the ovens. He must be at the river before daylight to get the best wood before the boys from the other households.'

Master was good at his work and knew the routines of everybody in the household. He made it all sound orderly, as if it were simply a matter of strolling along the river edge, selecting here a branch and there a log. He'd never seen the woodboys fighting each other for the wood, bodies black against red sunrise reflected in red water, doubly black from the mud. Serious fights they are, that leave shoulders dislocated, noses bleeding, sometimes boys drowned because to go back to your household with no wood, or only a bundle of twigs and dead rushes, means a beating. I am seldom beaten. Master is good at his work and I am good at mine.

'Has the boy reason to come inside the bakery?'

'Yes. When he has brought back the day's first bundle, he must carry the dried wood from three days ago inside and pile it beside the oven.'

'And that's what he was doing when he found Baker's body?'

'Yes.'

Eyes glanced at the neat pile of dry wood beside the oven. The oven was almost cold now, just a few ashes glowing. On the other side of the courtyard, Baker's deputy would be hurrying the slaves to fire up the oven in the old bakery, kept in reserve for emergencies such as this. Come frogs or murder, Pharaoh must have his bread.

'He stacked it there after finding Baker's body?'

'Yes.'

But Master blinked and looked uneasy. Although that was exactly what I had done – come frogs or murder, wood must be tidily stacked – Master had no way of knowing this.

321

'Very calm of him,' said Eyes.

And he looked at me as if he meant to draw the insides from me with that one look. I should have lowered my eyes, but sensed that he didn't want that, so stared straight back at him.

'You saw, I suppose, the knife sticking out of his chest?'

I nodded.

'It's the knife used for opening flour sacks,' Master said, annoyed that I should be addressed directly rather than through him. 'Baker usually left it on the edge of the kneading trough over there.'

Our eyes went to the stone trough, full of a plump cushion of risen dough. Normally by this time of the morning it would have been turned into sweet-smelling dises of bread, under the supervision of the man now lying on the floor. He was beginning to stink.

'Were you frightened when you found him?' Eyes said to me.

Either he was unaware of Master's annoyance or had decided to disregard it. I nodded again, hoping that was the answer he wanted. The true answer was that I felt very little, because my head was too full of the wonder of the frogs.

They came just before the sun rose. As I went down to the river I met the advance guard of them, hopping up to the city. When I came to the water, the mud was restless round my bare feet, then it became a whole sheet of frogs, moving slowly but purposefully up the bank, frogs up and down the river, as far as the eye could see. I shouted for the joy of them. I've liked frogs as long as I can remember. There is no picture in my mind of father, mother, brother or sister. As far as I know I never had any of them and might have grown out of Nile mud, with feet ready for wading and hands ready for grabbing wood. Yet I can remember as clearly as sunlight my first frog. I must have been quite small at the time, possibly crawling, because the frog seemed large and on a level with me. We stared at each other and I was aware of a great wisdom and gentleness. As I grew, I found out more about them. There were tiny frogs, so small that they could sit on the nail of my little finger and still have space round them. I thought I should like to see a mother giving birth to these small frogs and watched for many years before I found out the truth. When I puzzled it out at last – that the black dots inside the bubbles took on life and became strange little fish and the fish grew legs and hopped on land, I laughed and turned somersaults from sheer delight. The priests in our temples have their signs and wonders and understand the will of the Sun God. The Israelites have their great conjurer who, they say, can strike water from bare rocks and turn a stick into a serpent. But did any of them, priest or conjurer, ever do a marvel like this one? So when the world turned to frogs and I was there to see it, perhaps

I did not care as much as I should have done for the death of a man who in life had done me nothing but hurt. Before blaming me for that, consider the comparison between Baker and a frog, any frog.

One, a frog is sleek and pleasant to the eye. I have seen many thousands of frogs, but never one which is fat or greasy. Baker was both. Two, a frog smells cleanly of water. Baker, even in life, smelt bad. Three, a frog is temperate and regular in its habits. Once a year it mates, as is necessary. Baker was forever bothering the servants and slave girls. Four, a frog is peaceable and harms nothing but flies. Baker was always pinching, kicking and slapping his workers, usually without reason. Five, a frog is the calmest of creatures. Baker had a foul tongue and a worse temper. Six, a frog is honest. Baker cheated Master and we all knew it. Seven, a frog speaks no evil of other frogs. Baker was a tale-bearer. I mourned for the frogs being crushed under the beating brooms of the slaves, but not for Baker.

'Had Baker any enemies in your household?' Eyes said to Master.
  'None that I know of.'
  I looked at the floor, pitying Master. If he'd said yes, most people disliked him – which he surely knew was the truth – he would be admitting to Pharaoh's representative that the household was

less than harmonious and that would have shamed us all. When I glanced up again I thought Eyes looked annoyed. But then, it was his own fault for asking the question.

'Of course,' Master said, 'it may have been an enemy from outside.'

'Hardly likely, is it? I suppose you keep good guards.'

Yes, Eyes was certainly annoyed.

'My guards are personally selected and trained,' Master said stiffly.

'So would hardly let in a stranger.'

Master said nothing. Eyes thought for a while, hand to his chin.

'I must speak to members of your household.'

'Certainly. If you would care to come and drink a pomegranate juice in my rooms, we'll send for whoever you please.'

'I prefer to go my own way. I should be grateful if you'd let your people know that I have your authority to ask questions.'

'Certainly. Oh certainly.'

Eyes was merely being polite. A man with Pharaoh's authority behind him didn't need Master's. He walked to the door and turned.

'Are those the women's apartments overhead?'

'Yes. My wife's personal maids and some of the laundresses.'

'They are the most likely to have heard anything that happened. Would you kindly let your wife know that I should like to talk to some of them?'

'Yes. I'm afraid my wife is an invalid or I'm sure she . . .'

Master's voice trailed away. He looked more wretched than at any time since the body had been discovered.

'I'm sure the Lady won't object to my asking her maids a few questions. If you could arrange for me to do it in a room reasonably free of frogs it might save us some more screaming.'

He walked out. Master looked down at Baker's body.

'What am I supposed to do about this?'

I knew he didn't expect me to answer. He sent me to call one of the guards, to watch over Baker while he decided. I took myself off, joined twenty or so frogs sitting quietly in a shady corner of the courtyard and thought about Lady's personal maids, especially Lily.

Most of the maids are beautiful, but Lily is the best of them. She has a kind nature too. One evening, when she came down as usual to fetch Lady's bricks from the oven she saw my ear was bitten from a fight with the red boy from the scribe's household.

'It's nothing,' I said.

I was ashamed that the bite made me ugly in her eyes. She wrapped the two bricks in the cloths she'd brought with her and carried them upstairs. Soon she was down again, with a pot of ointment.

'Sit there,' she said.

I sat against the wall while she smoothed the ointment on my ear with her white fingers. It was as cool as Nile mud in the early morning and smelt of jasmine. Next evening she touched my ear very gently.

'It is better?'

'It is better.'

She reminds me of a frog, not in looks, only that so many of the good things about her are frog-like. Her skin is smooth and she smells clean. She moves silently and without fuss. She watches everything with her wide brown eyes but says little. She harms nobody and never bears tales or says unkind things about the other maids, though some of them are cruel to her because they envy her. So, on Lily's account, I wondered what Eyes wanted with Lady's maids.

I heard Master in the courtyard, giving orders to one of the slaves.

'You are to take a broom and stand at the doorway of the blue room. If the frogs try to go in you must beat them away. A very important person is inside and must not be disturbed.'

When Master walked away I slipped out to the courtyard and found the slave in tears. I asked him what was wrong. He was no more than a child and addressed even me with respect.

'Oh sir, I am so scared of the frogs, I don't know what to do.'

'You are a great baby,' I said. 'Still, I shall take pity on you and do your duty for you.'

I grabbed the broom from him and took up my post by the door to the blue room, a pleasant place where Master sometimes sits after his evening meal. A curtain woven from rushes hung over the doorway, but didn't quite stretch to the sides, so I was able to see in quite easily. Eyes was sitting on a stone bench by the wall with one of the maids standing in front of him. She had her back to me, but from the width of her hips and the coarseness of her hair I knew she was the one they called Parrot. Her voice was quieter than usual as she spoke to Eyes.

'Yes, Excellency, we sleep above the bakery. I heard nothing last night.'

'When did you last see Baker alive?'

'At noon yesterday. He was standing in the doorway to the bakery with Tallyman, counting in the flour sacks.'

'How long have you served your Lady?'

'Four years, Excellency. I have been here longer than any of her other maids.'

'So you know the household well?'

'Yes, Excellency.'

'To your knowledge, did Baker have any enemies in the household?'

'It is a well-run household, Excellency. We do our best to work harmoniously together for Master and Lady.'

Eyes tapped his foot impatiently, disturbing a frog that had been sitting quietly beside it.

'Please, let's take all that for granted. Did Baker have any enemies?'

A little silence. I couldn't see Parrot's face, but knew from the way Eyes' expression changed that she'd looked some kind of a message at him.

'He did?'

'It isn't my place to bear tales, Excellency.'

'Oh, but it is.' His voice had gone very cold. 'It is your duty, and everybody else's duty in this household, to tell me all they know about Bake's death. I ask you a third time, did Baker have any enemies?'

'She was very angry with him.'

Parrot said the words as if savouring a sweet pomegranate pip.

'Who?'

'Lily.'

Three frogs had arrived at the threshold. I banged the broom down, beside them but not on them, so that they hopped away. After they'd gone, I gave two or three more bangs. It was my only way of protesting, though my whole body was twitching with the urge to push the curtain aside, rush in and shout at Eyes: 'Don't listen to her, Excellency. She is an evil, lying bitch, jealous because Master takes Lily to his bed instead of her.' Unthinkable. The sky would fall if a woodboy spoke uninvited to the Eyes of Pharaoh. Through the rush of blood in my ears, I made myself listen.

'Lily being?'

'One of the other maids. She only came here last year.'

'And you say she was angry with Baker?'

'She told us she'd slapped his face.'

'Told who?'

'Me and the other maids.'

'When.'

'Yesterday evening, after we'd put Lady to bed.'

Eyes leaned forward.

'Tell me exactly what she said.'

'One of the other girls noticed that she'd been crying and wanted to know why. Lily said when she went down to the bakery to get Lady's bricks—'

'Bricks?'

'Lady suffers from pains in her side. When Baker has finished baking bread for the day, he puts two bricks in the oven. By evening, when the oven has cooled, they're just warm. We wrap them in clean cloths and put them in the bed beside her. It gives her some comfort.'

'I see. Was it always Lily who went down for them?'

'Usually. That evening, she said Baker had been waiting and caught hold of her when she went in. According to her, he wanted her to lie with him there and then on the bread table.'

'Had she been accustomed to lie with him?'

I banged with the broom again, though no frogs were near. I wanted to shout, 'No, of course she hadn't. Lily is a clean girl and would lie with nobody but Master.'

Parrot shrugged her shoulders.

'Answer me,' Eyes snapped at her.

'I don't know, Excellency.'

But the tone of her voice said something else.

'In any event, I take it that she refused to lie with him yesterday evening.'

'So she said. She said he tried to force her and she slapped his face, picked up the bricks and ran out.'

'Slapped his face, that was all?'

'All she said she did, yes.'

Eyes sighed.

'You may go for now. You are strictly forbidden to talk about this conversation to anybody else. Send Lily to me.'

As Parrot pushed her way out through the curtain I brought the broom crashing down within a hair's breadth of her squashy flat foot. She jumped, squawked and called me a bad name.

'Master's orders,' I said.

No sooner had Parrot gone than Master himself arrived, so hot and harassed he didn't seem to notice that I'd taken the child's place on frog duty. He pushed the curtain aside and went a little way into the room.

'Is everything in order, Excellency?'

Eyes looked at him, like a man turning a question over in his mind. Master's shoulders went tight.

'Yes, thank you. Tell me, did Baker have any particular friends in the household?'

'Friends?' The word seemed to puzzle Master. 'I don't think so.'

'Or any person he worked with particularly?'

'The bakery slaves, of course. Of his own rank, only Tallyman. They must be together several times a day because of accounting for the flour and the loaves.'

'How is the accounting carried out?'

Master took a deep breath and his shoulders relaxed. This was something he understood.

'In the morning, Tallyman has the flour sacks for the day brought out of the store. They are weighed and carried over to the bakery. Tallyman records them on his sticks and Baker makes . . . made . . . a mark on another stick to record that he'd received them. When the bread is baked, Tallyman counts the loaves and sends the allocation to Pharaoh's household.'

Eyes looked at him. Master grew nervous again.

'I hope there has been no short-falling in Pharaoh's bread.'

'As far as I know, everything is in order.'

There, for once, Master was wrong though I couldn't say so. Pharaoh's household would get its daily allocation, but there was a short-falling in Master's own household that we all felt in the pit of our stomachs. Over the past few moons, the loaves of the servants and slaves had been growing smaller and smaller so that we were hungry most

332

of the time and the sound of rumbling guts vibrated through the place like an animal growling in its sleep. We couldn't complain, but it made for general bad temper.

'Send Tallyman to me,' Eyes said. 'If the girl Lily arrives, tell her to wait outside.'

Master's head jerked back at Lily's name. I thought he was going to protest but he said only, 'Yes, Excellency.'

I expected him to send a slave for Tallyman but he went across to the storerooms himself, walking like a man giddy from fever.

Tallyman arrived some time afterwards, an unrestful kind of man, sallow of skin and thin as a dried rush, with a nervous way of moving his mouth as if always munching on something not very nourishing.

'I am sorry if I am late, Excellency. We were trying to get the frogs out of the cellars.'

Eyes gave him a cool look, but Tallyman babbled on.

'Nobody's seen the like of them, cellars knee deep in the filthy things, crawling over each other. People are saying it is a curse on us, Excellency, that we've displeased the gods. Do you think it's a curse?'

The frogs or Baker's death must have unsettled him badly, putting a question to a person so far above him in rank. Eyes frowned.

'We should leave these matters to Pharaoh and

the priests. I sent for you to talk about bread, and particularly your duties with Baker.'

'Yes, Excellency.

Tallyman's account for the first part of his day was almost word for word the same as Master's.

'So when the trays of loaves went to Pharaoh's household, was that the last you saw of Baker for the day?'

'No, Excellency. The empty trays must be counted back. The slaves bring them from Pharaoh's household every evening. I count them and return them to Baker, and Baker must notch the stick to record that he has received them.'

'In the evening?'

'Yes. The time before sunset.'

'And you did that yesterday evening?'

'Yes.'

'And Baker was alive?'

'Yes. He notched the stick. I can bring it if . . .'

'That won't be necessary. Was there anything unusual about Baker yesterday evening?'

'What do you mean, Excellency?'

'Did he seem scared or angry?'

'No.'

'Did he speak of having an enemy?'

'No.'

'So things were in every way as normal?'

'Yes. He was kneading the dough when I came in, quite as normal. He counted the trays, notched the stick. We spoke for a while.'

'What about?'

'One of the trays had been damaged by a slave's carelessness. He wanted to make sure he wouldn't be blamed for it.'

'So an entirely routine conversation?'

'Yes.'

'And you left him still kneading dough?'

'As I recall, Excellency, he finished kneading it while I was there. I remember him washing his hands at the water jar while we were speaking. The light was going by then.'

'And the dough would stay in the kneading trough till morning?'

'Yes.'

'And his knife on the edge of the trough?'

'I think so, yes.'

'Did you see Baker after that?'

'No. The next thing I knew was somebody shouting in the morning that Baker was dead.'

A soft step beside me and the smell of fresh river water round green rushes. Lily had arrived. Her brown eyes were wide and scared.

'Eyes of Pharaoh has sent for me. Is he in there?'

I told her that Tallyman was with him. Her little feet quivered on the ground from fear. I wanted to stroke her hair, like calming a frightened animal. All I could do was let my hand touch hers, so lightly that it might have been accidental. Then we had to move apart as Tallyman came through the curtain, blowing out his cheeks from relief at leaving the presence of Eyes.

'I should go in now?' Lily said.

She went through the curtain. A frog was sitting on the threshold, quite still, not trying to go anywhere. I squatted down beside it, to see and hear better.

'I believe you were angry with Baker last night,' Eyes said.

The tone of his voice was not unkind, but from the way she flinched he might as well have hit her.

'Speak up, please. Yes or no?'

'Yes.'

'Why?'

She was ashamed to tell him, though it was no fault of hers. He didn't become angry with her – not quite – just let her see that he might become angry if she didn't answer. He had the story from her, much as Parrot had told it, but without the malice and with things much worse against Baker. She'd gone in, not expecting to find him there. He'd hidden behind the oven, come out suddenly and tried to force her backwards onto the bread table, only she'd struggled free, hit him and run out.

'Only hit him?' Eyes said.

'Only hit him, Excellency. My hand on his cheek.'

'Not a knife in his chest?'

'I had no knife.'

'Did you not see the knife on the side of the kneading trough?'

'I don't remember one.'

'It was evening when you struck him?'

'Just before we helped Lady to bed, yes.'

'He was dead by the time the sun rose.'

'Yes.'

'So he died between evening and sunrise?'

'Yes.'

'Do you know of anybody who saw him alive after you struck him and ran out of the bakery?'

'No.'

Her voice was no more than the first stirring of the morning breeze among the reeds. I might have walked into the room then and said untruthfully that I'd seen Baker alive later, only there was a little commotion behind me in the courtyard. I turned and saw two big slaves carrying a chair between poles, another slave holding a sunshade over the person sitting in the chair. I hardly recognised her at first because it was so long since any of us had seen her outside her own rooms and she'd grown so thin and fine-drawn. Lady. The slaves brought her right up to where I was standing and set the chair gently down.

'Is my maid Lily inside with him?' she said, speaking directly to me as if I were somebody of consequence. Her voice was husky, but firm.

I nodded, not daring to speak to her.

'Take me inside,' she said to the front slave.

The slave with the sunshade and I held the curtain aside for them.

Eyes stood up as the slaves set her chair down in front of him.

'I apologise a thousand times for intruding on your work, Excellency,' Lady said. 'But I have something important to say to you about the killing of Baker. You will permit me to send my maid away for a while?'

He nodded and took his seat again on the bench. She told Lily to wait in the women's rooms until she was sent for again. Lily walked past me, eyes straight ahead. The chair slaves followed her and squatted in the dust in the shade of the wall. I kept my hand on the curtain, desperate to hear what Lady was going to tell him and full of fear for Lily. Lady would surely know about her and Master.

'It's about Lily,' Lady said.

Sure she was going to carry on the bad work Parrot had begun, I was too scared even to bang my broom.

'Lily is a good girl,' she said. 'A good, obedient girl.'

From the expression of Eyes, I knew that he'd heard about Master and Lily and was as surprised as I was. He simply nodded again.

'Is it true that you suspect her of killing Baker?'

He didn't answer at first, as if weighing up whether to trust her.

'She has admitted hitting him,' he said.

'And told you why?'

'Yes.'

'She is speaking the truth. She came to me straight after it had happened, distressed and crying.'

338

'With respect, she would have been distressed if she had killed him.'

'She had no blood on her hands or clothes.'

'She might have returned to do it later in the night.'

'No, she was with me all night, from the time she came to me crying to when the first of the frogs arrived in the morning.'

'I don't doubt your word, Lady, but can you be sure of that? She might have crept out while you were asleep.'

'I sleep very little, and more lightly than a dragonfly. Besides, waking or sleeping, I should know if Lily left the room. I keep her with me whenever I can because she soothes me and is more gentle than all my maids.'

When I heard that, I wished I could run into the room and kiss Lady's thin white feet in their gilded sandals. Eyes frowned.

'Lady, I hope your Lily is not guilty. Nevertheless, a crime has been committed against a servant of Pharaoh. It can't go unpunished.'

'Baker was a false servant,' she said. There was an edge of anger to her voice. 'He defrauded the household, everybody knows that.'

'Everybody?'

'I have nothing to do all day but listen to the servants' talk. Believe me, I know everything that goes on.'

'Everything? Do you know then who killed him?'

'No, but I know it can't have been Lily.'

He sat for a while, looking at the floor. When he spoke, his voice was sad.

'Lady, you have done me the honour to come to me and I accept that the girl Lily was with you all night. Still, she was the last person I know of to see Baker alive. Hands may be washed and clothes may be changed. I must do my duty.'

'And have Lily put to death?'

'The guilty person must die.'

'Lily is not guilty.'

Another silence. He sighed.

'Lady, will you have the kindness to go back to your rooms and tell Lily to come to me in the bakery.

'Where the body is?'

'Where the body is.'

I thought at first she was going to refuse. I was willing her to refuse. But at last she clapped her hands and the chair slaves came running in and carried her away. Her face was like stone.

Soon afterwards Eyes came out, deep in thought. He took a few steps past me and turned back.

'What are you doing here, Woodboy?'

'Keeping the frogs away, Excellency.'

'I was about to send for you. Follow me to the bakery.'

I followed him across the outer courtyard. Slaves scooping up crushed frogs or chivvying live ones looked at him sideways and some of them made the sign to turn away evil, keeping it small so as not to attract attention. But they needn't have worried because he walked head down, not looking round. When he stopped suddenly, halfway to the bakery, I almost ran into him.

'Go to your Master and tell him to come to . . .'

It showed how lost in thought he was that he'd almost given me an impossible order. How could I tell Master to come and go? He changed it.

'Go to Tallyman and tell him to give my respects to your Master and ask him to meet me in the bakery. Tallyman is to come as well.'

I ran to find Tallyman. He was in his office by the store-rooms, making signs on a clay tablet. He growled at me when he heard the message.

'You must have muddled it. Why should he want Master there of all places?'

I didn't contradict him, just went on repeating what Eyes had said. In the end he groaned, put on his sandals and went to do as he was told, saying to me in passing that I could expect a beating if I'd got it wrong. I went and waited by the door to the bakery. Lily arrived first, looking so alone and scared that I risked touching her hand as she passed. She looked up at me, eyes full of tears, then bowed her head and went inside. Master came next, with Tallyman hurrying after him. Once they'd gone in, I moved to the little store chamber just inside the doorway. They were all three of them standing by the oven, with Baker on the floor, covered now with a white sheet. The place smelt of him and of sour dough. Eyes stood by the kneading trough.

'The important question is when Baker died,' he said. His voice was calm and quiet. 'We know from Tallyman that at the hour before sunset he had finished kneading his dough and had left it in the kneading trough here.'

He gestured towards the dough. It had risen like a mass of white fungus to fill the trough. Because it had been standing much longer than usual there was a crust on it, but at some places the dough underneath had broken through the crust in paler bulges. It seemed a sinister thing, like another body.

'We know too, from the maid Lily, that sometime later in the evening, she struck him. She says he was alive when she left.'

I couldn't bear to look at Lily, so kept my eyes on the dough. A frog hopped on top of it and stared at me.

'At first light, Woodboy found him dead and raised the alarm.' He glanced in my direction. 'You had better come in, Woodboy. You are a witness too.'

I went in, shame-faced. Master and Tallyman glared at me. Eyes went on as if nothing had happened.

'As you see, Baker had not started making up the dough into loaves. I assume he would usually do that as soon as it was light enough.'

'Yes, soon after dawn,' Master said.

'So at sometime between the evening when Lily

struck him and when the light came back in the morning, somebody plunged his own knife into his chest.'

Master was looking at Lily, his eyes sad. I wanted to shout at him, 'Save her. Lady your wife tried to, and she had less cause than you.' He did nothing. I looked back at the dough. There was something sticking out from it, caught between the risen dough and the side of the trough. It looked like a piece of rush or leaf.

'We must also ask ourselves whether anybody beside Lily had cause to be angry with Baker,' Eyes said.

It was the wrong colour for a leaf, the wrong shape for a piece of rush. I moved quietly towards the trough. The frog blinked and hopped down behind it. The little noise it made was enough to make Eyes look my way.

'What is it, Woodboy?'

I touched the thing that was neither leaf nor rush, but something finer and softer than either. I looked up at Eyes, straight into his face.

'What have you found there, boy?'

He was beside me, almost as quick as a frog himself. With my eyes, I signalled to him to touch the thing. He touched it and frowned.

'A frog's foot. Turn the dough over. Tallyman, help him.'

It was below Tallyman's rank to do it, but he had no choice. Together we pulled the heavy cushion of dough towards us, hauled it over and flipped it back into the trough, with a glubbing noise like Nile mud. Master made a sound of disgust.

'Everywhere.'

There were three of them, two crushed as flat as sandal soles, the other nearly so. They were stuck to what had been the lower surface of the dough and was now the uppermost. Eyes turned to me.

'Woodboy, when did the frogs start coming up?'

'They'd already started when I went to the river before dawn, Excellency. I saw some tens of them on the paths as I went down to the river, hundreds as I came back.'

'That's what the priests tell us too,' Eyes said. 'The first frogs came into the houses in the hour before dawn.'

We all stared at the squashed frogs.

'So what do these three dead frogs tell us?' Eyes said.

Nobody answered. He looked at me.

'Well, Woodboy?'

'That the dough was taken out of the trough and put back again in the hour before dawn or after.'

I should have felt scared, saying so many words in front of Master, but there was something about Eyes that gave me courage. It seemed to have the same effect on Tallyman, because he gave an opinion unasked.

'Some frogs are around all the time.'

'Indeed, yes. It is just possible, though unlikely, in the normal course of events, that a frog might happen to be in the trough when Baker kneaded his dough there. But three? Not possible. Therefore we must assume that the dough was lifted out of the trough and thrown back in again with enough force to crush the frogs in the hour before sunrise or afterwards.'

'It couldn't have been afterwards,' Master said. 'Baker was dead by then and a guard on the door.'

'In the hour before sunrise, then.'

'When Lily was with my wife,' Master said.

His voice was full of relief, only I wished he'd spoken before, when things looked so black for Lily. She gave a little sob of relief and almost fell over. Eyes put out a hand to steady her and helped her sit down on one of the flour sacks. I had to look very hard at the dough and the crushed frogs to stop myself running to her. The dough round them was flat and quite fresh looking, as if it had been cut with a knife.

'What are you looking at now, Woodboy?'

Eyes seemed to notice every move I made. I gestured towards the cut surface, not able to put into words what I was thinking. He came past me, touched the dough.

'Cut. In the hour before sunrise, the dough was taken out of the trough, a piece was cut off it and the rest was thrown back into the trough with some force.'

'And in that same hour, Baker was killed,' Master said.

'Quite probably with the same knife. Since I can see no traces of blood on the dough, we may assume that the dough was cut first and Baker killed afterwards. Can you find any connection?'

He looked at Master.

'If somebody were stealing part of the dough . . . ?' Master said.

Master looked at Tallyman. Eyes nodded.

'Exactly. Let us imagine the scene. Baker comes in, just before it's light. He sees somebody hacking away a great lump of dough. Perhaps he has reason to suspect it has happened before and is keeping watch. He challenges the thief.'

Tallyman's face had turned whiter than the dough. Eyes went on speaking in the same calm voice.

'The thief already has the knife in his hand for cutting the dough. He knew the knife would be there where it always was, on the edge of the kneading trough. He had no need to bring one with him. That suggests a man who knows the routine of the bakery well, wouldn't you say?'

He was looking straight at Tallyman now. Tallyman stared at the floor, but that was no use because Baker was lying there under his sheet. Then Tallyman screamed. I'd only heard such a scream once in my life before and that was from a woodboy caught in a crocodile's jaws. Tallyman was screaming because the white cloth over Baker was rising and falling, as if the man were breathing again in gulping, irregular breaths.

'It was your idea,' Tallyman screeched at Baker's corpse. 'It was your idea all along.'

He was still screaming when a frog hopped from under the sheet and out of the door. He went on screaming when the guards came to drag him away.

The frogs stayed with us all the rest of that day and night. But by next morning, as I walked to the river before sunrise, they were streaming back again. It was like being carried on a moving carpet of frogs. I was sorry for the many that had been killed and especially for the two crushed by the dough. Yes, only two. The third that had been less squashed revived after all and hopped away. I was the only one to see it because Eyes, Lily and Master had left the bakery by then. Master was cast down because he should have known that Tallyman and Baker had been cheating him day after day for many moons, selling part of Pharaoh's dough every morning to a baker who kept a wretched little oven just outside the walls. Then, Eyes suggested, there'd been quarrels between the two of them over the division of the money. We could have told him that, all of the slaves and boys, but nobody asked us.

There is a new Tallyman now and a new Baker. Every evening, when Lily comes down for the warm bricks, I make sure I'm there to give them to her. She thanks me and sometimes lets her hand touch mine. As for the frogs, people say what a relief it is that they've gone. They still discuss why they chose to come that day and if they will come again. Some people say the Israelites' conjurer sent them as a sign to Pharaoh, but the priests say not. All I know is that the frogs have not gone at all. They're where they always were, in the mud by the river, living their own quiet magic. Which is a blessing in itself, because what would the world be without frogs?